The Short Stories of Frank Yerby

The Short Stories of

FRANK

YERBY

Edited by

Veronica T. Watson

University Press of Mississippi / Jackson

The University Press of Mississippi is the scholarly publishing agency of
the Mississippi Institutions of Higher Learning: Alcorn State University,
Delta State University, Jackson State University, Mississippi State University,
Mississippi University for Women, Mississippi Valley State University,
University of Mississippi, and University of Southern Mississippi.

www.upress.state.ms.us

The University Press of Mississippi is a member
of the Association of University Presses.

These stories by Frank Yerby were originally published as follows:
"Salute to the Flag" in *The Paineite*, 1936.
"White Magnolias" in *Phylon*, 1944.
"Roads Going Down" in *Common Ground*, 1945.
"The Homecoming" in *Common Ground*, 1946.
"My Brother Went to College" in *Tomorrow*, 1946.

All stories are reprinted/printed by permission of Frank Yerby's estate.

First printing 2020
∞

Library of Congress Cataloging-in-Publication Data

Names: Yerby, Frank, 1916–1991, author. | Watson, Veronica T., editor.
Title: The short stories of Frank Yerby / edited by Veronica T. Watson.
Other titles: Stories. Selections. 2020
Description: Jackson : University Press of Mississippi, 2020. | Includes
bibliographical references.
Identifiers: LCCN 2019058789 (print) | LCCN 2019058790 (ebook) | ISBN
9781496828514 (hardback) | ISBN 9781496828521 (trade paperback) | ISBN
9781496828538 (epub) | ISBN 9781496828545 (epub) | ISBN 9781496828552
(pdf) | ISBN 9781496828569 (pdf)
Subjects: LCSH: Short stories, American—20th century. | American
literature—African American authors. | BISAC: FICTION / Short Stories
(single author) | LCGFT: Short stories.
Classification: LCC PS3547.E65 A6 2020 (print) | LCC PS3547.E65 (ebook) |
DDC 813/.54—dc23
LC record available at https://lccn.loc.gov/2019058789
LC ebook record available at https://lccn.loc.gov/2019058790

British Library Cataloging-in-Publication Data available

CONTENTS

ACKNOWLEDGMENTS

This collection has been many years in the making. It truly would not have been possible for me to bring Frank Yerby's short fiction to the public if it were not for the impeccable attentiveness of my graduate assistants, Nedrick Patrick, Lisa Mazey, and Taylor Jones, who transcribed, proofed, and researched every story in this collection. I am forever thankful for their time, labor, and commitment to this project.

There are many, many partners who, without knowing all the reasons why it was important, supported this work every step of the way. Researching Frank Yerby has taken me to Augusta, Georgia, his native soil; Boston, Massachusetts, the home of his literary archive; and Madrid, Spain, where the world traveler remarried, settled, and spent the last thirty-six years of his life. Along the way, I have been supported by amazing scholars, friends, and institutions, who have been more generous with their time, resources, and expertise than I had reason to expect. My sincerest thanks go to Laura Delbrugge who helped to make my time in Madrid productive, and to Mireia Sentís, a photographer, researcher, and publisher in Madrid who generously shared her time and knowledge of Yerby's life in Spain with me. My research was also greatly facilitated by the faculty and staff of Paine College and community members of Augusta who helped me to understand the community landscapes that shaped Frank Yerby as a young man and artist; and the archivists at the Howard Gotlieb Research Center who, over the course of four years and multiple visits, brought boxes to my tables and responded to every inquiry I made as I worked to get a comprehensive understanding of Frank's short story production.

Financial support for much of my research has come from the School of Graduate Studies and Research, the dean of the College of Humanities and Social Sciences, and the Department of English at Indiana University of Pennsylvania. The Faculty Professional Development Council also provided a substantial grant that enabled my research in Madrid. Without these sources of support, this book would not be in your hands.

To Frank Yerby's children: thank you for your faith in my humble efforts to make a small portion of Frank's work available again. I know I have asked a lot, bothered you when you would probably rather not have heard from me, and asked you to claim a legacy you never thought of as yours. I hope you feel it was, in the end, all worth it!

And to my family, all my love and appreciation. Though I have wandered far to complete this work, you were always with me.

To God be the glory.

INTRODUCTION:
FRANK YERBY, WRITER

Born on September 5, 1916, in Augusta, Georgia, Frank Garvin Yerby was primed to write protest literature. As an African American man in Augusta, a town deeply rooted in the racist ideologies and practices of the segregated South, he certainly had had enough experiences with Jim Crow living, discrimination, and racial terrorism to fuel his writing for a lifetime. Indeed, as a young writer beginning to explore his craft, Yerby set off on a path that would have aligned him with many of his more famous contemporaries, including Richard Wright, Zora Neale Hurston, Langston Hughes, and James Baldwin. Yet, according to Yerby, when he wrote socially and racially conscious fiction, he collected a "houseful of rejection slips" ("How and Why" 146).

Interestingly, this statement, written over a decade into his publishing career, does not tell the whole story. In 1944 the author won his first literary award, the O. Henry Memorial Award, for "Health Card," a story about an African American soldier's attempts to enjoy leave with his wife in a small southern town.[1] The story was subsequently included in Langston Hughes's *The Best Stories by Negro Writers: An Anthology from 1899 to the Present* (1967), bringing him even further recognition. In fact, the success of this first story garnered him enough notice that he secured an advance to write a prospectus for a novel, which became his first best-seller, *The Foxes of Harrow*, published only two years later. Of the other eight short stories he is known to have published, seven of them also focus on the lives, identities, and psychologies of black Americans living with segregation, discrimination, and the threat of racialized violence. But, while writing about the American racial caste system was not completely a dead-end endeavor for him, Yerby was a person looking to make a living from his writing. Publishing short stories in literary magazines and journals would not necessarily have gotten him the outcome he envisioned for himself.

The first novel Yerby sought a publisher for, according to Bruce Glasrud and Laurie Champion, was a "race-based novel" centered on a "black man who is a steel worker as well as successful boxer, and exposes the problems of being an independent black man in racially-biased white America" (16). This manuscript, apparently reviewed by several publishers, never found a home. Yerby eventually destroyed it. Perhaps it was this experience that led him to conclude "the reader cares not a snap about such questions," and to change the direction of his writing for a significant portion of his career (Yerby, "How and Why" 146). He also commented in an interview with James Hill that "Jimmy [Baldwin] and other black novelists of his group and of his school . . . were preaching to the converted, that they had no possible way of reaching the people whom they needed to reach," suggesting yet another reason for the radical turn he took from writing about black lives ("An Interview" 211). Whatever the rationale, Yerby did decide to go a different direction with his writing and churned out a novel every one to two years for the next thirty-nine years of his life. Most featured white protagonists and would comfortably fit within the genre of romantic historical fiction, or what he termed the "costume novel" ("How and Why" 145). The decision led him to commercial success and financial stability. Claiming that "dealing with racial issues" was an "artistic dead end" for writers, he did not publish a novel that featured a black protagonist until the 1969 publication of *Speak Now*; it was his twenty-third novel (Yon 99). Two years later, *The Dahomean* (1971) became his first published novel that focused exclusively on a cast of black characters. But by the late sixties and early seventies, as Yerby complained, he was well outside of the interest or regard of most scholars, leading to the lamentable position we find ourselves in today: one of the most prolific and popular African American writers of his generation is also one of the least read or known writers of our times.

The Early Years

All indications are Frank Yerby was wickedly smart. James Carter, a local historian of black history in Augusta who knew the Yerby family personally, remembers his mother saying that Yerby was one of the brightest students she had ever taught in her forty-five years in the classroom (personal interview). In 1933 Yerby graduated from Haines Institute, a private black school founded by notable black educator Lucy Craft Laney, having been educated in a classical curriculum that included training in German, Latin, French, Spanish, business, and music for all students. From there he went on to Paine College, graduating in 1937 with a "record-high-grade average," and Fisk University where he earned a master's in English in 1938 (Yon 99). Carter believes Yerby was a fast thinker who could respond quickly and express things more eloquently than most. His quick intellect and aptitude, according to Carter, gave Yerby a "subliminal impatience" with most people because they were not as sharp-witted as he was (personal interview). Perhaps this explains why, as a young man, Carter remembers Yerby as being introverted and a loner, traits he apparently carried into adulthood.

The Yerby family was probably lower-middle class in terms of income, but they seem to have settled in the echelons of the black middle class in Augusta. Yerby's "much beloved" father, Rufus Garvin Yerby, was a hotel doorman who supplemented the family's income by hiring himself out as a carpenter (Yerby letter to Helen Strauss, October 13, 1962). His mother, Wilhelmina Ethel (Smythe) Yerby, was a seamstress and did laundry in their home to help provide for the family of four children. They provided private high school education for their children, Frank, Eleanor, Paul, and Alonzo, which would have been a necessity in 1930s Georgia since, according to the National Park Service report, "Public Elementary and Secondary Schools in Georgia, 1868–1971," it was not until 1937 that state funding was allocated to support African American schools beyond the elementary level (14).[2] They also owned their home and socialized with elite blacks in the Augusta community. Both of Yerby's parents were multiracial, with Rufus being part Seminole Indian and Wilhelmina being of Scots-Irish descent. Yerby would often refer to his heritage as a "mini-United Nations," but in the Augusta of his youth, fair-skinned though he was, he was regarded as strictly African American by whites in the city (Folkart 22). In the black community, on the other hand, he was not always considered dark enough. As he shared with *People Magazine* in 1981, "I was considered black there . . . even though away from home I could ignore the Jim Crow laws. When I was young a bunch of us black kids would get in a fight with the white kids and then I'd have to fight with a black kid who got on me for being so light" (Yon 99). The family's skin tones, however, might have afforded them a social mobility in the community that they would not otherwise have had. Such were the complicated politics of race and color in the segregated South. For an intellect like Yerby, the inconsistencies and contradictions of race were both frustrating and infuriating.

They were also dangerous. An experience that impacted Yerby significantly happened in the 1930s when, as a young man, he was harassed by an Augusta officer for "walking with a White girl" ("Author" 13). That young woman was his sister Eleanor, but the incident did not end before the outraged officer arrested Yerby for his perceived transgression (Schapp E1). Carter recalls that Yerby was beaten and needed medical attention after the encounter. Although Augusta of the early twentieth century had a thriving African American middle class comprised of entrepreneurs in the fields of education, the medical professions, insurance, and banking, these types of abuses were always a possibility in the segregated town. This was the context out of which Yerby emerged. It was a community that had to pull together to survive and provide for their collective human needs, but those community-forging pressures did not prevent intraracial conflicts from flaring up. The family and community expected and enacted excellence despite the fact that at any moment they might face the routine atrocities of segregation and white supremacy, and indeed might face physical violence for little to no reason at all.

No one is quite sure when Yerby began writing, but according to a letter from his sister, Eleanor, to the Howard Gotlieb Archival Research Center at Boston University, "Frank had a way of hiding things that he wrote, when I found them I should copy them into a notebook" (Boddie letter to H. B. Gotlieb, July 1, 1965). By college he was experimenting in a variety of genres, including poetry and drama. Taking advantage of his time at Paine College, in 1936 Yerby co-composed the Paine College school song, the "Paine Hymn," and published his first short story, "Salute to the Flag," in *The Paineite*. The story was quickly followed by a second, "Love Story," in 1937, which was also published in the school newspaper. That same year after beginning his studies at Fisk, he published "A Date with Vera" and "Young Man Afraid" in the *Fisk Herald*. Also while at Fisk, he "wrote and produced several plays, one of which toured several states on the Little Theater Circuit" (Hill, "Frank" 388).[3] After graduating with his MA, Yerby published five more short stories between 1939 and 1946: "The Thunder of God" (*New Anvil*, 1939), "White Magnolias" (*Phylon*, 1944), "Roads Going Down" (*Common Ground*, Summer 1945), "The Homecoming" (*Common Ground*, Spring 1946), and "My Brother Went to College" (*Tomorrow*, 1946). Notably, all of the stories published in the 1940s could fairly be classified as racial realism, protest fiction of the type that Yerby was said to have eschewed, and several others held at the Gotlieb (some of which are reproduced in this collection) would also fit that description. However, the fact that so many of Yerby's stories only appeared in small journals and magazines without wide circulation, or remained unpublished, clearly contributed to scholars' sense that he was a writer disengaged from issues and debates of his day on racism, social justice, and human rights. A deeper consideration of the corpus of work, however, does not bear out that evaluation. Mallory Millender, Augusta native and former faculty member and university historian at Paine College, asserts that Yerby had a "mission to interpret the world, particularly the world as it affected black people" (personal interview). Despite becoming best known, perhaps, for his prolific authorship of novels that focused primarily on white lives and characters, this assessment is one the author, himself, would seem to have supported. Yerby commented in an interview with Maryemma Graham, "In every novel I have written about the American South, I have subtly infused a very strong defense of Black history and Black people" (70). He also did that work in the genre of short fiction.

But there can be no doubt that Yerby was not a man with a singular artistic focus. Many of the stories in this collection cover themes completely unrelated to racism, inequality, or injustice. He explores the conditions of a life well lived, the meaning of freedom and courage, the role of luck in shaping human destiny, and the power of love. The stories also fall into an intriguing range of styles, from the historical fiction he is perhaps best known for, to ghost stories, noir, and racy murder-mysteries. For those who know him by his reputation as the "prince of pulpsters," or who have come to expect a rather formulaic approach to his writing, many of these short stories will come as a surprise (Bone 176).

Not much is known about Frank Yerby's short fiction. When asked by James Hill if he writes short stories "now" (1977), Yerby simply says, "I don't have time.... There is nothing more difficult than condensation, and since any story is at least five hundred pages long, to reduce ... [it] to two and a half or three is major labor.... [A] short story is much more difficult than a novel" ("An Interview" 239). So it would appear that by the mid-1970s he had abandoned the genre, suggesting the unpublished stories held at the Gotlieb were written before the occasion of the interview. They could very well have been part of the "series of short stories" that Yerby mentioned in 1955 when *Ebony Magazine* did a feature on him titled "Mystery Man of Letters" (31). But because he began his long and prolific career as a novelist when he signed with Helen Strauss in 1944, publishing a novel every twelve to eighteen months for the remainder of his career, it is simply not clear when Yerby wrote most of his short fiction.

The first five stories in this collection represent the span of his published stories, from those he wrote while in school to those that appeared just before his first novel. "Salute to the Flag" originally appeared in *The Paineite* in 1936 and is likely Yerby's earliest published story. Told by way of the monologue of an unnamed African American narrator who has served in the US military, the story slowly reveals why the speaker chooses to offer an unconventional "salute" to the flag as he dies from a gunshot wound. As he explains to the "Doc" who tends his wound why he does not show more respect to the American flag, readers are taken on a short tour of the physical and psychological violence experienced by soldiers during times of war. Coming in at around two pages the story is indeed short, but in that brief span it manages to question not only what constitutes ethical and humane action during times of war, but also to explore the politics of race, space, and national identity.

In 1944 "White Magnolias" was published in *Phylon*, a semiannual, peer-reviewed journal that was established by W. E. B. Du Bois in 1940. It is primarily the story of Beth, a young, southern white woman who is home from college in a southern town, who is looking forward to a visit from Hannah Simmons, an African American girl she met at a conference while at school. Demonstrating an early interest in whiteness that he would explore throughout much of his career, this story reveals the deep, troubling, and unreflected-upon foundation of Beth's identity as a white woman as she unexpectedly begins to imagine a social tea, such as the one they are enjoying, as it would have been held during the period of slavery. The story not only highlights her insensitivity, but also suggests the difficult journey she must undertake to become the progressive modern woman she believes herself to be.

The very next year Yerby published a story in *Common Ground*, a quarterly magazine that "included . . . both fiction and non-fiction that sought to educate the larger population about various aspects of the ethnic and immigrant experience" (Niiya). "Roads Going Down" focuses on the relationship between father and son, Rafe and Robert. Free-spirited and adventurous, Robert is coming into manhood, and his father, sensitive to the needs his son may have for friends and romantic interests, has suggested they move to the city. Before they leave, Robert wanders to a local lake at dusk to see it by moonlight, but he is privy to more than just lake views during his excursion and soon finds himself under attack and left for dead after witnessing a young white couple naked in the lake. The black gaze leveled upon whiteness is a source of terror and crisis, apparently for all involved. Robert immediately recognizes the danger he has stumbled into by his accidental act of witnessing, but the response of the white couple is also problematized when they lie about the incident, leaving the reader to wonder who feels more vulnerable in this chance encounter, and why. The next day, the two fathers—one white and one black—confront each other over the incident, and Robert's view of his father, and his life, is forever altered.

"The Homecoming," published in 1946 (also in *Common Ground*), follows Sergeant Willie Jackson, an African American military veteran, as he returns to his childhood home in the South after having served in World War II. When Jackson disembarks from the train, he immediately comes under the surveillance of a group of white men sitting nearby. But the soldier who returns is not the same young man who left. The tension of the story grows as Jackson refuses to silently submit to the racism and Jim Crow actions of the community, challenges that bring him into direct conflict with the white establishment, including a white benefactor who refuses to understand why he does not want to return to his former job on the plantation. Seeking to establish his sense of self through particular performances of black masculinity, Jackson struggles to extricate himself from the racism that refuses to acknowledge his emancipated self and that co-opts his performances of resistance and freedom.

Published in *Tomorrow* in 1946, "My Brother Went to College" has a more contemporary feel and centers on the reunion of two African American brothers, one who has led a nomadic life with little responsibility (Mark), the other who remained in their childhood community, pursued education, and became a doctor (Matt). Questions of race and class riddle the story. As Mark is introduced to and into the middle-class black community that his brother now inhabits, he ponders which of them had achieved freedom more fully through the choices they had made. Had Mark, through his care-free lifestyle, been more successful and happy, or had his brother achieved these attributes through his financial successes that seemed to render race irrelevant? Many years later when he is a successful pharmacist, family man, and business owner himself, Mark recalls a conversation between him and his brother that makes him question whether their "freedom" as black men is all that it appears to be.

The remaining stories in this collection have not been previously published and have been chosen for their diversity in subject matter and style. They truly demonstrate the range of interests and talents Yerby had as an intellectual and writer. Some themes are explored across a range of stories (and, in fact, novels), while others seem to evidence a willingness to experiment with genres, subject matter, settings, and voice. "Pride's Castle," for instance, is a story that echoes the style of the historical romance for which Yerby became famous, and may have even been an early exploration for a novel of the same name. It opens with a lush, multisensory description of a southern garden over which a lone woman, Sharon, gazes. The garden, as beautiful as it is, however, has something ever-so-slightly amiss that reminds

Sharon of its artifice, its imperfect attempt to appear perfectly natural. Sharon, too, feels like her life is off kilter, that the outward appearance of things is a façade that masks a painful and ugly truth. It is a theme that Yerby returned to many times in his career, especially in novels set in the antebellum and Reconstruction-era South, and especially in novels that focused on white lives. As is the case in this story, much of his work subtly challenges fictions about the South and contests white moral and cultural superiority through his complex and often unflattering rendering of whiteness. As Sharon stares thoughtfully at the garden, she sees her niece, Caprice, heading toward her, and soon it is revealed that a tragedy has struck their home and many family secrets are about to be made public. Sharon must decide whether to confront her life's choices or to keep up the façade she has been living.

Another consistency in Yerby's work, as several scholars have noted, is that he conducted meticulous research for his novels. When talking about his writing process, Yerby admitted that he researched exhaustively and "repeatedly loaded . . . [his novels] with history" (Yerby, "How and Why" 145). It is hard to know whether he was happy about the fact that "ninety-nine and ninety-nine one-hundredths of said history land[s] on the Dial Press cutting-room floor," but in the unpublished story "The Schoolhouse of Compere Antoine," much of the historical detail remained intact, giving the reader the feeling of being transported to a different time as the events of history unfold (Yerby, "How and Why" 145). This ability to immerse his reader in another time and place through his writing was a skill Yerby was known for. Set during and in the years following the Civil War, the story follows the saga of Compere Antoine, who is an old man when New Orleans is freed by Union soldiers in 1862. Antoine tries to live a quiet life until he witnesses a teacher from the North being harassed as she arrives in town. His intervention in the scene sets him on a path that he never anticipated for himself and has a profound impact on the community he calls home. In exploring a character who is not young, not dashing, and not able to steer the plot as a force of will, Yerby recognizes that questions of masculinity and manhood are not limited to people under a certain age. True to the historical realities of the time, the story questions the difference one man can make in a system designed to benefit the few over the many.

In the almost dream-like "Myra and the Leprechaun," the focus shifts to a female lead character, which significantly alters the trajectory of a story that is essentially about how to be true to oneself. Myra Tilden, a young teacher at a small, rural school, contemplates the direction she wants her romantic and professional lives to go. For a woman in her time, however, the two questions are interrelated, as Myra well knows. She is courted by the principal of her school who is much older and in whom she has no interest. The "Leprechaun" is Tony, a man around her age who frolics at the lake at night, playing a harmonica as a young deer skips and dances around him. She is immediately drawn to him; something about him is untamed and free and it resonates with her in ways she does not understand. While not a feminist manifesto, the story does at least ask the question of what brings joy to women, not presuming that the answer is inextricably tied to a respectable partner or career. Faced with pursuing respectability or passion, one of which will provide security while the other promises a different kind of fulfillment, Myra finds herself questioning not only her community's expectations, but her own sensibilities about who she is.

Reading like a gritty noir novel, "The Quality of Courage" begins as Johnny Saunders arrives home to witness his father being killed during a hurricane. This horrifying event sets him in motion to find the murderers and exact revenge. As he closes in on his prey, this crime fiction short story has him entangled in a lover's triangle, a sex-trafficking scheme, and the violence of a petty crime ring, causing him to question everything he knew about his father and the path he is on for his own future. The stark differences in masculine performances that Johnny witnesses and interacts with—from the beefy and brutal crime boss, Tim McCain, to Croaker, the seemingly reluctant enforcer who gives advice as a father would—forces the young man to decide which version of manhood he will embrace.

Kathleen and Rod are unhappily married in "Danse Macabre," but what begins as a modern rendering of a marriage headed for divorce unexpectedly turns toward the bizarre. Though Kathleen and Rod are antagonistic and overtly hostile to one another, they nevertheless plan an evening out at the Sepia Club, where all of the performers are black. As Rod overindulges in alcohol and becomes intoxicated, he becomes more inappropriate in his behavior toward his wife and one of the female dancers. Retaliation is swift, and for him as a white patron of the club, quite unexpected. He finds himself the object of an impromptu, primal number performed by a male dancer in the show. Unsure of what is happening within or around him, he flees the club with Kathleen trailing reluctantly behind him. Rod's insecurities and fears are exposed, his assumptions of power and privilege undermined, leading him to a reckoning fit for his misogyny and racism.

Also exploring the realities that cannot be easily understood, in "The Italian Ghost of Monte Carlo" we first meet John Bridges after he has made a mistake that could cost him his pride, his job, and his freedom. He had been hustled by a pretty girl who took a large sum of money from him, a deposit that he was supposed to have made for his company. He retreats to a hotel room to commit suicide rather than face prison. Pursuing courage at the bottom of a bottle to follow through on his plan, he is interrupted by a supernatural presence who says she can restore him in an unexpected way. In an unusual exploration of faith and fate, John must decide whether to believe the ghost who promises to help or to follow his original plan of action.

"Supper for Louie," a story set after a period of armed conflict for the US, centers on Annie May, a dark-skinned African American woman who learned to despise her appearance as a child. As an adult, she does not think herself beautiful and concludes she will never have a fulfilling relationship. When she meets Louie, a handsome West Indian man, she is immediately attracted to him, but does not feel herself worthy of his attention. In an unusually poignant presentation of a woman's heart, the story exposes Annie May's low self-esteem, which is the direct result of a society that refuses to see beauty that does not adhere to standards established by white society. Annie May begins a journey that might alleviate her insecurities, but is Louie the man who will love and appreciate her, or a charlatan out to take advantage of her lonely heart?

In a turn from the rural settings and historical periods that characterize many of Yerby's stories, "The Invasion on Chauncy Street" carries an unmistakable urban vibe. Woodrow is a young black man coming into adulthood. He is clearly of a different generation, using slang that his parents do not understand and wearing clothes that his father does not approve of, but the family is close and supportive of one another. Woodrow, however, is more impatient with the racism and discrimination that impact his life, and less willing to wait for the slow process of social change to improve his opportunities. One afternoon when he comes home from work, his parents tell him that the family is moving out of their apartment to a house just outside of the city. The neighbors, however, are not pleased about their arrival; they will be the first family to integrate Chauncy Street. When the family is attacked on their moving-in day, Woodrow and his father act to protect their home. But who will protect them?

Also exploring the meaning and importance of home, in "Drink the Evening Star" we meet Tad, an African American military serviceman from New England who has been stationed in the South. His homesickness is made all the more acute because, as an educated man, he does not find many men in his unit with whom he can relate, leading to even more isolation. He seeks the distraction of a woman's company but finds that not only is the casual encounter unsatisfying, but it also actually increases his despair. It is not until he acknowledges that he misses his wife and their life together, and that he longs to play the piano again, that a path is revealed to ease his pain. Home, it seems, can come in many different forms.

Taking a different lens to the experience of wartime service, "Land of the Pilgrims' Pride" reveals the toll that hatred and bigotry, this time in the form of antisemitism, can leave on the hearts of its most vulnerable victims. Hank Morrison is married to a decorated nurse serving in the armed forces. When Ella makes a promise to a dying mother to take care of her Jewish son, Hank unexpectedly finds himself a single father to a boy he does not know from a culture with which he is unfamiliar. Hank looks forward to Emil's arrival, though, and commits to follows through on Ella's promise that they will raise the child as Jewish in the United States. But racism knows no borders, and Harry and his new son must confront the evil that Ella is fighting overseas right in their own community.

The final story of the collection, "A Wake for Reeves O'Donald," is a multi-voiced eulogy. The titular character, Reeves, has died and his friends have gathered to remember him. As they tell personal stories of how they came to know, respect, and love him, he is called into being over and over again, haunting the story as an apparition would. A picture of a life lived with dignity, goodness, and freedom, emerges. Reeves's legacy is counted not in the money and things he left behind, but the complicated, messy people he touched, suggesting a different definition of what it means to live life fully.

A Writer's Legacy

Yerby married his first wife, Flora Helen Claire Williams, in March 1941, and together they had four children: Jacques Loring, Nikki Ethlyn, Faune Ellena, and Jan Keith. Almost as soon as his first novel, *The Foxes of Harrow*, earned him enough money, the family began to travel abroad and eventually moved to France in 1951. But the marriage fell on difficult times after their expatriation for reasons only those in the relationship would ever know, and Flora and the children returned to the US. If the writing "My Most Inspiring Moment" is to be believed, shortly after their departure and while he was still trying to escape the painful turn his personal life had taken, Yerby drove from his home in Nice to Madrid to visit a friend. He met Blanca Calle-Perez on the day he arrived. That was April 1955. They were married on July 27, 1956.

Divorce is always difficult, and is perhaps hardest on the children who often do not know why their family is suddenly changing. Yerby settled into a new married life and pursued his calling as a writer in Madrid—Franco's Spain—returning to the United States less frequently as time passed. In Madrid, doors were not rudely closed in his face because of his race, and the money he earned from his writing afforded him and Blanca more than a comfortable standard of living. He seemed to have remained in contact with his siblings but did not have much interaction with his children. Whether that was by choice, circumstance, or imposition one can only guess. But whatever wealth he earned did not seem to impact the lives of his children, and there can be little doubt that the family was estranged. His children did not know him well and never believed his prolific career was part of their inheritance. In fact, they were surprised to learn in 2013 that one of their names was listed as the permission holder for the archive at the Gotlieb. It has taken six years, as of the time of this writing, for them to become comfortable enough in their roles as custodians of a small piece of his legacy to allow this publication to proceed.

While Yerby never lost his interest in the US as the context and setting for much of his writing, his many years in Spain also profoundly impacted him. As an expatriate he became fluent in Spanish, took on citizenship of his adopted country, and settled in some of the most upscale neighborhoods and homes in Madrid over the course of his nearly forty years there. According to several sources in Madrid, he loved sports cars and raced them along lightly populated roads throughout the country. Though he never lost his passion for travel and immersing himself in other cultural contexts, he did not return to the US often and eventually his editor worried that his appeal to American readers would wane as he increasingly thought and wrote in Spanish and translated his drafts to English. But his ability to be at home anywhere in the world (except the US, it seems) served him well given the amount of travel that was required to support the translation and publication of his novels in so many countries. Mireia Sentís, a photographer, publisher, and researcher familiar with Yerby's life in Madrid, discovered that Editorial Planeta, now one of Spain's most important media companies, was saved from closure through their publishing arrangements with Yerby in the 1950s. His success and popularity throughout Europe and the US also supported translators, printing companies, illustrators, and distributors. He made an impact on many lives through the business side of his long career.

Despite his substantial and extensive business connections, however, when Yerby died on November 30, 1991, at the age of seventy-six, only Blanca was at his funeral. Ever the loner, at his request at least five weeks elapsed before any notices of his death were released. His tombstone at Cementerio de la Almudena reads simply, "Frank G. Yerby Smythe (Escritor)," followed by the name of his wife of thirty-five years, Blanca Calle Perez, who is buried next to him. By the time of his death he had published thirty-three novels with an impressive record: "[T]hree were translated into film, one for television; twelve were bestsellers; almost all were selections of the Book of the Month Club; they have been translated into over thirty languages; and, to date, over sixty million copies of them have been sold around the world" (Jarrett 197).

While clearly popular, most of Yerby's novels were not well regarded by critics, a fact that did not seem to bother him early in his career. But his desire to be considered a serious author rather than exclusively a writer of popular fiction asserted itself more strongly later in his life. By the early to mid 1960s, letters between him and his agent indicate Yerby was dissatisfied with the insistence of Dial Press (his long-time publisher) that he keep writing the formulaic fiction that had gained him an audience and commercial success. Yerby felt they had encouraged, and at times pressured, him into conforming to a particular style of writing to increase sales. By the 1960s, however, he was quite tired of the limitations being placed on his creativity and was pushing hard to write the great novel of which he felt himself capable. He wrote to his agent, Helen Strauss, "I should like to be allowed to make up for my literary sins by writing some good books before I die" (Yerby letter, April 16, 1964). It is not clear that he believed he ever accomplished that goal.

It is also not clear when or why he committed time to writing more than twenty short stories when his career was going so well as a novelist, or why they were never published individually or as a collection. Was it his idea to return to the genre that had launched his career, or a publisher's way to introduce him to a broader readership? Were stories too dissimilar from the fiction he was becoming known for, or did he have trouble finding a publisher willing to take a chance on a collection of short stories? These are questions we will perhaps never know, but as with so much of his work, Yerby had the foresight to have the stories sent to his archive, a repository for the future. Perhaps he sent them to the Gotlieb for a time such as this.

As slow as the critical engagement with Yerby's work has been, it will ultimately be incomplete—and thus an evaluation of Yerby as a writer and intellect incomplete—if we do not take stock of his short fiction. Here he grappled with the impact of race and racism on black and white Americans, the possibility of love as a redemptive force, the meaning of manhood and the performances of masculinity open to men of differing racial and ethnic backgrounds, and the role of fate and supernatural forces in human life. He explored different writing styles and genres and allowed himself to be vulnerable as a writer. Perhaps had more of his short fiction been published during his lifetime, he would have been taken more seriously. Unfortunately, that did not happen. But I believe it is not too late for Yerby's short fiction to save him from obscurity and redeem him as a writer.

Notes

Parts of this essay also appear in Matthew Teutsch, ed., *Rediscovering Frank Yerby: Critical Essays* (University Press of Mississippi, 2020).

1. The O. Henry Memorial Award is widely regarded as the most prestigious award for short fiction. Yerby was only the second black writer to be awarded an O. Henry Memorial Award. Richard Wright won the accolade for "Fire and Cloud," published in *Story Magazine* in 1938. He won it a second time in 1940 for "Almos' a Man," published in *Harper's Bazaar*.

2. As access to public education expanded at the turn of the twentieth century in the United States, it was strictly segregated in most states. One of Georgia's first publicly funded high schools for African Americans, Ware High School, was established in Augusta in 1880. However, it was closed in 1897 by the Richmond School Board, which argued the funds should be used to support African American *primary* schools instead. The case went to the Supreme Court as *Cumming v. Board of Education of Richmond County*, where the school closing was upheld. Augusta did not have another public high school for black students until 1945.

3. Yerby's experimentation with different writing styles and contexts continued throughout his career. Not only are twenty-eight of his poems preserved at the Gotlieb, but prospectuses for two television series are also held there, one entitled *County Sheriff* and the other called *Destination Danger*.

Works Cited

"Author Frank Yerby, 76, Dies; Buried in Spain." *Jet*, vol. 81, no. 14, 27 Jan. 1992, pp. 12–13.

Boddie, Ellena. Letter to H. B. Gotlieb. 1 July 1965. Frank Yerby Papers, Howard Gotlieb Archival Research Center, Boston.

Bone, Robert. *The Negro Novel in America*. Yale University Press, 1958.

Carter, James. Personal interview. 4 Aug. 2015.

Folkart, Burt A. "Frank Yerby; Novelist Felt Rejected by His Native South." *Los Angeles Times*, 9 Jan. 1992, p. 22. ProQuest Newsstand.

Glasrud, Bruce A., and Laurie Champion. "'The Fishes and the Poet's Hands': Frank Yerby, A Black Author in White America." *Journal of American and Comparative Cultures*, vol. 23, no. 4, Winter 2000, pp. 15–22. EBSCOhost Online.

Graham, Maryemma. "Frank Yerby, King of the Costume Novel." *Essence*, no. 6, October 1975, pp. 70+.

Hill, James L. "An Interview with Frank Garvin Yerby." *Resources for American Literary Study*, vol. 21, no. 2, 1995, pp. 206–39.

Hill, James L. "Frank Garvin Yerby." *Writers of the Black Chicago Renaissance*. University of Illinois Press, 2011, pp. 386–412.

Jarrett, Gene Andrew. "Frank Yerby (1915–1991)." *African American Literature Beyond Race: An Alternative Reader*. New York University Press, 2006, pp. 197–201.

Millender, Mallory. Personal interview. 5 Aug. 2015.

"Mystery Man of Letters." *Ebony*, no. 10, Feb. 1955, pp. 31–32, 35–38.

National Park Service. "Public Elementary and Secondary Schools in Georgia, 1868–1971. https://georgiashpo.org/sites/default/files/hpd/pdf/Historic_Schools_Context_0.pdf. Accessed 5 May 2019.

Niiya, Brian. "Common Ground (magazine)." *Densho Encyclopedia*. 31 Aug. 2015, 19:07 PDT. 4 May 2019, 15:4 https://encyclopedia.densho.org/Common%20Ground%20(magazine)/.

Schaap, Dick. "Frank Yerby, Expert in Pap Comes Up with an Angry Novel." *Detroit News*, November 7, 1968, p. E1.

Sentís, Mireia. Personal interview. 13 June 2014.

Yerby, Frank. "How and Why I Write the Costume Novel." *Harper's Magazine*, Oct. 1959, pp. 145–50.

Yerby, Frank. Letter to Helen Strauss. 13 Oct. 1962. Frank Yerby Papers, Howard Gotlieb Archival Research Center, Boston.

Yerby, Frank. Letter to Helen Strauss. 16 Apr. 1964. Frank Yerby Papers, Howard Gotlieb Archival Research Center, Boston.

Yerby, Frank. "My Most Inspiring Moment." 31 Aug. 1964. Frank Yerby Papers, Howard Gotlieb Archival Research Center, Boston.

Yon, B. "Expatriate Writer, Frank Yerby, Is Grousing Even Though His 30th Bestseller Is Coming Up." *People*, 30 Mar. 1981, p. 99+.

PREVIOUSLY PUBLISHED

Salute to the Flag

"Thanks, Doc; but it ain't no use. I've seen too many men gut-shot in my day. What we riding so slow for? You say that second slug ripped me across, and my guts'll come loose if we bounce? Funny . . . I saw a shell splinter rip a horse open outside of Fleville. He kept walking around in circles until his feet got tangled up in his guts and he fell down. God, how the poor beast screamed. What's that? You never heard a horse scream? They sound just like a child.

Sure I was in the War. Three hundred sixty-fifth, New York. Our officers were white though. Captain Smith, the finest white man, God ever put breath into. You say I mustn't talk? Hell, Doc, I might as well talk, I'm going out.. I know that; you don't get up and walk away with a forty-five through the guts. Sure I know it was a fool trick to thumb my nose at the flag, but I couldn't help it. Every time I see the damned thing I boil over. Thank those cops for getting me away from that mob, won't you? Why do I feel like that about the flag? That's a long story, Doc.

You see, we colored boys who joined up had a heap of crazy notions in our heads. We thought we were really making the world safe for Democracy and all that tripe. We had a feeling, somehow, that when we came back that the white folks would have changed their ideas about us. We didn't mind risking our lives. You see, Doc, we had hope. Hope that when we got back we'd find a different world; a world where there wouldn't be no Jim Crow, no lynching, where a man would be a man, no matter what color he was. Of course it was a pipe dream. I found that out before I even left France.

Thanks Doc, that sure makes me feel better. You see Doc, I had a pal. Young fellow* just out of college. Don't know why we teamed up. He was as smart as a steel-trap, and they had to burn the school down to get me out of eighth grade. He got to be Lieutenant. Name was Jones – Bob Jones. His mother used to come to the training camp and bring him cake. Called him

---

*Yerby's original spelling and punctuation have been left intact throughout.

3

Bobby. But he was all man though. Tall, handsome brown skinned boy. He was seasick all the way over. We got to Calais in August, 1918.

What you moving me for Doc? Oh I see you got to prop my middle up so I won't bleed so fast. What was I saying? Oh yes – we landed at Calais in August. Dirty, foggy places. They kept us in another training camp until the last of September. Then they shipped us to the front. Up to a little place called Vienne-le-Chateau. Yeah-it's just north of the Aisne right at the entrance of the Muese-Argonne forest. Yeah, we went through the forest. It was hell, all right. I remember one day, just before we got out of the woods, we got stopped by a machine gun nest. Bob and me wiggled through the brush 'til we got within twenty feet of the gun. Then Bob tossed a Mills. Yeah, a Mills is a hand grenade. You pull the pin out with your teeth and toss it quick. It goes off in five seconds. Well it put the gun out of section all right. But when we got there we found only one man. A little skinny Bavarian kid. He couldn't have been more than sixteen. He was chained to the gun. That grenade had certainly messed him up proper. Both his legs and a part of his chest was gone. But he was alive. He kept moaning and begging us to finish him. Bob took his pistol out, put it to the kid's mouth and blew the back of his head off. Then he sat down and cried like a baby.

Can't we go a little faster Doc? O.K. you know best. You see this, Doc? Well it's the Croix de Guerre. Bob got one too. Only his had palms. How? He saved Captain Smith's life, that's what he did. No, it was at Fleville. Yeah, Fleville is just out of the Argonne forest on the Aire river. We got cut off by those Bavarian Blue Devils, and a regiment of Prussians between Fleville and Exermont. We was caught down between our own barrage and the Prussian's. We couldn't move up or retreat. We was being cut to pieces. Captain Smith wouldn't ask for volunteers to try to get through. That's the kind of a man he was. He put Bob over the handful of men that was left and started back, himself. He didn't get ten yards. A Prussian sniper saw him and let him have it through both legs. Bob told me to take charge and started out after him. I passed the buck to Rob White and started after Bob. We got him all right. There was a Scotch regiment over to the East of us. How far? Oh about two hundred yards. Yeah. Bob carried him all the way. Neither one of us got a hit. A miracle I'll say it was. Two hundred yards on your belly, dragging a wounded man and nary a scratch. The Germans called those Scots, Frauleine von Holle. Yeah, that means Ladies from Hell. You see they wore kilts. Well the way they drove through to save our boys you would have thought that hell was too tame a place for them.

Any way we both got the Croix. And ten days leave to Paris. That's where I found out that it didn't make no difference if you waded through blood for this country if you was black. Ain't nothing you do can excuse your being born a nigger. You fight, freeze and starve, or get six inches of bayonet rammed through your guts and it don't make no difference. That' why I hate that flag. You see I'd been with Bob from the Aisne to the Aire, I fought with him, bled with him, been hungry and cold with him, and in the end I had to watch him bleed to death outside a dirty little estammet in Paris, knifed in the back by a dirty Georgia cracker.

How'd it happen? Well we was out walking. On the Rue des something or another. Well a pretty little French girl came up. 'Pardonez moi, M'sieur,' she says, 'mais ou l'Estammet de Monsieur le Pape?' Right this way honey, he says, 'Vienez vous – oh hell, I don't know how to say it, but come with me, bebe.'

Of course I tagged along. Then we ran into these Georgia crackers. They'd just got over. It was an all-Georgia regiment. Then they saw Bob and Jeanette. She was looking up at him and smiling at his goshed awful French. They forgot they were six thousand miles from Georgia. All they could see was a nigger and a white woman. They swarmed all over us. When the M. P.'s got there, Bob was on the sidewalk dying, and I was out cold. The crackers were gone. They arrested me, but Jeanette testified in defense and I got off. Every time I see that flag I think about it.

What's that Doc? We're passing one now? Raise me up Doc, I want to salute it! Yeah, my own salute: thumb to my nose and fingers waving. What you say? It'll start a hemorrhage? That's all right, I'm going anyway. Please, Doc, please – my last request.

Thanks, Doc, thanks. . . . What's. . . . that noise? Blood. . . . Blood in my throat? So. . . . long. . . . Doc. . . . . thanks. . . . The . . . . . stars and stripes forever . . . . damn it!

White Magnolias

"The magnolia," Clinton Thomas said, "is like a woman — a beautiful Southern woman."

"You mean 'Lady,' don't you, Dad?" Beth's voice was edged with the lightest touch of malice.

"Of course. The magnolia is like a high born lady of the old South Beautiful and refined and — delicate — like your Mother, Beth."

"But Mother isn't the least bit delicate, Dad," Beth grinned. "She can wear down a houseful of servants and run you ragged to boot. And I'm not at all sure that what passes for refinement isn't pure ignorance — the kind of head empty of everything but trivia that you men seem to prize so in a woman."

"Beth!"

"I'm sorry, Dad. I'm being rude again." She stretched out her long legs, tanned almost golden, and stifled a yawn with the back of her hand.

"Got a cigarette, Dad?"

"Beth, how many times have I told you that —"

"That you distinctly disapprove of young girls smoking. About a million, I guess." She got up and walked over to where he sat and dropped into his lap. Then she put her hand into his inside coat pocket and came out with the monogrammed cigarette case. She opened it, took out a cigarette and put it in her mouth.

"Got a match, darlin'?"

"Along with your bad manners," Clinton fumed, "your grammar is deplorable. Here!"

"A high born Southern gentleman would have lit it for po lil me," she mocked. "How do you like my Southern accent, Dad?"

"You sound like a nigger. Get up. You're mussing up my clothes. You know I promised to take your mother to the club this afternoon."

Beth stood up and shook her tousled head that always looked like it had sunlight tangled in it, even on cloudy days. She looked out to wards the big magnolia tree heavy with blossoms. The sunlight came down between the polished green leaves and picked out the huge flowers. They lit up when the light hit them, and blazed briefly with white fire. The air was drenched with their perfume. Somehow, it made Beth faintly sick.

"Aren't you a little late now?" she said to her father. "Shouldn't you be leaving?"

"Your mother isn't ready yet. It's her only fault."

"You're gallant, Dad; but you aren't a bit truthful. Mother has a million faults: She's forgetful; she's a sloppy dresser; she —"

"Beth!"

"Oh, all right, I'll shut up. But I do wish she'd come on!"

Clinton frowned. He half turned in his chair and looked at his daughter. "What are you up to, Beth? You sound like you want us to leave."

"Truthfully, Dad o' mine, I do."

"Why?"

"I'm having a guest here for tea this afternoon. I — I'd rather you wouldn't be here when she comes."

"When *she* comes? H-mmm — a girl. What's wrong with her? If it were some young whippersnapper — but a girl, that's different. Is she a bad girl, Beth?"

"No, Daddy, she's a lovely girl — one of the nicest girls I know."

"Then why the blazes?"

Beth turned to her father and the corners of her mouth climbed upward slowly. Clinton could see the little golden sparkles of mischief breaking the surface of her blue eyes.

"Her name is Simmons, Dad, Hannah Simmons. And she happens to be a colored girl."

"What!"

"I met her at a conference," Beth went on sweetly, "an interracial conference. And to think we'd been living in the same town all our lives and didn't know each other!"

"She won't come here!" Clinton said, "I'll see to that! I'll — I'll —"

"Clinton, you're shouting again."

They both turned. Martha Thomas was standing on the terrace looking at her husband with mild disapproval.

"My dear," Clinton said, "I'm sorry. But do you know what this idiotic daughter of yours has done?"

"No," Martha smiled, "no — what?"

"She's invited a—a Nigra girl to luncheon in my house!"

Martha reached up and patted her husband's tie back into place.

Her slip's showing, Beth thought irrelevantly. Poor Mom, she's always such a fright!

"There, there, dear," Martha cooed, "you always did get things wrong! What Beth means is she's hired this girl to serve her friends at luncheon. Isn't that right, dear?"

"No, Mom, that isn't right. I invited Hannah Simmons to be my guest at luncheon. She isn't going to serve anybody. She's going to be waited on. I want her to be treated decently. She's a very nice girl — she's a graduate of Fisk and vice-president of the International League — that's how I met her."

"But Beth," Martha said helplessly, "I'm afraid I don't understand —"

"She won't come in this house!" Clinton thundered.

"Now, dear, you know you mustn't shout. Why with your blood pressure —"

"Hang my blood pressure! I won't have a Nigra wench eating at my table!"

"Tildy does it," Beth observed, "and old George —"

"That's different! They're house servants, been in this family for generations — but this girl —"

"Is the daughter of one of your oldest and best friends. Why you and Doctor Simmons are just like that." And Beth crossed one finger over the other.

"This girl is Tad Simmons' daughter?"

"Yes, Dad. You don't seem to be bothered by his color —"

"Tad Simmons is a good doctor. If it wasn't for him half the white families in this town would be diseased."

"Now *I* don't follow you, Clint," Martha said; "what's this colored doctor got to do with the health of white people? You don't mean to tell me he treats white patients!"

"A few — poor whites mostly. But that's not what I mean. If he didn't keep the servants free of infection —"

"I see. And he sent this girl of his off to school and you met her at some kind of conference — what did you say it was, Beth?"

"An interracial conference. We used to get together to try to solve the race problem —"

"There isn't any race problem," Clinton said. "The South solved it years ago. Treat the Negro kindly, but keep him in his place."

The crinkles deepened in the corners of Beth's eyes.

"What is his place, Dad?"

"Just what you see around you. They make good servants, but their mentality is limited."

"Dad — Hannah's father learned medicine. And her brother is graduating this year — from Harvard."

"Exceptions. When this girl comes, Beth, I expect you to politely but firmly turn her away. Come, my dear."

"Wait, Clint, I want to see this girl. The old club can wait. I want to see what a colored girl looks like who's been to college."

"Martha, of all the idiotic notions —"

"You go on, dear; I'll have Henry drive me."

"No. I'll wait for you. I don't trust Beth. I'd better have a word with this girl myself."

"Daddy, you wouldn't dare!"

"Wouldn't I?" He settled down grimly in the big chair. Martha sat down beside him. Beth kept walking back and forth looking down the walk that curved past the magnolia tree. Clinton pulled out his big gold watch and looked at it.

"When is she coming?" he asked.

"Now," Beth said breathlessly and went flying down the walk like a colt.

Hannah was coming up the walk looking up at the magnolias. She was dressed in a trim suit of unbleached linen. It looked expensive — terribly expensive. Seeing it, Beth's heart sank. Dad will be furious seeing her dressed like that, she thought. But she extended her hand and took Hannah by the arm.

"I'm late," Hannah said; "I just couldn't get away earlier. There were so many people —"

"You're popular," Beth said. "You should be. You know, Han, you're the prettiest colored girl I've seen."

"You haven't seen many. The right kind I mean." She stopped still and looked up at the flowers.

"I hate magnolias," she said. "They always meant something to me something unpleasant — like useless beauty that can't even stand a breath. But I'm being silly. They really are beautiful, aren't they?"

"Han —"

"Yes, Beth?"

"Dad is at home — and Mother. Dad — just might be rude. He's a dear, but he's hopelessly old fashioned. — If he makes any cracks, just ignore him, won't you? He really is very kind —"

"So my father says. But perhaps I'd better not come in."

"Oh, come on! If Father doesn't meet you, he never will be cured."

The two girls came around the curve past the tree and mounted the steps, brown legs and white moving in unison. When they reached the place where Beth's parents sat, they stopped.

"Hannah," Beth said clearly, "I want you to meet my folks. This is my dad, Doctor Thomas, and my mother. And this," she said, drawing Hannah closer, "is Miss Simmons."

Clinton looked like he was strangling; but Martha managed a barely audible "How do you do?"

"My father speaks of you often, Doctor Thomas," Hannah said; "he admires you greatly."

"Huhmmurrumph," Clinton said, "Hmfmph."

"Sit down, Han," Beth said.

Hannah sank into a chair. A little half smile was playing about her mouth. One corner of her lips curved upward, but the other drooped a bit before it followed suit.

It makes her look mysterious, Beth thought, sort of wise and exotic —

Martha was looking the girl over from head to heel. Suddenly she found her voice.

"You know, Hannah," she said, "you're a very pretty girl."

"Thank you," Hannah murmured.

"I think it's going to be a handicap. Not many women in this town will hire a girl as pretty as you for a maid. They wouldn't trust you — or their husbands."

Beth's face crimsoned. She could feel the waves of heat traveling down her spine.

Hannah smiled.

"Oh, I shan't look for a job for quite a while," she said; "I'm going back to school."

"But I thought Beth said you graduated this year."

"I did. But Dad's sending me up to Boston U to do graduate work in the social sciences."

"Mother," Beth said pointedly, "isn't it getting late?"

Martha ignored her.

"You talk beautifully," she said to Hannah. "How'd you like to come to work for me? Just for the summer I mean — or longer if you'd give up this foolish notion about postgraduate study. I have the feeling you'd be quite a treasure."

"Mother!" Beth began, but Hannah silenced her with a small wave of her hand.

"I'm sorry, Mrs. Thomas," she said, "but I'm afraid it's quite out of the question."

"Why?" Clinton growled suddenly.

"I'm afraid I wouldn't make a very good maid, sir. I wouldn't know what to do and I'm quite sure I lack the proper humility."

"And what does your father have to say about that?" Clinton asked.

"I don't know. He wants me to be happy. He wouldn't want me different from the way I am."

"You father's a good man," Clinton said heavily. "There isn't a finer colored man in the state. He knows his place. You can't make me believe he'd stand for this sort of thing!"

"Yet," Martha said, "he's sent his boy to Harvard — where our Rod is."

"Dang blast it, Martha, I never thought of that! Making good money — so he's trying to buy his children out. But let me tell you — all the money and all the education in the world won't make a white man out of a nigger! All it does is to make the critter miserable. Wanting things he never can have. Forgetting he's black and trying to act white. Getting into all sorts of trouble —"

"Clint, dear," Martha said, "don't you think we'd better be going?"

"Yes, yes — just a minute. Young woman, you tell your father I want to see him. And I want it distinctly understood that I don't approve of this — visiting back and forth between you and Beth. No, no — don't get up. You can stay as long as you like — this evening, but after this —"

"I understand perfectly, sir," Hannah said.

The two of them went down the steps to the drive where Henry waited with the car.

"Oh Han," Beth wailed, "I'm so sorry!"

"It's all right; I should have expected it." She smiled quite suddenly. "You know, Beth, this is something very like social equality — and that would never do!"

"Come on," Beth said, "let's go inside. We'll have tea in the sun parlor."

They got up and walked through deep carpeted rooms and sat down before the little tea table in the glass enclosed parlor. Tildy came in with the silver service on a tray, but when she saw Hannah she dropped it. The tea made a brown stain on the carpet.

She gathered up the tray and the tea cups and fled from the room. Just outside the door she stopped.

"Mis Beth," she called, "Oh, Mis Beth!"

Beth got up and went into the hall. Hannah lit a cigarette and waited.

"Yo paw gonna kill you, chile," Tildy's voice came through the door; "he gonna skin you alive! Bringing dat gal in heah! You knows yo paw doan low no niggers in heah. Whut you thinkin bout, chile? Is you done lost yo min?"

"Hush, Tildy! Hannah's my guest and I don't want her feelings hurt!"

"Effen you doan git huh outa heah sumpin else sides huh feelins gonna git hurt!"

Beth looked at Tildy.

"Bring us some more tea, Tildy," she said very quietly.

"Yasm," Tildy mumbled, "yasm. I brings it right erway!"

Beth went back into the sun parlor and sat down beside Hannah.

"I could cry," she said. "I could bawl like a kid!"

"Please don't. It's nothing. After nineteen years you get a hide like a rhino."

"Why didn't you let me tell them? About your fellowship and the job with the Whitteby people? About your scholastic record?"

"What good would it have done? When you finished, your mother would have still offered me a maid's job."

"Oh, my God! *You!* You should have a maid yourself."

"I have had. But they don't stay. They think it's a disgrace to work for their own color."

"How stupid! But I still can't get over Dad and Mother —"

"I would look nice in a neat black uniform. With a white ruffled apron and a little cap. Your mother could see that. The rest — the rest is absolutely incomprehensible — like a monkey talking Greek."

"Oh, Han!"

"I'm sorry. I was being bitter. Forgive me, won't you? And for heaven's sake let's change the subject."

Beth sat across the tea table looking at her friend. She wanted to talk. She wanted horribly to say something clever, but she couldn't. And the silence lay between them like something that could be almost felt. The clinking of the spoons in the tea cups was drowned in it, reaching the ear faintly, unnoticed, forgotten.

Hannah put her cup down and looked out toward the front of the house where the magnolia tree was catching the last light of the evening. The big white flowers swam in a golden haze, silver white — immaculate.

"They *are* lovely," Hannah said.

"Dad says they're like a woman," Beth blurted, "a lovely lady of the old South. Delicate and refined — and pure. We aren't like that nowadays. It must have been a wonderful life. Hoop skirts and crinolines. Dancing on the terrace — and a gracious Southern gentleman bending over your hand. Duels under the old oak — you can see it from here, Han. And the scent of jasmine and white lilacs and magnolias —"

She stopped quite suddenly. The lovely ladies in the hoop skirts weren't there any longer. Instead there was only the long line of black men and women in their faded rags moving between the stalks of the cotton. And the auctioneer was holding open a black man's mouth to show his fine teeth. And the slow heartbreaking songs rose up from the little cabins and the stench of black flesh drowned out the jasmine.

Slowly Hannah's face relaxed and the stiffness flowed out of her limbs. She stood up.

"Yes," she said, "it must have been a wonderful life."

She walked through the house and out the front door. On the terrace she turned.

"Goodbye, Beth," she said. But Beth caught her arm and the two of them went down the walk together. Under the Magnolia tree, Beth suddenly stopped. She reached up and broke off a low hanging flower. Then slowly and ceremoniously, searching Hannah's face, she tore the heavy, waxen petals into shreds.

Hannah stood very still watching her, her eyes dark in her pale brown face.

"Thank you, Beth," she said, and she was gone, running down the walk, her high heels kicking up little spurts of gravel.

Roads Going Down

It is like this in northern Georgia: there are hills instead of the endless flatlands, and the pines stand up naked for more than a hundred feet before they are crowned with a crest of green. In the earth there are more stones than in all the broad sweep of cotton fields stretching out to the south, and the air is cooler. Up near the Tennessee line, the hills steepen into mountains. The fogs collect in the hollows in the morning, so that standing on a shelf rock you can look up at a clear blue sky and down at the pine tops poking their trunkless and disembodied tops through the swirling mists.

It was this that the boy Robert liked to do first in the morning, getting up early before his father was awake and climbing with long loping steps the trail that curved upward, going while it was still dark, moving upward over the fogwet rocks through the blue haze where the spruce and pine moved dimly in the air. "Chasin the sun up," he called it, smiling, showing all his teeth white and even in his black face. "I goes up while it still dark down below, an when I git to the top, I done raise up the sun, so I got daylight. Down there," pointing, "it still night."

The boy's father, old Rafe, did not stop him in his wanderings. He was an old man, old indeed even when Robert was born, and between them there was little communication. Rafe cut the trees, slash pine for the paper mills, cordwood for burning, and took them down the slow winding trails for fifty miles to Atlanta, driving all the way behind a mule as old and quiet as himself. Robert helped his father when he felt like it, and when he didn't, he simply wandered off. Old Rafe never checked him, and his mother was long since dead.

In the evenings, the old man sat before the big stone fireplace and read the Bible by the light of the pine knots. He taught Robert to read from it, and they took turns reading aloud to each other. Often they simply sat and stared into the flickering firelight, dreaming old dreams and young dreams, centuries apart.

"Oughta git erway frum heah," Rafe would say, "go down to the city, give you a chanct."

"What fur? We got everything. We got a house, we got vittles, an when we needs money you sells the wood. Whatcha wan to go fur? Ain pretty in th city. All dirt an smoke." He looked at his father, his voice softening, "An up heah, paw, we got—mountains."

"I knows, I knows," the old man said, "but you oughta have frens—young frens. You gitting big now. Fo long you be wantin you a gal."

Robert looked into the fire. "Be nice t have a gal," he said. "Be kinda nice to git some real booklearnin. Awright, paw, we go—next year. I'm sleepy. Bes be gittin to bed."

The fog crept down into the valleys and swirled around the boles of the trees. The sky purpled into night and pinned a tiara of stars above the low, rounded crests of the southern mountains. And the wind poured small, lost whispers through the dwarf spruce. In the cabin, the old man slept.

But the boy was kneeling by the glassless casement of the window looking out over the mountains. Already it was Spring and the air was warm, smelling of clover and cow dung, and the perfume of laurel. The fire, needless now for warmth, used only for reading, had burned itself out, so that in the cabin it was dark.

"Wonder how Loon Lake look right now," the boy whispered. "Never been there at night. Bright night lak this go there easy. Full moon now, bright as day. Paw woan know. Sleepin lak a log."

He stood up and tiptoed to the door. A little wind pushed against it as it opened, and the hinges creaked loudly. Robert drew in his breath sharply looking back through the darkness to where old Rafe lay on his pallet. The old man sighed, and the boy was frozen. Then it was still again and Robert was gone out of the cabin, running softly across the flat table rock on which it stood and dropping down the trail, his feet making a little scurrying on the rocks.

The lake was in a little valley that was not really a valley after all. It was a place where the steepness leveled off into a plateau, and the grass grew green and the trees were tall and untwisted by any wind. In the middle there was a large sink, into which all the mountain streams emptied themselves, making a little lake that rose until it spilled in the Spring over the last barrier of the rocks and cascaded in a narrow waterfall for three hundred feet into the real valley below.

Around it, the rocks were high like a wall, and the trees came down very close, dipping their branches into the water, so that, until you were very close, you could not see the lake at night. And sometimes, rarely, the great blue herons up from Florida rested there for a night, and sent their hideous booming out over the water. But no one had ever seen them there, and Robert had never been able to find anyone who had actually heard them booming, but still the story stuck (sometime in de night de ole loon come an bellow lak a mule—deys hants dere, boy, I tells you!) and the name.

The trails going down were steep, but the moonlight was very clear so that he could pick out every twig and every loose stone. Robert went very quietly, from force of habit rather than from any fear, moving as a woods thing moves, with grace and surety. Once when the trail curved sharply, he thought he caught a glimpse of the lake, gleaming with moonsilver, but the trees came up out of the blackness and hid it at the next step so that he was never quite sure.

Then at last the ground was leveling off, so that no longer could he merely lift his foot and let himself drop step by half-running-step down the trail; now he had to walk, loping along like a blacker shadow in a world of shadows picked out by the moonlight.

And now he could see the lake glimmering through the trees, washed with moonfire. But as he came close, the shimmering was broken by the two great splashes so close that almost they were one splash, the water rising up like white wings and the darkness shattered.

Instantly he dropped to his belly and started worming his way through the brush to a place where the rocks were broken through and he could see the water. The silver was dancing crazily, spreading out, out, out on little wave tops until it broke against the sides of the rocks (moss green and slimy) in a little lapping. Then a head broke the blackness and another, the moonlight glistening down upon bare shoulders. The water glued the hair down to their heads but even from where he lay Robert could see that on one head it was long and very fair, streaming down wetly over the neck, splaying out golden net over the bare back as she broke water and swam expertly toward the rocks a little way from the ones behind which Robert was hiding.

She. A girl. Robert drew his breath in sharply.

Then they were climbing out upon the rocks in the moonlight that was almost as bright as day and lying there in the brush the black boy saw that they were naked. He knew then at once that he should be gone, that for him to see this that now he saw could mean death and worse, but they were so close that he could not move without their hearing.

So at first he closed his eyes, the fear in him very deep and dark, and clutching at his throat from the inside so that his breath was a choking tangle burning in his lungs. But then he opened them again. The girl was standing up, and running her fingers through her long golden hair, pushing it out and back, away from her shoulders. And her whiteness was like the mountain laurel or, more, like the dogwood when you've been wandering all day through the green woods and round a turn, finding it there, leaping out at you, a cool seafoam blaze of white, stopping your breath suddenly.

Watching, unable to turn his eyes away, Robert saw how it was with a young girl, everything with a softness and a roundness, in spite of the sapling slimness and colt-like length of limb. He lay very still, measuring out his breath into the air so that there would be no noise; but then the girl turned, and the droplets of water still clinging to the fair skin caught the light, glittering like diamonds.

He stood up suddenly, recklessly. And all the little loose stones slid out from under his feet and cascaded off the bigger rocks into the water making a little silver splashes. The white boy was on his feet at the same instant facing him, and Robert was staring into a face he knew almost as well as he knew his own.

"Joey!" the girl cried, doubled up grotesquely. "He saw us!"

"Whatcha doin here?" the boy demanded. "Yuh dirty spying black bastid!"

"I ain spying, Joey," Robert said, "I jes come t—"

But the white boy hit him then, hard across the mouth, so that his full lips broke against his teeth, and his tongue was hot and salt with blood taste.

"Doan hit me, Joey," Robert pleaded, "I ain gonna tell, I swears fo Gawd—"

"Yuh damn right yuh ain't a goin to tell! You won't never git outa here alive!"

Robert's fists came up then, blocking the white boy's blows, riding the punches, ducking under them, bobbing, wheeling, sidestepping. And the girl watching, forgetting to hide her secret body with her hands, whispered to herself, "He seen me! Like this he seen me! God almighty!"

Then, suddenly, all the fear was gone from Robert as though it never was, and he struck out in a fury, hooking Joey's head from left to right to left again. Then he sent his fist whistling into the white boy's stomach, and Joey went down abruptly upon the rocks. The black boy wheeled then and started to run, scrambling across the rocks.

But the girl dived into the bushes where their clothes were and came out with the bottle.

"Here," she cried, "he seen me! Don't let him git away!"

The rocks there were steep, and Robert had to turn and twist. Joey waited until he was scaling the side of one a few yards away, then he ran up close and threw the bottle. It turned over end by end catching the moonlight, gleaming silver. Then it crashed against the side of Robert's head in a bright shower, and afterwards came the blood. His hands clawed briefly against the rock, then he dropped down into the tall grass. The pair approached him, shivering a little in the rising wind.

"Is he daid?"

"Yeah—reckon so. C'mon, git your clo's on. We got to git th hell outa here!"

They went back toward the lake, and afterwards, clearly, came the rustle of garments. Robert lay very still until he could hear their footsteps going down. Then he was up, pressing his hand to his head where the hot, sticky ooze was slowing and stumbled blindly up the trail.

In the morning, the sun was hot and golden. Robert lay on the pallet with his head bandaged with clean sheeting. He twisted miserably under his father's eyes.

"Ain'tcha gonna tell me?" Rafe asked gently.

"I done tole you, Paw," the boy said. "I cain't tell you, I jes cain't!"

The old man went to the doorway and looked out down to where the trail went curving down the mountainside. Above the cabin, the laurel were beginning to whiten, and lower down the dogwood made Spring snow.

"You ain hurt bad," he said. "I jes doan want you in no trouble. You ain in no trouble, is you son?"

"Naw, Paw," Robert said softly.

"Awright, son, you go to sleep now. I go out an git some stuff to make a poultice."

Robert heard him moving away from the door, his ancient footsteps dragging.

Afterwards it was very still in the cabin. The sun crossed the mountains stretching the shadows out long and cool blue, then shortening them inch by inch until finally there were no shadows at all. Then again there were short shadows starting this time pointing east, lengthening into evening, the coolness coming down, and the little wind talking.

Old Rafe came back to the cabin with his hands full of fresh green leaves. They gave off a clean smell. Then he was bending over his son, unwinding the bandage, and pressing the leaves against the torn scalp. Almost at once, Robert could feel the fever leaving. He felt stronger.

The old man stirred up the fire, putting the iron pot over it, tossing in the greens and the hunk of salt pork. After a time it began to simmer, filling the room with a rich, dark smell. Rafe bent over it stirring rapidly. Then he straightened. From the door had come a hard, clear knocking.

Robert sat bolt upright. His head crashed and throbbed.

"You're here, Rafe?"

"Yassuh, Mr. Walters!" Rafe beamed, "yassuh!" Then he was flinging his door wide, saying, "Come in, suh! Come right on in!"

"Naw," the white man said, "reckon I'll stay out here. I got something to talk over wit you, Rafe."

"Yassuh," Rafe said, and his voice was puzzled, "Yassuh?"

"Thet boy o yourn. Las night he did something bad, Rafe, powerful bad." Rafe's voice was a dry whisper.

"Yassuh," he croaked, "Yassuh?"

"Las night my boy was out walkin with his girl. He says that boy o yourn come outa the bushes an grabbed at her. Say he acted like he were drunk."

"But my boy doan drink, Mistuh Walters! He doan never tetch a drop."

"Be better to think he were drunk, Rafe," the white man said quietly. Rafe's chin was sunk into his chest, and his old form seemed to shrink.

"Yassuh," he quavered.

"Well my boy beat him off. Had to hit him over the haid with a bottle fore he'd leave. Rafe, you know what'd happen if I was to spread this eroun?"

"Yassuh."

"You been a good nigger, Rafe," the white man said slowly. "Ain't never had no trouble outa you."

"Nawsuh, Mistuh Walters, you sho Lawd ain't!"

"But he got to be punished, Rafe. You got to punish him." Rafe's voice was loud with relief.

"I punish him, awright, Mistuh Walters! I tek the hide offen him!" The white man looked at Rafe.

"Now, Rafe," he said quietly.

"Right now, suh? He kinda sick—that bottle—"

"Right now, Rafe."

Rafe came back into the cabin. His breath was coming out in thick gasps, and the whites of his eyes showed yellow in his black face. He walked through the house and out on the back porch where the heavy razor strap hung. Then he came back, his eyes glittering.

"Git up!" he roared at the boy, "go in yo maw's room!"

"Paw—" Robert said. "Paw—"

"Do lak I tells yuh!"

Since she had died, they, neither of them, had disturbed this room. The magnificent brass bed, brought all the way from Atlanta by wagon, still gleamed golden in the sunlight. Then old Rafe was bending the boy over, tying his wrists to the bedstead, lashing them so tight that they hurt. He stepped back then and swung the strap.

"Doan never say nuthin to no white man!" he chanted, and the strap came down with a broad clear whack. "Doan you never say nothin," he grunted out, "to no white folks! Never no mo!" And the big strap sang through the air and bit and again and again and once more again until Robert lost all count of them, the blows being blended in one sickening welter of pain that rode in upon his vitals in wave after wave of sickness.

"You gonna do hit eny mo?" the old man cried, bringing down the strap, "You gonna do hit eny mo?"

But something else was rising up in Robert's throat, something black and nameless, rising so thick and hot that gladly, willingly, he would have died there before loosening his bitten lips to utter a word.

His father brought the strap down once more.

"An roun er white gal," he chanted hoarsely, "doan even breathe!"

But this time the pain had bitten down too deep. The boy opened his mouth wide, the corded muscles of his belly heaved, and he was sick upon the floor. Rafe let the strap fall. Then he fished in his pockets for his knife and cut the boy loose.

"You go lay down," he said harshly. Then he walked through the house to where the white man waited.

"Awright, Rafe," the white man said, "you sure give him a hidin! Stop by my place when you're down that way. Got a couple o little jobs I want you to do."

"Yassuh," Rafe croaked. "Yassuh." Then he sat down on the steps and watched the white man striding off, down the trail. He sat very still, hunched up on the steps, while the dusk deepened into night, and a string of stars trailed out over the mountains.

And after it was dark, the boy came out, dressed, wearing his shoes and his hat. He stopped beside the old man, leaning with his eyes closed against the post, and stretched out his hand. Rafe did not move or speak. Leaning close, Robert could see the slow tears streaking from under the heavy lids. But now, finally, it was too late. He went past his father without speaking, the little bandana-tied bundle in his hand, and started down the trail to where the trains were, where they snorted to a stop under the water tower, pluming the night with whiteness.

The old man stood up suddenly and called out: "Robert!"

But the boy plunged on unheeding down the dark road, his hard heels making a great clatter on the rocks. And as he went, the moon rode out of a cloud, but still the road was dark, all the roads going down were dark, drenched in night—darkness within darkness—all down the darkened trail.

The Homecoming

The train stretched itself out long and low against the tracks and ran very fast and smoothly. The drive rods flashed out of the big pistons like blades of light, and the huge counterweighted wheels were blurred solid with the speed. Out of the throat of the stack, the white smoke blasted up in stiff hard pants, straight up for about a yard, then the backward rushing mass of air caught it, trailing it out over the cars like a veil.

In the Jim Crow coach, just back of the mail car, Sergeant Willie Jackson pushed the window up a notch higher. The heat came blasting in the window in solid waves, bringing the dust with it, and the cinders. Willie mopped his face with his handkerchief. It came away stained with the dust and sweat.

"Damn," he said without heat, and looked out at the parched fields that were spinning backward pass his window. Up on the edge of the skyline, black against the sunwashed sky, a man stopped his ploughing to wave at the passing train.

"Huccome we always do that? Willie speculated idly. "Doan know a soul on this train - not a soul, but he got t wave. Oh well --"

The train was bending itself around a curve, and the soft, long, lostlonesome wail of the whistle cried out twice. Willie stirred in his seat, watching the cabins with the whitewash peeling off spinning backward pass the train, lost in the immensity of sun blasted fields under a pale, yellowish white sky, the blue washed out by the sun swarth, and no cloud showing.

Up ahead, the water tower was rushing toward the train. Willie grinned. He had played under that tower as a boy. Water was always leaking out of it, enough water to cool a hard, skinny little black body even in the heat of summer. The creek was off somewhere to the south, green and clear under the willows, making a little laughing sound over the rocks. He could see the trees that hid it now, the lone clump standing up abruptly in all that brown and naked expanse of the fields.

And now the houses began to thicken, separated by only a few hundred yards instead of by miles. The train slowed, snorting tiredly into another curve. Across the diagonal of the bend, Willie could see the town, all of it - a few dozen buildings clustered around the Confederate Monument, bisected by a single paved street. The heat was pushing down on it like a gigantic hand, flattening it against the rust brown earth.

Now the train was grinding to a stop. Willie swung down from the car, carefully keeping his left leg off the ground, taking all the weight on his right. Nobody else got off the train.

The heat struck him in the face like a physical blow. The sunlight brought the great drops of sweat out on his forehead, making his black face glisten. He stood there in the full glare, the light pointing up the little strips of colored ribbon on his tunic. One of them was purple, with two white ends. Then there was a yellow one with thin red, white, and blue stripes in the middle, and red and white stripes near the two ends. Another was red with three white stripes near the ends. Willie wore his collar loose and his uniform was faded, but he still stood erect with his chest out and his belly sucked in.

He started across the street toward the monument, throwing one leg a little stiffly. The white men who always sat around it on the little iron benches looked at him curiously. He came on until he stood in the shadow of the shaft. He looked up at the statue of the Confederate soldier, complete with knapsack and holding the musket with the little needle type bayonet ready for the charge. At the foot of the shaft there was an inscription carved in the stone. Willie spelled out the words:

"No nation rose so white and pure; none fell so free of stain."

He stood there, letting the words sink into his brain.

One of the tall loungers took a sliver of wood out of the corner of his mouth and grinned. He nudged his companion.

"What do hit say, boy?" he asked.

Willie looked past him at the dusty unpaved streets straggling out from the monument.

"I axed you a question, boy." The white man's voice was very quiet.

"You talkin t me?" Willie said softly.

"You know Goddamn well I'm talkin t you. You got ears, aincha?"

"You sed boy," Willie said. "I didn know you was talkin t me."

"Who th hell else could I been talkin t, nigger?" the white man demanded.

"I dunno," Willie said; "I didn see no boys eroun."

The two white men stood up.

"Ain't you fergittin sumpin, nigger?" one of them asked, walking toward Willie.

"Not that I knows of," Willie declared.

"Ain't nobody ever tol you t say sir t a white man?"

"Yas," Willie said, "they tole me that."

"Yas what?" the white man prompted.

"Yas nuthin," Willie said quietly, "jes plain yas. N I doan think you better come eny closer, white man."

"Nigger, do you know where you at?"

"Yas," Willie said, "Yas I knows. N I knows you kin have me kilt. But I doan care bout that. Long time now I doan care. So please doan come no closer, white man, I'm axin you kindly."

The two men hesitated. Willie started toward them, walking very slowly. They stood very still watching him come, then, at the last moment, they stood aside and let him pass. He limped across the street and went into the town's lone Five and Ten Cents store.

"Huccome I come in heah?" he muttered; "Ain got nobody t buy nothin fer." He stood still a moment, frowning. "Reckon I'll git some postcards t sen th boys," he decided. He walked over to the rack and made his selections carefully: The New Post Office Building, The Memorial Bridge, the Confederate Monument. "Make this look like a real town," he said, "keep that one hoss outa sight." Then he was limping over toward the counter, the cards and a quarter in his hand. The salesgirl started toward him, her hand outstretched to take the money. But just before she reached him, a white woman came toward the counter, so the girl went on pass Willie, smiling sweetly, saying, "Can I help you?"

"Look a heah, girl," Willie said sharply, "I was heah first!"

The salesgirl and the woman both turned toward him, their mouths dropping open.

"My money th same color as hern," Willie said. He stuffed the cards in his pocket. Then deliberately he tossed the quarter on the counter and walked out the door.

"Well I never!" the white woman gasped.

When Willie came out on the sidewalk, a little knot of men had gathered around the monument. Willie could see the two men in the center talking to the others. Then they all stopped talking all at once and looked at him. He limped on down the block and turned the corner.

At the next corner he turned again, and again at the next. Then he slowed. Nobody was following him.

The houses thinned out again. There were no trees shading the dirt road, powder dry under the hammer blows of the sun. Willie limped on, the sweat pouring down his black face, soaking his collar. Then at last he was turning into a flagstone driveway, curving toward a large, very old house, set well back from the road in a clump of pine trees. He went up on the broad, sweeping veranda and rang the bell.

A very old black man opened the door. He looked at Willie with a puzzled expression, squinting his red mottled old eyes against the light.

"Don'tcha member me, Unca Ben?" Willie said.

"Willie!" the old man said; "Th Colonel sho be glad t see yuh! I go call him - rat now!" Then he was off, trotting down the hall. Willie stood still waiting.

The Colonel came out of the study, his hand outstretched.

"Willie," he said, "You little black bastard! Damn! You aren't little anymore, are you?"

"Naw," Willie said, "I done growed."

"So I see! So I see! Come on back in the kitchen, boy. I want t talk to you."

Willie followed the lean, bent figure of the old white man through the house. In the kitchen, Martha, the cook, gave a squeal of pleasure.

"Willie! My, my how fine yous lookin! Sit down! Wheah you find him, Colonel Bob?"

"I jes dropped by," Willie said.

"Fix him something to eat, Martha," the Colonel said, "while I pry some military information out of him." Martha scurried off, her white teeth gleaming in a pleased smile.

"You've got a mighty heap of ribbons, Willie," the Colonel said; "What are they for?"

"This heah purple one is th Purple Heart," Willie explained. "That was fur m leg."

"Bad?" the Colonel demanded.

"Hand grenade. They had t tek it off. This heah one's a fake."

"Well I'll be damed! I never would have known it."

"They mek em good now. N they teaches yuh fore you leaves th hospital."

"What are the others for?"

"Th yaller one mean Pacific Theater of War," Willie said, "N th red one is th Good Conduct Medal."

"I knew you'd get that one," the Colonel declared; "You always were good boy, Willie."

"Thank yuh," Willie said. Martha was back now with coffee and cake.

"Dinner be ready in a little," she said.

"You're out for good, aren't you, Willie?

"Yassuh."

"Good. I'll give you your old job back. I need an extra man on th place."

"Beggin yo pardon, suh," Willie said: "I ain't stayin heah. I'm goin Nawth."

"What! What th clinking ding dang ever gave you such an idea!"

"I cain't stay heah, Colonel Bob. I ain suited f heah no mo."

"Th North is no place for niggers, Willie. Why those dang blasted Yankees would let you starve t death. Down here, a good boy like you always got a white man to look after him. Any time you get hungry you can always come up to most anybody's back door and they'll feed you."

"Yas," Willie said, "They feed me awright. They say thas Colonel Bob's boy, Willie, and they give me a swell meal. Thas huccome I got t go."

"Now you're talking riddles, Willie."

"Naw, Colonel Bob, I ain talkin riddles. I seen mens kilt. M frens. I done growed inside, too, Colonel Bob."

"What's that got to do with your staying here?"

Martha came over to the table bearing the steaming food on a tray. She stood there holding the tray, looking at Willie. He looked past her, out the doorway to where the big pines were shredding the sunlight.

"I done forgot too many things," he said slowly." I done forgot how t scratch m haid n shuffle m feet n grin when I doan feel lak grinning."

"Willie!" Martha said; "Doan talk lak that! Doancha know you cain't talk lak that?"

Colonel Bob silenced her with a lifted hand.

"Somebody's been talkin t you," he declared; "teaching you th wrong things."

"Nawsuh. Jus had a lotta time f thinkin. Thought it all up m self. I done fought n been mos kilt n now I'm a man. Cain't be a boy no mo. Nobody's boy. Not even yourn, Colonel Bob."

"Willie!" Martha moaned.

"Got t be a man. M own man. Cain't let m kids cut a buck n wing on th sidewalk f pennies. Cain't ax f handouts roun th back door. Got t come in th front door. Got t git it m self. Cain't git it, then I starves proud, Colonel Bob."

Martha's mouth was working, forming the words, but no sound came out of it, no sound at all.

"Do you think it's right," Colonel Bob asked evenly, "for you to talk to a white man like this -- any white man -- even me?"

"I dunno. All I knows is I got t go. I cain't even say yassuh no mo. Ever time I do, it choke up in m throat lak black vomit. Ain comin t no mo back doors. N when I gits ole, folks gonna say Mister Jackson - not no Unca Willie."

"You're right, Willie," Colonel Bob said; "You'd better go. In fact you'd better go right now."

Willie stood up and adjusted his overseas cap.

"Thank yuh, Colonel Bob," he said; "you been awful good t me. Now I reckon I be goin."

Colonel Bob didn't answer. Instead he got up and held the screen door open. Willie went pass him out the door. On the steps he stopped.

"Goodbye, Colonel Bob," he said softly.

The old white man looked at Willie as though he were going to say something, but then he thought better of it, and closed his jaw down tight.

Willie turned away to go, but Uncle Ben was scurrying through the kitchen like an ancient rabbit.

"Colonel Bob!" he croaked; "they's trouble up in town. Man want yuh on th phone rat now! Say they's after some cullud sodjer -- Lawdy!"

"Yas," Willie said, "maybe they after me."

"You stay right there," Colonel Bob growled, "an don't move a muscle! I'll be back in a minute." He turned and walked rapidly toward the front of the house.

Willie stood very still looking up through a break in the trees at the pale, whiteish blue sky. It was very high and empty; and in the trees no bird sang. But Colonel Bob was coming back now, his face very red, and knotted into hard lines.

"Willie," he said, "did you tell two white men you'd kill em if they came nigh you?"

"Yassuh. I didn say that, but thas what I meant."

"And did you have some kind of an argument with a white w o m a n ? "

"Yassuh."

"My God!"

"He's crazy, Colonel Bob," Martha wailed; "He done gone plum outa his min!"

"You better not go back t town," The Colonel said; "you better stay here until I can get you out after dark."

Willie smiled a little.

"I'm gonna ketch me a train," he said; "two o'clock t day, I'm gonna ketch it."

"You be kilt!" Martha declared; "They kill you sho!"

"We done run too much, Martha," Willie said slowly; "we done run n hid n enyhow we done got caught. N then we goes down on our knees n begs. I ain runnin. Done forgot how. Doan know how t run. Doan know how t beg. Jes knows how t fight, thas all, Martha."

"Oh Jesus he crazy! Tole yuh he crazy, Colonel Bob!"

Colonel Bob was looking at Willie, a slow thoughtful look.

"Cain't sneak off in th dark, Colonel Bob. Cain't steal erway t Jesus. Got t go marchin. N doan a man better tech me." He turned and went down the steps. "Goodbye, Colonel Bob," he called.

"Crazy!" Martha wept. "Outa his min!"

"Crazy," the Colonel echoed. "That's it!" Then he was racing through the house toward the phone.

Willie went on around the house toward the dirt road where the heat was a visible thing and turned his face in the direction of town.

When Willie neared the one paved street, the heat was lessening. He walked very slowly, turning off the country road into Lee Avenue, the main street of the town. Then he was moving toward the station. There were many people in the street, he noticed, far more than usual. The sidewalk was almost blocked with men with eyes of blue ice and a long slow slouch to their walk. He went on very quietly, paying no attention to them. He walked in an absolutely straight line, turning neither to the right or the left, and each time they opened up their ranks to let him pass through. But afterwards came the sound of their footsteps falling in behind him, each man that he passed swelling the number until the sound of them walking was loud in the silent street. He did not look back. He limped on, his artificial leg making a scraping rustle on the sidewalk, and behind him, steadily, beat upon beat, not in perfect time, a little ragged, moving slowly, steadily, no faster nor slower than he was going the white men came. They went down the street until almost they had reached the station. Then, moving his lips in a prayer that had no words, Willie turned and faced them. They swung out into a broad semi-circle without hastening their steps, moving in toward him in the thick hot silence.

Willie opened his mouth to shriek at them, curse at them, goad them into haste, but before his voice could rush pass his dried and thickened tongue the stillness was split from top to bottom by the wail of a siren. They all turned then, looking down the road to where the khaki colored truck was pounding up a billowing wall of dust, hurling straight toward them.

Then it was upon them, screeching to a stop, the great red crosses gleaming on its sides. The two soldiers were out of it almost before it was still, grabbing Willie by the arms, dragging him toward the ambulance. Then the young officer with the single silver bar on his cap was climbing down, and with him, an old man with white hair.

"This th man, Colonel?" the officer demanded.

Colonel Bob nodded.

"All right," the officer said; "we'll take over now. This man is a combat fatigue case - not responsible for his actions."

"But I got t go!" Willie said; "Got t ketch that train. Got t go Nawth wheah I kin be free, wheah I kin be a man. You heah me lieutenant, I got t go!"

The younger officer looked Willie up and down. Then he jerked his head in the direction of the ambulance.

"Lemme go!" Willie wept, "lemme go!"

But the soldiers were moving forward now, dragging the slim form kicking and twisting between them with one leg sticking out very stiffly, the heavy heel drawing a line through the heat softened pavement as they went.

My Brother Went to College

When I was very young, the land was a hunger in me. I wanted to devour it all: plains, mountains, cities teeming with men. Therefore I left the three rooms above the little shop where my father cobbled shoes, crawling over the still sleeping form of my brother, Matt, and tiptoeing pass the great brass bed in which my father snored. As I went by he turned over and murmured, "Mark," but he was still sleeping, so I crept by him very quietly and stole down the creaking stairs. Mark was my name. I suppose that father was planning to have two more sons and name them Luke and John, but mother died before he could accomplish it. Afterwards Matt and I used to argue over whether father, if he had been blessed with three more sons, would have called the fifth one, "The Acts," Matt holding that he would not, and I that he would. Acts of the Apostles Johnson. It had a very satisfying sound.

I was ten when I ran away from home. When I came back, I was twenty. For ten years I wandered upon the face of the earth, hearing the long, sweet, sad, lostlonesome cry of the train whistles in the night until the sound was in my blood and part of me. I wandered through the Delta while the sun soaked into my black hide, and sat on Scott's Bluff near Baton Rouge and watched the Mississippi run golden with the mud of half a continent. I grew a lean belly and a knotty calf and the black wool on my head kinked tight as cockle burrs. I drank Moonshine in the Georgia swamp country, and rotgut in the Carolina hills. I worked for spells until I would wake up in the night to hear the trains crying, then I was off, pushing the earth backward under my feet. I listened to the Whippowill at night, and sang with the Mocking bird in the morning.

I wasn't worth a damn and I didn't care. I was free. I couldn't keep a job because of that. Sooner or later the boss would find out that I could jump to do his orders and still stay free, that I could be polite and still be free, that you could kick me and cuss me and I could still stay free because freedom was inside me. I had soaked it up from the blazing sun in Texas, I had breathed it in with the cool mountain air in Tennessee, I'd drunk it down with all the tepid, muddy, fishtasting river water I'd devoured along with ten thousand miles of timeless space.

I whored from New Orleans to Memphis, and gambled from Louisville to Miami. I was worthless, useless, a ne'erdowell, a disgrace to my family and I didn't give a damn. But after a while, as I grew older, the hunger lessened in me, and in its place came a great longing to see again the face of my brother, and walk down streets where people would call out to me as I passed, knowing me, knowing my name. Beside, I had decided to settle down, get me a good job, maybe in the post office, and take a wife.

It took me four days to get there. I didn't even stop to eat. I swung six freights and a fruit truck, and did twenty miles afoot. Then I was walking down the streets of my city, all the well loved streets sniffing the smell of garbage like bouquets of roses, and laughing all over my self. A woman leaned out of a window and said:

"Where you going, pretty brown?"

"Home!" I laughed, "Home!"

"Come on up and I give you luck sho. Two ways for a dollar. Come on up, pretty brown."

"Hell," I said, "I'm black and I sure ain't pretty and what you got ain't worth no dollar. Leave me be, sister, I'm going home!"

I went around the last corner very slow, making the pleasure last, and there was the old shop just like I left it, only a little more run down maybe. Then my heart stopped beating altogether because the man hammering away at the thick, mostly cardboard, halfsoles sure Lord wasn't father, or even the half of him.

I walked in the door and I asked him where Deacon Johnson was who used to keep this shop and he looked up at me and said:

"He dead. Mighty near six years now since he was laid to rest."

I sat down weakly on one of the high stools.

"And his son – Matt Johnson?" I asked.

"Oh he here awright. He Doctor Matt Johnson now. Finished up his schoolin at Mo'house and taken up medicine at Meharry. Fine man, Doctor Johnson. He my doctor. Other night I was taken with a misery in my---"

"Where he live?" I demanded; "I got to see him."

"Way cross town. Over there on Westmoreland Drive. What's the matter son, is you sick?"

"Naw," I said; "Naw, I ain't sick. I'm ever so much obliged to you, Mister."

When I left town, ten years before, only white people lived on Westmoreland Drive, and Big Shots at that so I wasn't at all sure that the new Cobbler wasn't stringing me. But that other part sounded all right--all that about the schooling and being a doctor and all. That was just like Matt. There wasn't but one place for him and that was at the top. That's the way Matt was.

It took me more than a half hour to get over to Westmoreland Drive. I had to go pass five points and through all the city traffic, and after ten years I wasn't exactly clear as to where it was. But I reached it at last and stood on the corner looking down the shaded street at all the big brick houses sitting high on their green terraces with the automobile driveways curving up and around them and I drew in my breath and let it out again in one big whoosh. Then I went up to the first house and rang the bell. A young girl came to the door. She had brown skin and soft black hair that curled down over her shoulders. She was so doggoned pretty that I couldn't get my mouth shut.

"Yes?" she said; "Yes?"

"Doctor Johnson," I said; "Doctor Matthew Johnson -- do he live here?"

"No," she said, "He lives four houses down on the other side."

Then she smiled at me. I wanted to stand there and just look at her, but then I saw my old rusty shoes and the worn out fringes at the bottom of my britches, so I mumbled, "Thank you, M'am," and went back down the walk to the street.

I stood in front of my brother's house a long time before I got up the nerve to climb up the inclined walk to the door. It was just about the biggest and the best looking house on the street. Matt had got somewhere, he had. I pushed on the bellbutton and held my breath, then the door popped open and a young woman, prettier'n an angel out of glory, and so lightcomplextioned that I looked at her three times and still I wasn't sure, stuck her head out and said:

"Good evening?"

"Howdydo," I said: "Is Matt home?"

"Yes," she said, and her voice was puzzled; "Whom shall I tell him is calling?"

"Just tell him, Mark," I said; "he'll know."

She went back in the house, leaving me standing there like a fool. The sunlight slanted through the shade trees on the walk. Where it hit the leaves, it made a kind of blaze. Then it came on through and touched the side of the house, making it a kind of salmon pink.

I heard Matt's big feet come hammering through the hall, then the door banged open and there he was big as life and twice as handsome. He had on a dark blue suit that must have cost plenty, and his hair was cut close to his skull so that the kink didn't show so much, and his black face was shavened, steamed, and massaged until the skin was like black velvet. He took the pipe out of his mouth and stood there staring at me, his Adam's Apple bobbing up and down out of the collar of his silk shirt. Then he grinned and said:

"Mark, you crazy little bastard!"

I put out my horny paw and he took it and wrung it almost off. I was ashamed of myself because all the time I had been standing there thinking that maybe he wouldn't want to see me now, but I should have known better. Matt wasn't like that at all.

He took me by the arm, rags and all and drew me inside the house. It was a palace. I had seen houses like that in the movies but no body could have made me believe that there was a black man anywhere who owned one. The rugs were so soft and deep that they came up to my ankles, and the combination radio-phonograph filled up half of one wall. Sitting in one of the huge chairs was the light girl and with her were two fat, copper brown children with soft brown hair almost the same color of their skins curling all over their little heads. I just stood there and I couldn't say a word.

It came to me then that Matt had done what I had tried to do and that he'd done it the right way. He'd built himself a world, and he was free. I had run away from everything, and slept in the open fields, hunting for something, and Matt had stayed at home and fought for the same thing and he had got it. I felt less than two inches high.

"Martha," Matt was saying, his voice full of laughter; "this bum you were telling me about is my little brother, Mark."

"Oh," she said, "Oh -- I'm so sorry -- I didn't know--"

"It's awright, Ma'm," I said; "You was right. I am a bum. I just wanted to see Matt one more time, and now that I have, I reckon I'll be on my way agin."

"Like hell you will!" Matt roared. "You come on in the back and have some supper. I promised paw on his death bed that I'd find you, and now that I have, you aren't getting away. Come on now."

He took me back in the kitchen and began to pull stuff out of a huge electric refrigerator and pile it on the table. There was so much food there that I couldn't eat. For the life of me I couldn't. I barely tasted the cold chicken, and ate a tiny piece of cherry pie. And all the time, Matt sat there and looked at me.

"Why didn't you write?" he growled at me. "Anytime in the last four years I could have had you back in school -- well, it isn't too late now. You're gonna bone up, do you hear me – college preparatory - we'll skip over high -- you're too damned old. You'll take pharmacy along with college, and when you're out we'll open a drug store. And Gawddamnit, if you fail, I'll break every bone in your stupid body --- running off like that!"

I just sat there like a fool and gulped and said "Yes, Matt, no, Matt, that's right, Matt, that'll be swell." When I had finished he took me upstairs to the bathroom and drew a tub full of water hot enough to scald the hide off of me.

"Get in," he said, "and give me those clothes." I did as I was told, and he took them out into the hall. I heard him calling the old woman who was his housekeeper. When she got there, I heard him say:

"Take these rags out back and burn them!"

When I got out of the tub he gave me his robe and slippers and there on the bed was one of his suits and a white shirt and tie and handkerchief and socks and shoes and silk underwear – silk mind you!

"Get dressed," he growled; "we're going for a walk."

I put on the things and they fitted except for being a little too big here and there; then we went back down the stairs. Matt put on his hat and kissed his wife and the children and then we went out on the street. By that time it was dark and the stars hung just above the street lamps. I tried to talk.

"The kids," I said, "Geez, Matt ---"

"They're allright," he said; "Martha's swell too --"

"I'll say," I said; "Where'd you find her?"

"College. You'd better do as well."

"Not me," I said; "She's too light. I wouldn't feel comfortable. I want me a tall brown with white teeth and wide hips. Fat chance, though."

"You get what you go after," Matt said, "and doggoned it, I'm gonna see that you go after it! We go in here."

I looked up and saw that it was a barber shop. All the barbers grinned when Matt came in.

"Howdy, Doc," they said; "back so soon?"

"Tom," Matt said to the oldest barber; "This is my brother, Mark. Get out your clippers and give him a close cut. Take that rosary off his head!"

When they had finished with me I was somebody else. I looked like Matt. I looked prosperous and well fed. I looked important – and just a little I began to feel important too.

"Tomorrow night," Matt said, "there's a dance. You're going with us. I want you to meet some nice girls. And for Christsake watch your grammar."

"That girl," I said, "Four houses up the street on the other side, will she be there?"

"Elizabeth? You catch on fast, don't you? Yes, I imagine so. But you won't get a look in there – she's doggoned popular, I tell you."

"Ain't no harm in trying," I said.

They were nice to me, but I felt strange. Martha went out of her way to make me feel at home. Little Matt and little Martha crawled all over me and called me Uncle, but still I didn't feel right. The mattresses were too soft. I couldn't sleep. The food was so good and so rich that my stomach refused it. And every doggoned one of them including Matt talked English like Yankee whitefolks so that half the time I was saying "Huh? Whatcha say?"

They said "Courthouse -- Courrrthouse - not Co'thouse, like a body ought to. They said "sure -- not sho." And they never said "ain't." They talked like the people in pictures – like radio announcers. I admired their proper talk, but it didn't sound right. Martha – allright, she looked the part, but I couldn't get it through my thick skull that anybody black as Matt and me ought to talk like that.

And that dance. I stood by a pillar and looked at the girls -- they had on evening dresses that trailed the floor, and there were flowers in their hair. And they were all the colors of the rainbow: soft, velvety nightshade girls, chocolate brown girls, coppery brown girls, gingerbread brown girls, lemon yellow girls, old ivory colored girls, just off white girls, and snowy skinned octoroons with blonde hair and blue eyes.

"Jesus!" I said; "Jesus! Old Saint Peter done gone to sleep and left open the gates." But I didn't dance. The couples drifted pass me in stately waltzes. No body jitterbugged. If anybody had started to, they'd have been thrown out. I felt stiff. I felt frozen. I felt like the Deuce of Spades against a King High Flush. I was a lost ball in high grass. I was a cueball smack up behind the eight and the side pocket was miles away.

I got to get out of here, I thought. I got to catch myself a freight and highball it down the river. I can shuffle in a Beale Street Juke Joint where the girls are wide across the beam and you can count every knee in the place. Where you hang a cigarette out the corner of your mouth and shove your hat back on your head and tickle the ivories while you squint your left eye so the smoke won't blind you. Where your sweetgal dances with you up against you til her thighs scald you and you smell her hairgrease under your nose along with the bodysweat and cheap perfume. But in here I can't breathe, not here where they drift along like something you dreamed about and the perfumes don't come from the dime store and the girls move on the air halfway out on your arm. No, by God!

I started toward the door. When I got there I saw a blackboy in a Zoot suit standing there looking in. I felt a great rush of fellow feeling for him. I was outside looking in, too, although I was inside the hall. But as I got close I saw the white policeman that a city ordinance required that they have at all negro dances no matter how respectable they were, standing there breaking matches into little pieces and flipping them into the broad brim of the boy's Big Apple hat. And the boy was grinning all over his flat face. I turned around and went back into the hall.

Then she was coming toward me, smiling. I wanted to run. I wanted to hide. I wanted to kick a hole in the floor and pull it over me.

"Hello," she said; "I've been looking all over for you."

"You - you been lookin all over for me?"

"Yes - Doctor Matt told me you were here. My, but you've changed! Why you're positively handsome with a haircut."

I pulled out a hankechief and mopped my brow.

"Well," Elizabeth teased, "aren't you going to dance with me?"

I took her in my arms and we moved off. It was like floating. Like flying. Like dreaming. And I didn't want to wake up. Matt had me. He'd won. The Juke Boxes in the riverjoints died away out of mind into silence. I was lost. I could never go back again and I knew it.

"Oh my God," I groaned, "Oh my God!"

I took Elizabeth home after the dance, and went through hell wondering whether or not I should try to kiss her, but in the end I decided against it, and watched her running up the stairs laughing all over herself. Then I walked home through the grey dawn on Westmoreland drive that was like no other dawn I'd ever seen. And I thought about how it was with Matt and Matt's crowd: the men in tuxedoes and tails, the women in evening gowns, all very correct, no body laughing out loud or dancing with their entire bodies or yelling across the dance floor, or saying ain't, or ever doing anything that wasn't on page one of Emily Post, and I wondered if it really felt good to be like that. And while I was wondering I pushed open the door to the bathroom and found Matt standing before the mirror shaving with a tiny gold plated safety razor cussing with quiet violence.

He turned around and saw me and slowly his eyes lit up.

"You," he said, "you can do it!"

"Do what?" I said.

He put his hand down in his pocket and came out with a ten dollar bill.

"You go down town today and buy me an old fashioned straight razor. I hate these damn little things!"

"Alwright," I said.

"I've been wanting a straight razor for five years," Matt said, touching his jaw with his fingertips.

"Yeah," I said, thinking about Elizabeth.

"I can't always wait to go to the barber shop," Matt said.

"Five years," I said; "why didn't you just go and buy one?"

Matt turned and looked at me, one half of his face still covered with lather.

"You know I couldn't do that," he said.

"Why not?"

"You know what they'd think I wanted it for."

I looked at Matt and I began to laugh. I laughed so I lost my breath. When I went out into the hall, leaving him there, staring at me, I was still laughing. But I shouldn't have laughed. Even then I must have known it wasn't funny. Now, when I think about it (after all these years, watching my wife, Elizabeth, with her beautiful hands serving ice cream sodas over the counter of our drugstore, remembering that Matt did this too) I realize that it was really sad, one of the saddest things, in fact, that I ever heard of.

NEW
STORIES

Pride's Castle

Sharon pushed open the casement window and looked across the green sweep of the lawn toward the hedgerows. The asters were clustered around the pool and from a break in the mossy surface of the rocks the water fell in a tiny, white silver cascade, making a noise curiously like laughter. The willow bent low over the unruffled surface of the water, like a sorrowing woman trailing her hair before her; and hollyhocks stood along the rough hewen surfaces of the stonewall. There were lilacs, slimstalked, standing in clumps here and there amid the rocks, and between them were queenly roses, the whole thing having that air of studied unconcern which betrayed the fact after a time that here was a masterly deceit, that the whole garden had been planned to give the impression of utter naturalness which unaccountably always missed in small, indefinable ways . . .

Sharon wondered how and why the garden missed its aim. God knows Pride had spent time and money enough upon it. The gardener had been brought all the way from England; the stones had been carted fifty miles from the district around Lake Mahopac; and the willow had traveled, its roots encased in rich black loam, bound tenderly about with burlap, from a plantation in Virginia. You could not see, Sharon knew, that the silver water tinkled from a pipe of the finest, softest copper; it seemed to bubble up from the earth itself. Yet, the sound it made was faintly derisive. It was as though, looking up suddenly, she half expected the whole thing to vanish, to see again the livery stable that had occupied the spot upon which Pride had built her garden, to smell the harsh, nostril stinging odors of animal dung, and wet straw and steaming hair. . . . She shook her head, as if to clear it. The garden would not vanish. Faked though it was, it was permanent.

False though my life is, it, too, is permanent – at least until death. And after that? Punishment, swift and terrible, for my faithless, for my dishonor, for my shame? Or have I not already had here my lovely hell, here in my small and perfect garden hidden on a sidestreet, where the voice of the fishmonger and the junk dealer roar through the branches of my far travelled willow, and the iron hoofs on the cobblestones outside, drown out the breeze that makes the lilacs nod? Is not my God, truly, a subtler God than the ancient thunderer? Might He not prefer this endless waiting here in this artful wilderness for a step, a breath, a word, to leagues of sulphur and oceans of brimstone? And is my cage not none the less a cage for its gilt; my prisionhouse a prison still, for all its lack of bars?

Her hand reached out and gripped the casement as though to close it; but she stopped quite still, the motion arrested abruptly, and peered toward the break in the hedgerows. For a girl had come through the opening in the hedges, a tall girl with silvery blonde hair piled atop her small, queenly head.

"Caprice!" Sharon muttered. "Ah, Caprice!" She leaned forward, half through the window, all her being caught up in a wild surge of love for the slim, silvery creature walking through her garden, for this fairy princess who should have been her daughter, but who was not: Caprice Dawson, Pride's child – not hers. Caprice came toward her, walking slowly, with a curious stateliness, totally unlike the spring dance of her usual gait. Caprice, at nineteen, ran still, skipped still, was mercurial and virginial, and wildwoods-thingpure, nymphlike, faerylike, a little beyond comprehension so that the coldly critical faculty suspended judgement while what was left of youth in Sharon looked upon her with joy.

But now, today, there was no joy. Caprice's small feet (what on earth possessed Esther to name her, Caprice?) moved one before the other, slowly, and her small head was bent. Sharon never knew how the feeling of terror started. But suddenly it was there – there like the hand of winter in her garden, there like the weight of death upon her heart. She leaned out now, far out from her window, and called the name, hearing her own voice wintery and sere, rustling like dead leaves about that slim and lovely head:

"Caprice!"

The girl's head came up. There was something awful in the deliberation of the motion. Her blue eyes widened, held level, and caught Sharon's gaze in a shaft of utter finality.

"Auntie Sharon," she said, her voice, high, clear, toneless. "Auntie Sharon, I came to tell you. . . . . . ." (That time can stop between a child's need for breathing, that death can stand in a garden, skeletal, at a lovely girl's right hand)

"Yes," Sharon's own voice was high and sharp, harshtoned, ugly, "Yes, Caprice?"

"That Pride's dead. He shot himself."

Sharon stood there, staring down at Caprice, her own mind off on oblique, idiotic paths: (I saw Bernhardt once, receive news like this in a play. Her grief was titanic; it was unbearable to watch her. But I – I have no words. I stand here and do nothing. I am not crying. I'm quite sure I'm not going to faint.... Is it because, at times like this, we are unequipped with the means to express that which, finally, is perhaps beyond expression?)

She settled her weight down upon her thin arms and stared at Caprice.

"Come in, child," she said gently. "Please come in."

Caprice started for the door. Sharon raced down the stairs to meet her. She threw open the garden door, and put out her arms. Caprice walked into them (how many times have I held her thus? Her, the lost, the loved, neither bone of my bone, nor flesh of my flesh; but of my heart's blood, and my rebellious spirit, truly, the child?).

"Auntie Sharon," she said, "Don't cry. Pride wouldn't like it. I haven't cried. I'm not going to."

Wildly Sharon shook her head.

"I won't," she promised. "You've told your mother?"

"No."

"You," Sharon whispered, spacing the words one after the other, with great pauses in between, "have not told Esther?"

"No."

"But why, Caprice? Why?"

"Pride loved you, Auntie Sharon – not mother. I think he'd want you to know first."

Sharon looked up toward where the gaslights were sputtering, their gauze like filaments glowing white. Then she looked back at Caprice's still face.

"You know," she said flatly, calmly, "that this is a dreadful thing. You should have told Esther first."

"Dreadful?" Caprice's voice had the first thin entering note of hysteria in it. "What isn't dreadful in the world? Wasn't it dreadful for father to know you first, to love you from the hour he set eyes upon you, and yet to marry mother – because she was rich? Wasn't it dreadful for him to get me in that big empty place where there is no love, where the silences echo at you, by a woman who has been tortured into a serpent of hatred? Wasn't that dreadful?"

"And what I did," Sharon whispered, "that was not dreadful?"

"No. Pride belonged to you. Mother should have given him up."

"Caprice!"

"Sorry. But there is no time. I came here to tell you because you must be ready. You're going to be troubled – more troubled than mother or me or anybody else – God but father was a cruel man!"

"Caprice, you mustn't! You don't know...."

"I do know! There're going to be reporters, Auntie Sharon! I don't want them writing about you! Pride Dawson's Fancy Woman! – That's what they'll say. And it wasn't like that. It wasn't like that at all."

"No," Sharon said slowly, "it really wasn't like that. But the papers know nothing of me. Who'll tell them. . . ."

"Mother," Caprice said flatly, "with great joy. Besides," the blue eyes measured Sharon's brown ones, "father shot himself with a little pocket pistol that has your name engraved upon the barrel. It – it's still in his hand. . . ."

She looked at Sharon, the high white courage in her face crumbling into splintery planes and angles of pure grief. "I tried to take it away, but I couldn't! He'd gripped it so tight, and held it so long . . ." She swayed forward suddenly, violently, and Sharon caught her to her breast, feeling through the warm and trembling flesh, the earthquake upheaval of the girl's pain.

Sharon rocked her back and forth in her arms, murmuring wordless, ancient, motherthings. Finally Caprice straightened up.

"I wasn't very brave, was I?" she whispered. Her small, pink mouth brushed Sharon's thin face. "Goodbye, Auntie Sharon, I have to go now . . ." She stood up, dabbing at her eyes with a wisp of a handkerchief. "You'll be ready, won't you?" she asked anxiously. "They'll be here, soon."

Sharon got up and put her arm about Caprice's slim waist.

"I'll be ready," she said, and together they walked out into the garden.

The Schoolhouse
of Compere Antoine

When the Yankee gunboats ran pass the guns in Forts Jackson and St. Phillip and anchored off Canal Street in the pouring rain, it made very little difference to Compere Antoine. He was already an old man, and although as black as the shoes he cobbled, he had always been free. He went on singing very softly to himself in his native Gumbo patois and making the tenth or twelfth repair upon the dainty shoes of Creole ladies who before the War had been able to throw away a pair of shoes every fortnight. The only other difference was that now the ladies could not pay for repairs, but Compere Antoine made them just the same.

The ladies said: "God bless you, Compere!" and some of them gave him huge bundles of Confederate money for which the old man thanked them politely and took home and papered the walls of his little house down on Rampart Street with it, for that was all it was good for now.

On the day that the gunboats arrived, however, Compere Antoine closed his little shop. It would have been very dangerous to keep it open. The crowds of white men were running through all the streets of New Orleans and smashing the windows of all the shops and setting them on fire. Down on the levee thousands of bales of cotton were burning so that the whole sky was blotted out by the billowing smoke, and the wine and molasses were running through the cypress lined gutters of the banquettes like water. Some of the Negroes had buckets and were dipping up the wine by the pailful and drinking it just as fast so that by night they were all drunk and happy while the whole waterfront blazed. Compere Antoine stole through the roaring streets like a black ghost. He was looking for his five tall sons and fearing that by now they all had drunk their bellies full of wine and had got into trouble. He searched all night and by morning he had rounded them all up, yanking them for the most part from the sides of comely mulatto wenches and booting them soundly down the street before him. The fact that they were all tall, stalwart blacks who could have broken him in half with one hand apparently never occurred to either him or them, for they went along sheepishly with never a cross word.

The cobbling business was very bad for the next five days, so Compere Antoine spent them all in the streets trying vainly to keep up with his boys. Being a simple man, it never occurred to him that these five days were history. He was present when W. B. Mumford hauled down the Federal Flag from above the Mint, and he ran with the mob when the Pensacola opened up with her maintop howitzer. The shooting was very bad, but it was the first time that the old man had ever heard cannon fire, other than the curfew guns of his youth.

"It sound different when it's aimed at you, yes!" he said, and thereafter he avoided crowds. But something of the excitement of the day was gradually working within him. Old as he was, he limped along the banquettes over the entire parade route when General Butler's troops marched into New Orleans on the first of May. Down the levee they went, with Compere Antoine and all his boys trying to keep step beside them. They turned into Poydras Street, with the Negroes swollen into a mob, singing and cheering beside them. On Poydras to St. Charles, down St. Charles past the St. Charles Hotel to Canal, and on Canal to Custom House Street, and Compere Antoine kept up with them all the way.

After that, life was never the same for Compere Antoine. His oldest boy, Jean, who, like all Compere Antoine's sons, could read and write, got mixed up in politics. But the old man never got used to the smooth white men who came around to his little shop and called him Mister instead of Compere, which in old New Orleans was a title roughly equivalent to the 'Uncle' that Southern whites call old colored men to this day. They tried to buy his vote, or pay him to influence the other Negroes who listened to him when he spoke or came to him for advice. But Compere Antoine wouldn't sell. He asked the opinions of Oscar J. Dunn, a black man whom even the Democrats admitted was incorruptible, or of Antoine Dubuclet, a Creole mulatto, whose books, after he became State Treasurer, were examined and re-examined without anyone's finding a penny out of the way even through error. And he read the bible of the Louisiana Negroes, the *New Orleans Tribune*, owned by the Roudanez brothers of San Domingo, and edited by the brilliant black man, Paul Trevigne, who spoke seven languages. But he had no dealings with Pinchback.

"He too near white, him," Compere declared; "Can't be honest!"

His son, Jean, got a seat in the legislature and acquired a cabriolette with two spanking bays, and wore a big diamond in his red cravat. He sat by day with his feet upon a mahogany desk that cost three hundred and sixty five dollars and spat into a polished brass spittoon and pounded upon his desk with a hardwood gavel and bellowed: "Orduh!" at little or no provocation. He voted upon an immigration bill which included provisions for importing one thousand Chinamen and two thousand thugs from India, and five hundred Arabs and five hundred monkeys in order to solve the labor situation because the freedmen were damned sure not going to work any more because after all weren't they free? And he drove all over the Vieux Carre with an Octoroon mistress who had blue eyes and red hair and whom he covered with cheap jewelry until she looked like a Christmas tree. But he got very little real money. The carpetbaggers and the scalawags took care of that. They doled out the cigars and the champagne to the colored brethren, but they kept the hard cash for themselves.

And old Compere Antoine shook his head sadly and said:

"Can't no good come out of it, no! You watch what I tell you, me."

He was right. On July 30, 1866, he marched with his legislator son in a parade on Dryades Street on the way to Mechanics Institute. Somewhere up near the head of the line a few whites jostled the marching Negroes and somebody started cursing and after that somebody hit a whiteman in the mouth. So the whites came out with their guns and started shooting and the Negroes ran into the Institute. But the whites kept on shooting and two or three Negroes shot back, so the police came up and opened fire, and when they got through there were forty eight dead Negroes on the floor of the building, and sixty eight more dying, and ninety eight with gunshot wounds. And among the dead was Compere Antoine's oldest son.

The old man gathered his four remaining boys together and got out of New Orleans. He went up into Natchitoches Parish and opened another shoe shop. But even here there was no chance for a quiet life. Every time there was an election people got killed. Since nobody paid dollars and cents for Negroes any more, the native whites declared open season upon them the whole year round. Compere Antoine hid with his sons in their cabin while the Ku Klux or the Knights of the White Camelia or the Sicilian Innocents rode by singing:

"A soul I have to save,
A God to glorify,
And if a nigger don't vote for us
He shall forever die!"

But Compere Antoine was a brave man so he kept on trying to vote. He believed in the power of the ballot, the right to hold land, and the necessity for an education. Voting in the upstate parishes was quite a trick for a black man. Compere had to get up in the middle of the night and trail the white men to find out where the polling places were. Then in the morning he would ride up on his mule with his four sons only to find most of the time that the polling booth had been moved again. And no matter what time he reached it, it had just been closed. But Compere kept on trying.

After a while, being human, he got discouraged and gave it up. Voting hadn't done any good anyway, because they tore up his ballot the minute his back was turned and voted his name and that of his four sons on the Democratic ticket. Then they took it down to New Orleans where the Republican Returning Boards declared that there had been fraud and violence, as of course, there had, and reversed the decision so that there were always two Governors, two senates, and two houses in Louisiana. What made Compere sad, however, was the knowledge that the Republicans were just as crooked as the Democrats, and that who ever won, the black men lost.

So after a while he went back to minding his own business and cobbling shoes, and the Democrats decided that he was a good nigger after all and brought him their business and the Republicans did too so he prospered. He bought two young mules and a wagon and a barren stretch of land out in the piney woods. He put his four sons to work clearing the land and planting cotton which he hauled up to Shreveport in his wagon and sold.

Life became peaceful for him again -- as peaceful as a black man's life could be in the bulldozed parishes during the Reconstruction, which wasn't so peaceful after all. But Compere Antoine shrugged with true Gallic grace and bore it with African fortitude. Then late in the fall in the early seventies he drove once more into Shreveport, sold his cotton, and was driving away when he saw a crowd of white men surrounding a lone white woman. Cautiously he pulled up his team.

As he came to a stop he could see that the woman was young and that she was struggling to keep back her tears. All the men were laughing. One of them turned around and saw Compere Antoine. Instantly he turned back to the woman and said:

"So you come down here to teach niggers. Well, here's yore chanct. You kin start wit Uncle here!"

"Oh Mandy!" another man cried, "is you git yo Greek yet?"

All the others roared with laughter.

Compere Antoine looked at the young woman and smiled timidly. She looked up at him, then she said to her tormentors:

"Thank you, I will!"

She started forward and all the men stood back and let her through. She came straight up to the wagon and looked up at Compere Antoine.

"May I come up, sir?" she said.

"Sir!" the white men laughed. "Lookit the Sir! Sir Darky! Why Uncle, where's yore manners? The lady is axing fur a lift!"

Compere Antoine sat there without moving. The young woman put one foot on the wheel hub, exposing a well turned ankle, and all the men made catcalls. Then the old man put out a trembling hand and the young woman took it. With one convulsive jerk, he drew her into the wagon, and brought the whip savagely down upon the mules. They bounded off and the white men ran alongside the wagon laughing and making jibes about niggerloving Yankees until they were out of town.

When the last townsman had fallen back, Compere Antoine looked at the young Schoolmarm.

"If you tell me where you wants to go," he said; "I take you there, me."

She turned to him and her eyes were bright with tears, but she managed something like a smile.

"That's just it," she said. "I don't know. I just got here this morning. There was supposed to be a school, but it isn't there any longer -- and the superintendent is gone too. Those men said -- that they horsewhipped him!"

"Ain't surprised," Compere Antoine said.

"Then what on earth. . . . ."

"Lemme think, M'am," the old man said. They rode along in silence for a long time. At last Compere Antoine turned to the woman. He opened his mouth and closed it at least three times before he got it out, for after all what he was thinking was impossibly bold.

"Please M'am," he said, "don't be mad wit me. I been thinking, me, that maybe . . ."

"Yes?" the Schoolmarm said.

"That maybe you come down in our parish an teach us. We ain't got no school, us; but we build you one. And we build you nice house where you kin stay, yes. Can't nobody down there read and write but me and my boys, so all the time the folks git cheated, yes. They gives em Dimocrat votes and tells em they's Republican, an poor niggers don't know the difference. An they charge em double for everything. We pay you good, us. We work hard and git the money, yes. But mebbe you don't want. . . . ."

"Don't want?" the schoolmarm said. "Try and stop me!"

A week later a schoolhouse of handhewn pine boards stood on Compere Antoine's land. In all those seven days and nights neither Compere Antoine nor any of his neighbors had slept an instant. All other work had been totally neglected. The young schoolmarm boarded with a quadroon woman until the school was finished and afterwards they built her a home. Then Compere Antoine drove all the way down to New Orleans with a sack of half dollars, picayunes, and pennies which he had collected from his neighbors and bought books for the children.

There was never before on earth a hunger like the hunger of the freedmen for learning. Grownups came with their children and shared with them the slates. They came early in the morning and stayed until night. Whenever the weather was too bad for planting the men came too and listened with awed faces to the young Yankee Schoolmarm. Compere Antoine fairly lived in the school. Miss Varrick, the schoolmarm, soon found it necessary to delegate some of her simpler classes to the old man, for already she was hovering at the point of exhaustion. The news spread over the entire parish and many families moved into the neighborhood from distances of fifty miles away to be near the school.

Finally Miss Varrick took a weekend away from her duties and went to visit the Freedmen's Bureau down in New Orleans. When she came back she brought with her a written order granting appropriations for the school's support.

After that the school ran beautifully for almost two years. And all around Compere Antoine's place there grew up a widening island of black folks who could write their own names and read their Bibles and count money. They were very quiet and very dignified, but they weren't very popular. They had the bad habit of reading the papers that were brought to them for them to sign, and if they didn't agree with what the paper said, they would ask for time to "pray over it" which meant that the papers never would get signed after all. And it was kind of hard to cheat people who could count money.

But little by little things got bad again. Compere Antoine never knew just how it started. All he could do was to shake his head and say: "Blood thicker than water, yes!" By which he meant that even if the Yankees had fought the Confederates, they were after all whitefolks too, and sooner or later they were going to get together again. And when they did that would be the end of the blackman's chance.

He was right. One day he went up to the school and found the Yankee Schoolmarm sitting at her desk and crying like a little child.

"What's the matter, M'am?" he asked. "Ain't nobody done you nothing, no?"

She didn't say anything. Instead she stretched out her hand and gave him the letter. Compere Antoine took it and spelled out the words. As near as he could figure, it meant that the Freedman's Bureau wasn't going to spend any more money on the colored schools and that the state taxes for their support had been withdrawn.

The old man stood there a long time with his brow furrowed with thought. Then he said:

"Don't worry yourself none, you. I fix this, me. You watch."

That night Compere Antoine disappeared, riding away into the Piney Woods on his old mule. Three weeks later he turned up in New Orleans at the office of the Yankee General. He had a roll of paper thirty feet long. It was pasted together with flour paste and stuck together with pins. It had thousands of X's on it, where the black folks had put their marks to the petition that Compere Antoine had written out asking the Yankee General to please collect the tax and offering to pay extra so that the schools could go on in Louisiana for the black children and the white children too.

The general was touched. He sent Compere's petition up to the Legislature and they voted a small tax so that the schools went on after a fashion.

But by this time there had been the massacres at Bossier Parish, and St. Landry and St. Bernard and Colfax and Coushatta and in New Orleans the White Leaguers had killed forty four policemen and captured two gatling guns and one twelve pounder and thrown the Kellog Government out of office. But a few days later President Grant put Kellog back in office and the war went on. For the Civil War didn't stop in Louisiana or anywhere else in the South with the surrender at Appomattox Court House; it went on until 1877 and finally the South won. In 1876 the presidential election between Tilden and Hayes was in dispute and Florida, Louisiana, and Oregon held the balance of power. The votes had been counted and recounted but neither man had a clear cut majority. Oregon came out for Hayes early, but all the time Louisiana and Florida sat back holding the trump cards. Then the South sent men* to Washington to make a deal. If the Federal Troops are withdrawn, she promised, if the Yankees let us handle the blackmen as we see fit, then we'll cast our vote for Hayes.

And since this was the day of the Tweed Ring, of the Whiskey Ring, of the Credit Mobilier, and of the Star Route Frauds, when the National morality

---

* Senator John B. Gordon of Georgia and Congressman J. Young Brown of Kentucky

[note by Yerby]

was about on the level of a better class of New Orleans bawdy house, the deal was made.

And all this was a part of Compere Antoine's story because he had lived through it all during the years when for a black man to stay alive at all was a victory. Twelve hundred Negroes were killed in Louisiana between 1865 and 1877 and some of them were Compere Antoine's friends and one of them was his son.

But Compere Antoine wasn't bitter about it all. He kept the earnest sweetness of his nature until the night in 1877 when the last of the Yankee troops marched away. Then he stood by the side of the Yankee schoolmarm – alone, for he had hidden his sons to save their lives, and watched the White Leaguers setting his schoolhouse afire. All over the state the schoolhouses were burning. After they had burned the school, and chased Miss Varrick, the Yankee schoolmarm away, and whipped Compere Antoine, not too long or hard, for he was very old and they didn't want to kill him, they rode away and the night settled down, and it was very dark.

Compere had a feeling about that darkness. He thought maybe that the sun would never rise again. For the South had won its war and the things that it had fought for: aristocracy, the belief that one man was born better than another, and that men with black skins and poor men with white skins had no rights, that they, the rich and powerful, need respect, was the order of the day again. Elsewhere the world would go forward: There would be labor unions and the working man would strike for decent pay and shorter hours and better conditions. But in the South the clock had been stopped; the pages of the calendar had been turned backward. The South had won, and in winning, she had lost.

Compere looked at the last red embers of his schoolhouse smouldering feebly against the dark. And the bitterness entered his soul like iron and acid. He sat down on the ground beside the embers of his schoolhouse and wept. And this, of course, was nothing at all: just old black Compere Antoine, crying in the gathering night.

Myra and the Leprechaun

Mister Miles, the principal, bowed his head deeper upon his chest and the last words of the prayer came out in an inaudible mumble. Then he growled, "Amen," and opened his mouth to say "Class dismissed," but there was no need to. The children boiled out of the doorway of the little three room school and went running down the trail, shrieking with laughter so loud that the rocks threw back echoes. Myra looked across the big room at Miss Wilson, the other teacher, then at Mister Miles.

"Miss – ah – Tilden," Mister Miles said, "I'd like – ah – a word with you -- " Miss Wilson's eyebrows rose.

"Oh excuse me!" she said archly. Then she gathered up her books and marched out of the room.

"Darn!" Myra thought; "this is it. What on earth can I tell the old goat?" She turned briskly to her books and papers, murmuring, "One moment," in her soft, throaty voice. I have no doubt that you're a dear, Mister Miles, her irreverent mind went on, but you're rather an old dear, and besides I don't want my family ready made. I want the fun of getting my own brats with a young and lusty man. I should tell you that. It would shock the pants off of you. Only I don't fancy the sight of you <u>sans</u> trousers. Or with trousers for that matter. In fact, I just don't fancy you at all, Mister Miles. She dawdled over the papers.

Mister Miles crossed the room, and laid his hand lightly upon her shoulder. She dropped the shoulder slightly and went on gathering up the papers with great attentiveness.

"Myra," Mister Miles began.

Myra looked up at him, and her wide blue eyes were disconcertingly clear. Mister Miles swallowed thickly. Then he squared his shoulders.

Myra saw this gesture of resolution.

"Oh my God!" she murmured.

"My dear Miss Tilden," he said, but the shrill, childish voice was piping from the doorway:

"Miss Tilden!"

"Tina!" Myra said delightedly, and running to the doorway, she gathered the child up into her arms.

Mister Miles frowned.

"I – ah – had something I wanted to discuss with you," he said pompously. "You – ah – are not leaving for the city immediately?"

"No," Myra said, "not until tomorrow."

"Then may – ah – I have the honor of calling upon you tonight?"

Myra nodded dumbly. Still holding the child, she scooped her books and her handbag and disappeared through the doorway without even saying goodbye.

"I don't like that old Mister Miles," Tina said.

"Sssshh!" Myra said, holding the little girl closer, "you blessed, blessed child!"

"Why am I blessed?" Tina piped.

"Because you're my good fairy," Myra told her gravely. "You appear just at the right times and wave your wand and make everything all right."

"But I haven't any wand," Tina said.

"Oh but you have!" Myra said. "It's invisible, that's all."

"Really?" Tina said. She looked up into the face of her teacher. "I wish you didn't go away in the summertime," she said; "I wish you stayed with us always -- forever and ever and ever."

"So do I, darling. But I can't. I have to go away and study and learn new things to teach you. You don't mind that, do you?"

"W e ll," Tina hesitated. "New stories? Beautiful new stories about Knights and princes?"

"And elves and gnomes and fairies, and wicked old witches."

"I like the princes better," Tina said.

So do I, Myra thought. Only there aren't any anymore. Nowhere in the world. There are nothing but aging widowers with three fiendish ghouls howling about the house. Oh well --

The Svensen's farmhouse, where she boarded, was the first one down from the school, lying aslant on the slope of the hills with the beautifully tilled fields curving up and around the rock strewn mountain slope. She went in, holding Tina by the hand, and all the Svensens grinned happily at her.

"Ach!" Peter Svensen said; "tonight you eat good. Your last night with us. It will be sad to have you go. Then afterwards you play the fiddle and sing for us? Please?"

"I'm sorry," Myra said, "really I am. But tonight I must go out. You'll forgive me this time, won't you, Mister Svensen?"

"Where you go?" Peter demanded. "To the village? I go with you. Is not good you go alone – so youngt as you are."

"But I'm not going to the village," Myra laughed. "It's a secret, and I won't give it away."

"S-o –o," Hilda, Peter's plump wife said, "who is he – this youngt man? Why does he not come to the house?"

"There's no young man," Myra said. "Please don't tease me. Nobody wants an ugly old schoolmarm."

"You aren't ugly," Tina said. "You're just beautiful."

"Thank you, darling," Myra said. "But I'm not. Am I Mister Svensen?"

"No," Peter said gravely; "You're not pretty. You are something better than pretty. You are good. All the way through you are good. Your youngt man will be lucky."

"Oh my goodness!" Myra said. "That imaginary young man again. Please, Hilda, may I have some hot water. I need a bath the worse way."

"Sure," Hilda said, "right away!"

The round tin tub was small even for so slim a girl as Myra. She got out of it quickly, and dried herself with the rough towel before her mirror.

At least I have a good figure, she thought. She touched her plain oval face with the great blue eyes set a trifle too far apart, and her full, generous lips turned upward at the corners. She sat down before the mirror and began to comb out her long, pale wheat colored hair. "Not a curl in it, darn it!" she said. "But my figure is nice ----- much good it does me!"

Out of the corner of her eye she caught sight of the clock.

"Judastree!" she said; "I meant to be two miles away by now. Cowardly to run out on the old goat, but I can't let him get sticky on my hands." Hurriedly she got into her clothes – a serviceable two piece suit, heavy stockings, and comfortable, low heeled shoes. Outside, it was already night, and the wind was talking darkly with the trees. Myra went back up the trail toward the mountain, walking with long, loping strides, putting the miles between her and the house. As she topped the first rise, the moon was out, and the green-ish white blossoms of the apple trees were shredding the light into a feathery silver blaze. Her shadow stretched out behind her, blueblack on the trail.

It was an amazingly warm night for even late spring. Myra found it nec-essary to wipe her forehead with her handkerchief, but she kept doggedly onward, moving up the trail to where the laurel was, whiter than seafoam among the somber spruce. Then she was dropping downward into the hollow in which the cold, clear mountain springs came together and formed a great pool, almost a small lake, before it spilled between a crevice in the rocks down

into the valley below. She sat down upon an outcropping of granite, and let
her fingers trail in the water. It was warmer than she thought. Quickly she
bent down and removed her shoes and stockings.

"I could go swimming," she said, "but people do pass here – even at night.
Wading is bad enough --- " She tried the water with her toe, then, gathering her skirt in her hands she waded out into the pool. Slowly she splashed
through the cool water, feeling the sandy bottom firm under her feet, then,
suddenly, half way out she stopped, holding her skirt high, the water laughing
about her knees. She stood very still, listening.

"I'm crazy," she said, "I must be!"

But the sound was clearer now, a swirl of wild music, spinning dizzily
down from the mountain top. She turned her face toward the place that it
seemed to come from, but the echoes made it difficult to find the exact spot.
Slowly she moved her head from side to side, while the music laughed and
exulted and mocked in playful little runs and trills. Then it burst out, louder
than ever from a place almost directly above the pool, and lifting her head
she saw him coming, in gigantic, soaring leaps, and gamboling whirling
turns. And beside him, matching leap for leap was a tiny, spindle legged faun.

The two of them floated down in a beautiful curving arc, landing weight-
lessly upon a table rock just above the pool, then the boy went up on one toe
and whirled so rapidly that her eyes blurred following him. She stood there
unmoving, her skirt held at hip level, and stared at him. He stopped dancing suddenly, but there was no abruptness in the halting of the motion. He
drifted to a stop, so that one instant he was dancing and the next he was still,
but even the stillness had the quality of motion, like action arrested by the
hand of the sculptor, so that he seemed suspended in space, looking down
at her with great dark eyes. Seeing him, clearly now, fully for the first time,
she let her breath out slowly, in a long, long sigh.

Nothing, she thought stubbornly, nothing alive could be that beautiful.
I've read too much, and dreamed too much, and now I'm cracking up . . . .
But he came down to the edge of the pool, coming as a deer comes, soaring
over the rocks in one great effortless leap.

When he was close, she saw that he had on ragged overalls and a tattered
shirt that was open in front down to his broad belt. His hair fell in heavy
curling black masses over his forehead, and he kept pushing it back with one
slim, brown hand. As he half turned she caught a flash of white, and saw the
great white flower that he had shoved behind his ear. The faun came with
him, sniffing at his footsteps.

"H'lo," he said; "why don't you swim? It's warm enough."

Myra didn't answer. She was staring at the singing breadth of shoulders and the beautifully muscled arms, slim and unknotted, but flowing with power. His chest was broad in proportion to the rest of him but his waist, tightgirt with smooth muscle was no larger than her own. Myra's blue eyes widened.

"Does he always follow you?" she asked idiotically, although she wasn't the least bit concerned about the faun.

"Sure. Can't you swim? Wading's no fun."

Myra's face reddened.

"Nothing to swim in," she said.

"Oh," he said, "I forgot. Girls are silly. You don't care if I swim, do you?"

"No," Myra said, "not at all." Then she gasped, for already he was loosening the broad belt. She whirled away from him, and a moment later she heard twin splashes as he and the faun split the white water. Then he was lying in the shallow water almost at her feet. He looked up at her and his white teeth flashed in his tanned face.

"You're pretty," he said. "Come and swim with me, won't you?"

"No," Myra said, "no!"

Two strokes took him out into the deep water. He swam up the pool then down again, with the little faun bobbing along after him. Then he bounded out upon the rocks, and stepped into his overalls. Myra waded over to where he stood, and he reached down a slim, brown hand and helped her out of the water. He draped himself effortlessly over a curving rock, and Myra sat down beside him. The faun came up out of the pool, and shook itself. Then with no hesitation at all, it came up behind Myra and lay its head across her shoulder. Myra put up her hand and stroked the tiny head.

"You live around here?" she said to the boy. "I've never seen you before."

"I live there," he said, pointing. "Up over the top and down the other side."

"But I've been there," Myra said.

The boy frowned darkly. The water dropped out of the heavy black curl that fell over his left eye. He shook it back and away, so that a fine silver spray curved out from his moving head. He pushed the great white blossom closer down behind his ear, and looked at Myra.

"I'm sorry," she said; "I didn't mean to pry." She stood up. Instantly he was on his feet, the long cool fingers locked about her wrist.

"No," he said; "don't go ---- please don't go."

"Oh all right," Myra said, and sank down again. He bent forward, holding on to her wrist until she was entirely seated, then he released her.

"I don't go out in the daytime," he said. "Only at night."

"Oh," Myra said.

"People," he said; "I don't like people. I'm afraid of them."

"But I'm a person," Myra said.

The boy threw back his head and laughed. It was a clear, ringing sound, echoing out over the pool.

"No," he said, "no, you're not!"

"I'm not?" Myra gasped.

"You're a wild thing," the boy said. "Wild like me. See – Mike likes you."

The faun was nuzzling affectionately against Myra's hand. She smiled and stroked its head gently. Then she took hold of one of the tiny forelegs.

"Howdy, Mike," she said. "Glad to meet you."

"He doesn't like people," the boy said. He stood there looking at her a long time. "My name is Tony," he volunteered at last.

"Mine's Myra," she said.

"Myra," he said softly, "Myra. I like that."

She stared at him frankly, seeing the slimness of him, the unbelievable, wild-woodsthing grace. A dozen questions were trembling just back of her tongue tip. She couldn't hold them back, not all of them.

"Why do you wear that flower?" she burst out. "Why do you dance in the moonlight? Where did that music come from?"

Tony shook his head sadly.

"You too?" he said. "Maybe you really are people --- like the others."

"No," Myra said desperately; "I'm wild – I'm very wild. I just wanted to know about you."

He appeared not to be listening.

"They say I'm queer," he said. "But they're the queer ones. They don't like flowers, and they don't like to dance, and they don't know it's beautiful at night."

"It is," Myra said. "It's very beautiful."

"You see," Tony said triumphantly, "You are wild – I told you so!"

"Dance for me," Myra said.

Tony's slim hand went down into his pocket and came out with a battered mouth organ.

"It's no good," he said regretfully. "The birds do lots of things it can't. I've tried and tried ---"

Myra took the harmonica out of his hand.

"What you need," she said, "is a chromatic harmonica. This one doesn't have sharps and flats. I'll get you one."

"Will you?" the boy said breathlessly. "When?"

"Tomorrow. Please dance for me."

He put the instrument to his lips and began to blow. The wild, sweet music floated out, filling all space. Then he went up on one toe and whirled, the heavy black mass of his hair clouding his head. He came out of his turns and soared up and over the rocks. It was like floating, like flying, weightless, effortless, incredibly swift. And beside him the little faun cavoted all four legs off the ground at once.

"Beautiful!" Myra sighed, as he sank down again beside her.

He lay very close to her in the darkness, so that she could feel his breath stirring her hair. She got up abruptly.

"I've got to go now," she said.

Wordlessly he dropped down the trail with her, until they reached the place where the creek wandered across the upper fields. A little white fog hung over the water, no higher than a man's head.

"You'll come again tomorrow night?" he asked.

"Of course," Myra said, and ran across the log bridge, still holding her shoes and stockings in her hand.

She sat in her room a long time, poring over the mail order catalogue. And she wrote out the order for the chromonica and sealed the envelope before lying down to sleep.

The next morning she was at the post office before the window opened, feverishly scratching at the money order blank with the miserable desk pen.

"Staying with us a little longer, M'am?" the postmaster said as he banged the window open.

"Yes," Myra said nervously. "How much will this be?"

"That'll be eighteen cents extra," the postmaster said. Myra fished in her pocketbook for the change, and laid it on top of the crumpled bills. When, at last, the postmaster stopped his laborious scratching on the blue money order, she took it and stuffed it into the envelope.

"I'll take it," the postmaster said.

Myra shoved the letter through the window and went out upon the sidewalk, walking so fast that she almost bumped into Miss Wilson before she saw her.

"You lucky girl!" Miss Wilson cooed. "I suppose good wishes are in order?"

"Good wishes?" Myra echoed blankly. "For what?"

"Don't tell me he didn't propose!" Miss Wilson said. "He was getting up his courage all week."

"Oh!" Myra said. "To tell the truth, Martha, I didn't even see Mister Miles last night."

"You didn't see him! But he told me he was calling on you -- "

"I didn't wait," Myra said; "I didn't want to see him."

"Myra!"

"He could be my father, or even my grandfather. I don't want an old man, Martha."

"But Mister Miles is a big man. He's considered quite a catch," Miss Wilson said.

"For Pleasant Corners," Myra said: "But I'm not Pleasant Corners, and I never will be. You catch him, Martha."

Miss Wilson's little eyes narrowed still further.

"I suppose you'll leave for the city right away now," she said.

"No," Myra said, "No, --- I'm not going away at all."

Funny, she thought, as she strode away, leaving Miss Wilson staring after her, I didn't intend to say that. I didn't intend staying either. But I am --- and that makes it the truth. But God knows I didn't know it until just now. So this is what it does to you ---

Back at the farm she passed Tina with barely more than a preoccupied nod and went into her room. The child looked at her retreating back and the great tears rose and spilled over her lashes.

"She doesn't love me anymore," she wept. "What did I do bad, Miss Tilden?" But Myra was gone into her room and the door was shut behind her. A few minutes later old Peter paused by the door. The sound of the violin was clear in the hall, singing aloud in a swift swirl of gypsy music that stirred even his old blood. He frowned, listening. That music wasn't exactly proper, especially for a girl like Myra to be playing. She shouldn't even know the things it was suggesting. Perhaps she didn't. Maybe she was just playing the notes as it was written. "Ach!" he muttered sadly, and went on down the hall.

When it was early dark, Myra came out of the house lugging the heavy violin case. But before she had reached the gate she saw Mister Miles' flivver chugging up the road. "Oh my God!" she said, and measured the distance to the upper trail with her eye. It's no good, she thought. He's sure to see me. Oh well, it had to be done sooner or later. It'll be a relief to have it off my mind. She stood quite still and waited. The flivver crawled up the road and coughed to a stop beside her. Mister Miles got down from the driver's seat.

"Miss – ah – Tilden," he said. "You – ah – weren't at home when I called."

"I know," Myra said. "I'm sorry, Mister Miles. But you see, I knew why you were coming, and I needed time to think."

"And have you – ah – thought?"

"Yes," Myra said crisply. "The answer is no, Mister Miles."

Mister Miles frowned.

"I know I'm rather – ah – old for you," he said; "but I thought that in time -- "

"No," Myra said. "You're a good man, and I'm honored that you asked me. But I couldn't marry a man merely because I respected him. I'd have to love him, too, Mister Miles."

"That, too, would come in – ah – time," Mister Miles said.

"No," Myra said, "no!" and fled upward along the trail.

She waited by the pool until she heard the first laughing notes of music, then she lifted her bow and swung into a wild gypsy dance. He came spinning down the rocks, whirling dizzily on tiptoe. Then he bounded upon the table rock and sculptored her music into windlight motion. Mike, the faun, scampered all around him, his tiny feet twinkling over the rocks.

Myra put down the violin and looked up at him, and he floated down to earth at her feet.

"Beautiful!" she whispered.

"Play for me," he said.

Myra picked up the violin and began to play a soft, sad tune. He listened attentively for a long moment, then his weightless body began to curve through space in great, brooding arcs. The music sang and sighed its way into silence. Tony put out his hand to Myra.

"Now you must dance with me," he said.

Without any hesitation at all, Myra got to her feet. Tony played a few bars on his harmonica, then he whirled into the dance. Myra danced with him, whirling on tiptoe, swaying just out of reach. Time and time again the boy curved over her, his face bent down so that his lips were almost touching her own. But always at the last instant he drew back until Myra's young breasts were full and tight and there was an ache at the base of her throat. Then he hovered bird like above her, his slim hands moving up and down her body without ever touching her at all until the ache spread down from her throat and covered her whole body and her limbs were melting and scalding her. She spun up on tiptoe and her lips brushed his, just once, lightly, then she was gone, running down the trail, leaving the violin on the ground, and the boy and the beast Medusa touched, arrested into frozen motion, stood staring after her until she was out of sight.

Myra was breathless when she reached the farmhouse, but she kept on until she reached her room. Slowly she undressed. Then, just before she lifted her nightgown to put it on, she turned to the mirror. She stood there a long moment looking at herself, passing her hands lightly over her young breasts, feeling them visibly pointing.

"I never knew I had a body before," she said; "but I've got one now -- and darn it, I'm stuck with it!" Then she slipped the gown swiftly over her head and lay down but she did not sleep. I shan't go again, she decided. What's on his mind, he dances -- even when he doesn't know it's on his mind. But what's in mine I know, so I mustn't go again – I mustn't!

But three days later a letter came from the mail order house stating regretfully that they no longer had any chromatic harmonicas in stock. Myra threw a few clothes in her smallest bag and caught the next train down to the city without saying a word to anyone. It took her almost a week to find the instrument, battered and rusted in spots, lying dust covered in the window of a pawnshop. With it in her hand unwrapped she started uptown to her little hotel. Then she picked up her bag and caught the next train back to Pleasant Corners.

It was night when she got there, so she trudged the long trail to the Svensen's, and opened the door with her own passkey. She tiptoed down the hall, hearing the chorus of snores coming from old Peter's and Hilda's room, and Tina's deep, quiet breathing. Quietly, she undressed for bed. Out of the bag she drew her one useless possession – a gown spun of silver white cob web, so light that it drifted in her hands from a breath. She drew it over her head and sat down before her mirror. Picking up her brush she went to work on her pale hair, her mind busy.

No, I shan't see him again. I'll take it up there and leave it where he can find it, then I'll go back to the city and look for a job. Never come back again -- no, never. It's no good and I mustn't think about it or let it get me not ever ----

The brush spun out the long fine hair into glossy strands. Stroke, down stroke, out and down, one two three four five six ---- long way to go to reach a hundred. Then the brush was still in her hand, because the slight noise from the window had caused her to look up into the mirror. The soft muzzle of the faun lay across the sill, and Tony crouched in the window, staring at her, the great white blossom glowing behind his ear.

"You came back," he said. "Come --- "

Myra stood up, her hair spilling down over her shoulders.

"No," she said, "I can't -- I mustn't --- "

The boy crouched there, looking at her, seeing the pale white gold hair and the gown that was like a white mist over the creek at the time when the moon was just topping the apple trees. Then the patter of tiny feet was very clear in the hall.

"Tina!" Myra said. "She's waked up, you mustn't --- "

And he was across the room in one stride, gathering her up into his arms. Strange how strong he is, Myra was thinking, feeling his arms cord with the lifting, then they were gone through the window, and he was running cleanly, effortlessly across the high fields, carrying her like a child while the faun scampered along ahead of them.

And Tina stood in the open window staring after them, her great eyes saucer round and very bright. Just as they went into the dark where the trees lay their night shadow across the first rocks, the twin beams of the headlights butted around the bend, and Tina ran through the house to the front porch and waited for the car.

"It's very late," Mister Miles said. "It's – ah – after eleven."

"Well," Miss Wilson said, "it is sort of an emergency. We didn't know about the rally until this afternoon. Myra'll be glad to serve -- if she's back yet. She's getting so mysterious here of late -- running off to the city and all ---"

"Lovely girl," Mister Miles sighed. "I – ah – did have hopes --- "

Miss Wilson patted his arm.

"I know," she said. "Myra's just young, that's all. Give her time. She'll come around."

"You think so?" Mister Miles said, but Miss Wilson's hand tightened upon his arm.

"There's somebody there," she said. Mister Miles stepped down upon the brake, and the two of them got out and walked toward the porch. But before they reached it, the little white nightgowned figure came flying down the path and Miss Wilson bent and picked the child up, hearing, feeling the tiny body shaking with great, convulsive sobs.

"She's gone!" Tina wept. "He took her!"

Miss Wilson patted the thin little body.

"Now, now, Tina," she said, "catch your breath. Who's gone? Where?"

"Miss Tilden!" the child sobbed. "Up there!"

Mister Miles looked toward where the little finger was pointing.

"Up there?" he growled, "Who?"

"That wild boy! He came and he picked her up and ran up there!"

"The child's raving," Mister Miles said.

"No," Miss Wilson declared grimly, "she isn't raving. What wild boy, Tina? What are you talking about?"

"Tony," Tina said. "She goes up there lots – by herself. But she always comes back. But this time he took her – so now she won't never come back and I won't ever see her no more and maybe she doesn't love me!" She buried her little head against Miss Wilson's shoulder and shook all over.

"Tony?" Mister Miles said.

"Old man Boswell's son. You know, the queer one. I think we'd better look into this."

Mister Miles looked at Tina and then at Miss Wilson.

"Yes," he said slowly, "I – ah – expect we'd better."

"You run along to bed, Tina," Miss Wilson said. "We'll be back in a little while."

"You'll bring her back?" Tina said. "Please, Miss Wilson, please!"

Miss Wilson looked at the child. When she spoke her voice was very gentle.

"Yes," she said. "Yes, Tina, we'll bring her back." Then the two of them started upward, across the higher fields.

Tina didn't go back to bed. She curled up in the big rocker and waited. She fought her heavy eyelids for a long time, but it was no good. Her sleep was light and fitful, so that it seemed only minutes later that she heard the voices.

"Oh my God!" Miss Wilson was saying, "Oh my God!"

"I – ah – don't know what to -- ah -- say," Mister Miles said.

"Shameless," Miss Wilson said, "utterly shameless! Dancing in the moonlight with that lunatic -- in a gown as transparent as window glass!"

"Beautiful," Mister Miles said.

"Mister Miles!"

Mister Miles' face reddened in the darkness. "Sorry," he said.

"The question is," Miss Wilson said, "what are you going to do?" Tina thought her voice sounded fierce.

"I guess," Mister Miles said sadly, "We'll – ah – have to call a special meeting of the school board."

"Yes, yes!" Miss Wilson said. "But how will we let her know?"

"Leave her a note with Tina. Yes, I – ah – guess that's best. Dear me! There's the child now – asleep in that chair."

Miss Wilson picked Tina up, but the little girl did not snuggle up to her again. She lay rigid in the teacher's arms and stared straight into her face, while Mister Miles got his briefcase from the car and laboriously scribbled a note by the glow of the headlights. He folded it carefully and gave it to Tina.

"Give this –ah – to Miss Tilden," he said; "when she – ah – comes back."

Then they went back to the flivver and backed out of the yard and turned into the road. Tina took the note and went back to Myra's room. Then, still holding it, she lay across the bed and fell asleep.

It was dawn when Myra stole back into the room and found her there, still holding the note in her tiny hand. Myra tried to ease it out without awakening her, but Tina sat straight up without a word and watched her while she read it.

"It's – it's bad?" she quavered.

Myra looked at her and smiled sadly.

"Yes, Tina," she said; "it's bad – very bad. I'll have to go away now – far away. And I doubt that I can ever come back."

Instantly the child hurled herself upward into Myra's arms.

"I did it!" she wept; "I told them! I thought you weren't coming back! Oh how wicked I am!"

"Hush, Tina," Myra whispered. "It isn't as bad as all that. Maybe someday I'll see you again." She put the child down, and began opening drawers, pulling out her clothing. Tina watched her with great round eyes. Then she fled from the room leaving a trail of half stifled sobs behind her.

At a little before ten o'clock, Myra came out of her room. She was dressed for traveling, and she carried her little bag. Tina saw her go into the front room, and heard a few scraps of muffled conversation. She edged closer.

"The express man will call for my other things," Myra was saying. Tina didn't wait to hear more. She skipped down the steps and started running upward, toward the place where the apple trees were and beyond.

Myra hesitated only a moment before the school. She could see them sitting around the walls, the loose faced men, and all the thin, acrid women with tight, grim faces. They're all here, she thought, all the vultures! Well, this time, I'm going to cheat them. Then, raising her chin into the air, she strode into the schoolhouse, swaying like a young willow on her high spike heels. The minute she came in the buzz of talk died, and something like a gasp ran around the wall. Myra took the envelope out of her bag.

"I came here," she said clearly, "to submit my resignation in writing. I have no doubt that it will be accepted. But I don't intend to be examined by any of you in regard to my morals or my personal affairs or anything concerning me. So now I'll say goodbye to you all and I hope -- "

They heard it at the same time, the banging, metallic clatter of the truck on the road, and the screech of the brakes.

"And I hope," Myra went on, with the barest perceptible pause, "that you enjoy yourselves!"

She heard the light skittering of noise of the footsteps at the door as she turned, and Tony was there in the doorway, his black eyes darting fierce bright from face to face stunning them into silence.

"You old buzzards!" he spat, then his arm was around Myra's waist, drawing her through the door. Outside the engine of the truck pounded raggedly.

"That's paw in the truck," Tony said; "and I got a license, and paw called up the preacher. You ain't gonna be disgraced!"

Myra looked up at him, seeing the store bought clothes that fitted him so badly, blue, with bell bottom trousers and a light powdered blue vest with dark blue lapels, and a dark blue strap that ran across his stomach. The big, light grey hat sat high on his head, and those tight shoes must have been giving his feet agonies.

"You came out in the daytime," Myra said. "You came around people ---"

"I forgot. I'm not afraid anymore. I got mad. Come on now!"

"No," Myra whispered, "no."

Tony stood looking at her blankly while Mike, the faun, pushed his head over the back end of the truck, and Tina looked out from the seat beside the old man.

"You're free," Myra said; "You don't need a wife. You don't want responsibility."

Tony's black eyes clouded.

"I want you," he said. "You're my kind. Nobody can stop us now. If we want to dance, we can dance, or swim in the pool, or -- "

"You're a wild thing," Myra said, "remember? You're free---"

Tony took off the big hat.

"If you go away," he said slowly, "I shall never dance again."

"And if I stay?"

"We'll dance! And all our kids'll dance. And nobody'll tie us down -- not nobody!"

Myra didn't say anything. She stood there looking at him, then the laughter started down deep in her throat. She reached up and took off his hat and sailed it across the street, over the truck. Then she yanked at his bow tie and threw it after the hat. She loosened the buttons of his vest.

"Take it off!" she said. "It and the coat!"

Tony looked at her wonderingly, then he obeyed.

"Now the shoes!"

He sat down upon the curb and drew them off while all the board members gaped from the windows of the schoolhouse. When he stood up, Myra rolled up his shirt sleeves and loosened his collar. Then she stood back and looked at him.

"Just one thing more," she said, and ran across the lawn to where the white roses were in bloom. She bent down and broke off a blossom, stripping the thorns from the stem. Then she went up on tiptoe and he could see her eyes were tearbright, but the deep laughter still gurgled in her throat. She put the rose behind his ear, and looked up at him, holding him by the shoulders, swaying lightly from side to side.

"Now I'll marry you," she said. "Now!"

Then she slipped one arm down low around his waist and the two of them went across the sidewalk and out into the street toward the place where the truck waited, a wisp of vapor standing straight up from its radiator cap like a plume.

The Quality of Courage

The hurricane came in from the South from beyond the Keys, and whatever it struck, it destroyed. It shattered the plate glass in the expensive storewindows on Biscayne Boulevard, and wrecked the little fishing shacks on the fringes of the Everglades. A hurricane does not play favorites. It is as remorseless as the hand of God.

It lifted the sign which read "Saunders' Fruit Farm" from above the gate of the little citrus grove about twenty miles North of Miami and turned it end over end, lifting it higher and faster, until young Johnny Saunders could not see it anymore. He came out of the house, then, bending over against the wall of the wind, his oilskin standing straight out behind him, his red hair pulling against his scalp, and started for the orange groves. Beside the road, the wind was laying the coconut palms down in rows, splitting them halfway up their trunks, then breaking them raggedly in half and sending them down. It was curiously like watching a newsreel, for although the palms struck the earth with tremendous force, Johnny could not hear them. The wind slammed against his eardrums like gigantic cupped hands, so that after the first minute there was no more sound for Johnny – nowhere in the world.

He stopped when he reached the orange groves. It was no good. The trees were down – everyone of them. He turned and started back toward the house, angling off toward the road.

The house was still there. Even the roof had not yet let go. Beyond it, off the point, the sea boiled white and angry, and now and again, when the wind slackened, he could hear it booming. But now there was a new thing: for a black sedan stood on the road beside the house. Little white wisps of vapor pumped from its exhaust and were snatched away by the wind. A man sat behind the wheel, waiting. Then Johnny saw the others. They were standing before the house with their hands pointing downward at something on the ground. As he watched, Johnny saw the black shapes in their fists jump jerkily, and the yellow orange tongues of flame spat. The little mound on the walk quivered under the impact. Then one of the men kicked whatever it was that lay on the ground, and they turned back to the car, walking slowly, calmly.

Johnny started running toward the car. But, long before he reached it, it moved off, its tires throwing up bright circles of rain spray. Johnny ran after it a few steps, but it pulled away effortlessly. He stopped and turned toward the drive. Then he was bending over the object on the walk and the breath in his lungs was a slow, sick gurgle.

"Paw," he whispered, "paw . . ."

It wasn't pretty. They had shot Monk Saunders seven or eight times at very close range. And they had left him there, face up in the rain, with his eyes wide open and staring. Johnny knelt down and gathered him up, feeling him light and frail and wetcold to the touch, awkward to carry, looseswinging. He got the door open at last, and lay the body of his father down upon the bed. The rain water dripped off him, wetting the sheets. Where there was blood, the stain was pink.

Johnny stood back and looked down. Then, very gently, he pressed the eyelids shut, and tied up the jaw with a fishline. Then he sat down and lit a cigarette, seeing the matchflare jerking in his trembling hands. He sat there all night while the wind caught at the eaves of the house and shook it like a terrier shakes a rat. The mound of burned out butts grew in the ash tray, and after a while the cigarettes were all gone.

First in the morning, the wind died. Johnny got up stiffly and opened a drawer. He took the Colt automatic out and looked at it, feeling it heavy in his hands, cold and deadly with a lovely deadliness, then he stuffed it inside his shirt, and breaking open the cartridge boxes, emptied them into his pockets. He pulled on his oilskin, and started for the door, but at the bedside he paused.

"Goodbye, paw," he said. Then he went out into the greying morning.

He had to walk all the way into town to reach the police. All the telephone lines were down. But when he was there, he made a wide detour into the wilderness of splintered wreckage that had been shanty section where the Negroes lived, and found Midge's house. It and all the houses on the same side of the street were untouched. On the other side, fifteen feet away, not a shanty was left upright.

When the big black man came to the door, Johnny took the pistol out of his pocket and handed it to him without any ceremony.

"Here," he said, "keep this for me for a while."

"Mister Johnny –" Midge began.

"Don't argue. Keep it." Then, seeing the worry and fright in the big Negro's face, he added. "Paw. They killed him. Got to see the police – and I don't want them to take away my gun. Get it?"

"Yessir," Midge rumbled. "Who done it, Mister Johnny? Tim?"

"Somebody he sent. Here, take these, too." He passed over the bullets. "I'll be back."

But it was three days before he got back. It was only after the coroner found that the bullets that killed Monk Saunders came from guns of two different calibers, a thirty two and a thirty eight, that the police, reluctantly, let Johnny go.

"Bird in hand," Johnny said grimly. "Wrong bird."

He stood on the highway with the Colt slung beneath his armpit in a crude rope holster, and thumbed the passing cars. The cars moved northward along U.S. One, coming very fast, their tires singing over the pavement, one after another in a long line. They went by Johnny without stopping until his shoulder ached from holding up his beckoning arm. Then, finally, one of them stopped and Johnny was speeding northward, looking out at the wind bent trunks of the palms. The man who was driving the car saw the look.

He said: "Some hurricane, eh?"

Johnny looked at him before answering. He measured the seasonal red tan of the round face, the dark glasses and the yellow sport shirt with flying fish on it that in one form or another was a uniform of the winter people.

"Yes," he said. "Some hurricane."

"Did a lot of damage?"

"Some," Johnny said.

The conversation died. The tires sang on. The light spilled over the rim of the land and the dusk came in with a coolness, the wind rising.

Johnny turned to the driver.

"This is it," he said. "You can let me off here."

The brakes complained briefly and the car slid to a stop.

"I don't see anything," the driver said.

Johnny pointed to a sign, nailed to the trunk of a palm. "Pinelawn," the sign read.

"Down the road apiece, I reckon." His head jerked toward a dirt trail that lost itself in the brush twenty yards from the highway. "Thanks for the lift."

"Don't mention it," the driver said. Still he sat there for a brief moment, watching Johnny move off, his shoulders broad, lean thewed, slim of belly and buttock in the faded G. I. fatigues, and sighing he remembered his own lost youth.

Johnny had forgotten the car and the driver before they were out of sight. He walked slowly under the palms through the palmetto brush, swiveling his legs out of reach of the bayonet leaves of yucca, following the ancient road. As he walked, the shadows moved in upon him, and finally, when he lifted his head, he saw the first pale glimmer of a star.

He rounded the next bend, and then, abruptly, he was there. The roadhouse sprawled in a pinewood, with the little tourist cabins trailing out from it on both sides. Before it in a neat semicircle, the cars nuzzled, everyone of them bearing the yellow square of a Florida license. This he could see plainly, because the roadhouse was ablaze with light, and most of the tourist cabins were lighted, too. The sound of music beat in faintly upon his ears, harsh and tinny, and with it the muffled scrape of dancing feet. Now and again laughter shrieked through the other sounds, feminine laughter, high pitched and night crazed – like the swamp birds in the 'glades.

Johnny took off his jacket, and slid down and out from under the rope that held the holster to his armpit. Then he took out a wide square of oilskin from his pocket and wrapped the gun in it carefully. He stood quite still for a while holding the yellow burden in his hand and gazing at the trunks of the trees around him until he saw what he wanted – the black triangle of hollow trunk. He moved through the brush toward it, and kneeling down, thrust the oilskin wrapped Colt far inside. Then he stood back and looked at his work. It was good. Even if you looked for it, you wouldn't know the gun was there.

Johnny straightened up and went down the gentle slope toward the roadhouse coming directly to it across the open road, making no effort at concealment. On the wide veranda, he hesitated a moment; then he pushed open the door and went in. Sound blasted both his eardrums, juke box blare and the rumble and titter of many voices, glasses rattling, and the scuffle of shoeleather on the pinefloor. Smoke tugged and stung his eyes and a solid wall of odor assaulted his nostrils: perfume, whiskey reek, sweat stench, stale beer . . .

He walked uncertainly through the wall of vapors toward the bar. The bartender looked up.

"What's yours, son?" he growled. "Name yer pizen."

"Looking for Tim," Johnny said. "Sent for me. Said he had a job . . ."

The bartender stared at him. Then his head jerked backward.

"In back," he said. "Knock before you go in."

Johnny walked over to the stout door and raised his hand.

"Go ahead," the bartender said. "Knock. Tim won't eat you."

Johnny brought his knuckles down, hard, upon the door. It flew open so suddenly that he fell back two paces. The man who had opened it was tall, grey, a ghost of dignity lingering on in his face.

"Yes?" he said.

"You Tim?" Johnny said. "Mr. McCain, that is?"

"Hell no!" another voice boomed. "Stand aside, Croaker, and let me see what in hellfires alookin for me now."

The grey man stood aside. Behind him a mountain of a man sat upon a bench. His little black eyes were lost in puffy rolls of fat. His big head sank down amid greasy jowls upon his shoulders, his neck lost in oily mounds of hairy flesh, and below that he was all belly. On his lap a woman sat, her white arms locked about his nonexistent neck. A young woman, blonde, lacquered, expensive. Like the winter people. Then she spoke and Johnny knew she was one of the winter people, for her voice was crisp, swift, pointed, with no sun in it anywhere.

"Hello handsome," she said. "You're cute."

"Who in hellfires might you be?" Tim growled.

Johnny ran the tip of a dry tongue over drier lips.

"Johnny," he said. "Johnny Saunders . . ."

The big man was up then, moving with a speed unbelievable in one of his bulk. Johnny felt rather than saw the inch long muzzle of the bellypistol thrust into his middle. Tim's big head moved to one side in the direction of the man named Croaker.

"Frisk him," he ordered.

Croaker's hands moved over Johnny's hard young body with weary expertness.

"Nothing," he said quietly. "No cannon, Tim. The Kid's clean."

Johnny saw the little expression of puzzlement creep into Tim's eyes.

"Please," he said. "What's wrong? I come here looking for a job, and you . . ."

Tim's little pig eyes opened wider.

"You come here looking for a job?" he echoed. "Ain't you Monk Saunders' boy?"

"Yes," Johnny said. "He always told me to come to you if I needed anything. And the other day when the tree fell on him . . ."

The muzzle of the pistol came away from Johnny's middle. Now he could breathe again. He dragged the stale, fetid, smoke laden air into his lungs. It tasted like wine.

The big man stood there like an obscene idol, the gun that was thicker about the barrel than a standard police pistol and shorter than a man's extended hand dangling from his fist.

"Lemme git this straight," he said. "Monk's dead. He was kilt – by a tree that happened to fall on him . . ."

"Yessir," Johnny said. "That's right. Paw was growing oranges. We had a little place down on the Keys. Saunders' Fruit Farm, Paw called it. Then there was this hurricane. Kilt Paw, and wiped us clean at the same time. So I remembered what Paw said about coming to you. And I did. That's all."

Tim looked at Croaker.

"Croaker," he said, "this kid's telling the truth – ain't he?"

Croaker smiled – a thin, sad smile that seemed to mock the whole world.

"Yes," he said, quietly, "he is."

"Why th' dirty, double crossing sons of . . ." He looked at Johnny, seeing the look of well feigned surprise on the boy's face. He grinned suddenly. "'Scuse me, Kid," he said. "This ain't got nothing to do with you. Croaker just told me something. Two mugs I paid five hundred smackers to do some nice easy work ain't done it – and collected just the same. Things like that git me riled up. Sorry I shoved that lil tinker toy in your belly, but a man's got to be careful." He stuck his big head through the doorway and bellowed:

"Harry! Bring us another Fifth of Scotch. Th' best. I got company." Then he sat down, rearranging the blonde on his lap.

"So you want a job," he said to Johnny. "Well I kin use you. With your build you'll do all right. Monk Saunders' boy. Well, well, well . . . Good old Monk. Him and me was in business once. He told you that?"

"Yes," Johnny said, "Yes."

"Business?" the blonde said.

"Running rum in from Cuba," the man called Croaker said wearily, "and guns back to Havana, and anywhere else where the little brown brothers had a mad on with their government. Good business. Profitable."

Tim glared at Croaker. But, when he spoke, his voice was calm.

"One of these days, Croaker," he said, "I'm gonna git too tired of you. Just a little too tired." He turned back to Johnny and his fat face creased into a grin.

"You know, Kid," he said, "I'm mighty glad to have you – yeah, mighty glad." He attempted to rise, his breath fluttering noisely through his flabby lips. "Jinny," he grunted, "git th hell offen me. Gotta see something."

The blonde slid easily to her feet, her short dress trailing so that Johnny could see her legs. Legs were nothing. Winter people always went nigh onto naked. But in here it was different. Outside in the clear air and the sunlight was onething. But here, somehow, it was different.

"Nice gams, eh, Kid?" Tim guffawed. "Don't let em git you. You'll git yore bellyfull o' gams here. Gams and whatever else you wants . . . Stand up straight."

Johnny stiffened. His quick eye saw Tim's hand double into a fist, big as a shoulder ham. Then the fist whistled out, straight for his jaw. His forearm came up instinctively, and he rolled with the punch, letting it ride harmlessly over his shoulder. He dropped into a crouch, both hands ready.

But Tim was roaring with laughter, his big belly shaking.

"Good!" he bellowed. "You'll do!"

Slowly Johnny straightened up, wonder in his eyes.

"Part of yore job. Now an then somebody fergits his manners. Can't have nothing like that in my place, now kin I? You gonna help Harry mix drinks. He'll learn you how. Slack nights you waits tables – when the gals are off. But every night. . . ."

"You see that the gentlemen who visit this elegant establishment conduct themselves with decency and propriety," Croaker finished for him in his weary voice.

"Damn!" Tim said. "That sounds right good, Croaker. Write that down for me. Gonna have a sign made up like that. Hang it over the bar."

"And in the cabins?" Croaker said, a slow smile lighting his melancholy eyes.

Again Tim's bullbellow beat against the ceiling.

"Cabins is their own damn business," he said. "Come on Kid, might as well git you started."

Johnny trailed behind him into the tavern. A minute later he was clad in a white apron, and juggling ice and scented liquids while the bartender snarled instructions at him out of the corner of his mouth. And that was how it began.

By the middle of the next week, the coolness had gone out of the air and the heat settled down like a blast furnace over the land, so that the palms drooped listlessly above U.S. One and the cars grew fewer – so few that there were minutes when Johnny heard no tires whining upon the highway at all. And when the hot wind blew in from the sea it stank of dead things and salt flats and rotten weeds.

Johnny came down to his steaming little cubbyhole of a room, half dead of fatigue, only to find Croaker sitting upon his bed waiting for him.

"Don't mind me," Croaker said. "Sit down." He pulled a huge bottle from under the bed where he must have hidden it earlier, for Johnny had no liquor. "Have a drink?" he said.

Johnny shook his head. "Never touch it," he said.

"Good," Croaker said. "Look Kid, I'm going to talk to you. First I'm going to tell you to get out. But you won't listen to that. So I'm going to tell you why."

Johnny settled back listening.

"First the things you'll have to do. You've been lucky. You haven't seen a really ugly drunk yet. But this is how they handle them here: You don't play with a drunk. You hit him very fast and hard, in the pit of the belly or lower, and chopp the back of his neck as he goes down. If you give him time, very often he comes out with a gun or a knife and that's bad for business. After you've hurt him as bad as you can, you drag him out, search him, and dump him into the station wagon. One of the other boys will drive him off, and drop him miles away. Like it?"

Johnny shook his head. "No." he said. "No, I don't like it."

Croaker grinned at him.

"Didn't think you would. Number two: the girls who wait on the tables have several functions: They wait tables, try to talk the customers into a mood of free spending, and they engage in certain other activities in the so called tourist cabins behind the roadhouse. You can make a pass at them if you want to. Tim doesn't mind. Only they won't respond – because they're dead on their feet from sheer weariness; and also because by now they've all acquired a ferocious dislike for the entire race of man . . ."

He tilted the huge bottle ceilingward, and his adam's apple jerked in his thin neck. Then he wiped his mouth, not with the back of his hand like everybody else, but with a snowy handkerchief. There was something different about Croaker.

"Number three. You don't talk to me too much. I'm a subversive influence. Tim doesn't like my ideas. Number four: you keep your hands off Jinny. Tim doesn't like that either."

"That," Johnny declared, "will be easy."

"No it won't. Or rather, it won't be easy to keep her hands off you. You and anything else that breathes and wears pants . . ."

He took another long pull from the bottle.

"Jinny," he observed tiredly, "is a tramp. Only that's an insult to the noble tribe of hoboes – male and female."

"I see," Johnny said. Then: "Why do they call you Croaker?"

"Doctor," Croaker said. "Maker of stiffs extraordinary. I came here two years ago looking for something. Been here ever since. Tim likes having me around. I amuse him."

He leaned forward, looking at Johnny.

"Get out!" he spat. "Get out of here while you can."

Johnny lit a cigarette and studied him through the thin wreath of smoke.

"You," he said. "Why don't you go?"

"Can't. Got something to do."

"Like what?"

"Like putting a fort five slug through that obscene monstrosity's guts." The words were spoken very quietly and without any expression at all. But Johnny was convinced. Completely convinced.

"Why?" he said.

"Jinny."

"But you said. . . . ."

Croaker got up and walked toward the door. He paused a moment, look-ing at Johnny. "That she's a tramp?" he answered. "She is. But she is also – my wife." Then he walked very quietly out of the room, ducking his head a little to avoid bumping into the tiny, yellowish light bulb that dangled from a frayed cord in the hall.

Johnny threw his cigarette down on the floor, and ground it out under his heel. Then he got up and went back into the darkened roadhouse, pausing long enough to gather up a pail and a mop. But, once he was inside, he placed them carefully in a corner and went out of the door into the dark. He went straight to the tree where he had left his gun. He stood there for a long time, looking about him, before he knelt down and thrust his arm into the deep hollow in the trunk. His fingers had already closed over the oilskin wrapped bundle when he heard the voice.

"What you got there, sweetiepie," it said. "Buried treasure?"

Slowly Johnny's fingers loosed their hold. He brought his hand out without the gun and straightened up. Jinny stood there in the moonlight, a cigarette dangling out of the corner of her too red mouth, the smoke making her left eye squint.

"What do you want?" Johnny growled.

"You," Jinny said.

Johnny stared at her, his brow held in a frown so hard it hurt.

"Look, Jinny," he began.

"I'm looking, sweetiepie," Jinny whispered, "And I like what I see. . . ."

"Oh for pete's sake, Jinny," Johnny said, "leave me be, will you?"

"No." She walked toward him. Johnny took a step backward, but the tree was directly behind him. Jinny's arms came up and her hands locked behind his head. Her lips parted little by little so that the cigarette fell from their corner without any effort on her part, then they caught his and worked until he felt the triphammers start in the pit of his stomach, and he was being scalded from the inside by the beat of his own blood. Furiously he brought his hands up and broke her grip. Then he turned and ran like a man whose life was in danger. But, as he tore through the underbrush, he heard the sound of her laughter, low, eager, mocking; and never before in all his life had he felt himself so completely and utterly a fool. . . .

Back in the roadhouse, he picked up his mop and pail and began to work with terrible energy, washing away the leavings of last night's hilarity and brawls. The work quieted him. He kept at it steadily until it was almost done. Then he heard the door open quietly and straightened up quickly over the mop handle. But it wasn't Jinny. It had been, he guessed, more than an hour before he had left her in the woods. Surely she had come back by now. He stood very still, staring at the doorway, until, a long moment later, the men came in. They had a girl between them. Johnny looked at the girl. Even in the semidarkness of just before dawn, he could see she was not like the others. Like they had been, perhaps, before they came to Pinelawn. Young. Not a day over eighteen. Thin and unformed, her breasts under the tight dress as small as seed oranges, her hips as slim as a boy's.

"Where's Tim?" one of the men said.

"In back," Johnny said.

The man released the girl and walked across the room. From ten feet away, by the light of one dim bulb, Johnny could see the red marks his fingers had left upon her slim wrists. The other man caught her and held both her arms, half twisting them behind her back. The girl did not struggle. She looked at Johnny and the mute appeal in her blue eyes was too much, so that he had to turn away his face.

Behind him, Johnny heard the soft shuffle of Tim's bare feet. For all his bulk, Tim moved as quietly as a cat. He walked over to the new girl and looked at her.

"Wanted a job as a night club singer," the man who held her grinned. "So she ran away from her maw. I ask you, Tim, was that nice?"

"Oh don't bother me!" the girl wept. "Let me alone!"

Tim didn't say anything. He looked at Johnny out of the corner of his little eyes as though he were thinking of something. Then he said:

"Hang onto her, Blackie. Got to tell th Kid, here, something." He put his ham like hand on Johnny's arm and led him into the back room. He closed the door.

"Look, Kid," he whispered, "them two bums who just brought that little tramp in is the two what pulled that fast one on me. Collected five hundred for a job they didn't do. Didn't expect em tonight or I'd have had some of the boys around. But I'm going to take 'em. You with me?"

Johnny nodded grimly. These two had killed Monk. Not out of anger or hatred or out of any feeling whatsoever. They had done a job. And had been paid for it. Five hundred dollars. The price of Monk Saunders' life. And Tim, who had paid them, was going to pay them again. The real price this time. The ancient, Biblical price. Afterwards, he, too, would be paid. Johnny would see to that.

They came out the room very slowly and casually. Johnny's fingers were gripped tight around the blackjack Tim had given him. They walked until they stood close to the two men, spread out a little so that the men were between them.

"Give th little gal to the Kid," Tim said.

The man half turned the girl in Johnny's direction. Johnny saw Tim's big fist go up, the brass knuckles on it glinting in the light. Then it crashed down and the man crumpled like a thing of rubber, bonelessly to the floor. The other man whirled tugging at his armpit. Johnny hit him then, hard across the face, feeling the bones splintering under the blow, drawing the ugly, loaded little club of leather back, and the man following it as it came, bending over grotesquely in a curious bow that ended only when he stretched out full length at Johnny's feet.

"Nice going, Kid," Tim grinned. "Wanta drive th wagon?"

Johnny shook his head.

"Got no stomach for that," he said weakly. "Might foul it up for you."

"Okay," Tim said. "I'll call Harry and Bobo. You take th gal out to Thirteen. Lock her up." He paused a moment, then a grin spread over his fat, oily face. "And lock yoreself up with her. You earned a little fun." He turned then and picked up the phone.

Johnny gave the girl a little push to start her walking. The girl's black hair, under his nostrils, was very clean, and the scent of a dime store perfume rose from it. She didn't struggle or cry out or do anything at all but walk ahead of him like one half asleep. Johnny took the key ring from his belt and fished for the key. He unlocked the door and turned on the light.

The girl looked at him, her face blank, wooden.

Johnny grinned at her suddenly.

"Sit down," he whispered. "I can't leave right now. 'Tain't safe."

"You mean," the girl said, "that you ain't gonna . . .?"

Johnny shook his head.

"I ain't gonna," he said. Suddenly he crossed to the window and drew the curtain aside. His breath came out in a hard rush, and he knelt beside the window, watching. The girl came over to where he knelt and sank down beside him.

The station wagon stopped behind the roadhouse. As they watched, Tim came out, and after him Harry and Bobo. Harry and Bobo bore something between them - something long, inert, loose-swinging. Tim waited very quietly until they had dumped their burden into the back of the station wagon. Then they went back into the roadhouse and came out with another.

This time the burden stirred, tried feebly to get up. Tim's big fist rose and fell, and there was no further motion. The motor whirred, coughed into life. The station wagon moved off, gathering speed as it went. Then it screeched around a curve and was gone. Tim yawned and went back into Pinelawn.

The girl turned to Johnny, naked terror in her eyes.

"They said they was Movie Scouts," she whispered. "They promised me a job . . . Then they bought me here - to this place - where they kill people!"

Johnny nodded.

"I reckon you know now what kind of job they had in mind for you," he said.

"Yes," the girl said dully, "Yes, I know."

"What's your name?"

"Martha," the girl said. "Martha Jennings."

"Mine's Johnny Saunders. Come on now, I'm gonna get you outa here."

Very quietly, Johnny unlocked the door and pushed it open. There was no moon, but the stars stood above the pine trees, very high and clear. They made a wide circle to the rear of the roadhouse and came out on the road beyond the bend. Johnny put his hand in his pocket and came out with his savings - all of his savings. Then he took out a ten dollar bill and put it back. The rest of the money he gave to Martha.

"Take this," he said. "Walk, or hitch your way into town. Then get a bus for Jacksonville. Go to the Roseland Hotel. It's cheap. Wait there for me. It may be a couple of days before I can get away."

"I'll walk," the girl said. "I'm never gonna hitch again as long as I live." She looked at him, her blue eyes very soft. "What did you say your name was?" she whispered.

"Johnny," he said, "Johnny Saunders."

"Johnny," the girl faltered, "you know I ain't – that I ain't like those other girls I saw at that place . . ."

"I know," Johnny said.

"And Johnny," the tears were in her voice now, choking it off, "Thank you - for everything. I'll be waiting at that hotel. No matter how long it is, I'll be waiting..."

Johnny opened his arms and she came into them very simply. Then he kissed her, hard. She didn't know how to kiss. It was like running into a post.

After she had gone, Johnny walked very swiftly toward the hollow tree. He knelt down and thrust his hand inside and his fingers closed on - nothing. There was no gun in the hollow anymore. There was nothing in the hollow but dampness and dark and the feel of rotting wood.

He stood up and let his breath out in a long sigh.

"Jinny!" he exploded, "that little nogood. . . ." Then he was running hard toward Pinelawn. He stopped beside the row of garbage pails and dug into them furiously, his mind working clearly, cleanly. After a while he found what he was searching for, a bottle still more than half full. There was always a few like that, thrown away by men too drunk to know that the bottle was not yet empty.

"I took on too many, Tim," he would say. "While I was sleeping, she took my keys and beat it . . ." Tim would be mad: but not too mad. Then, after the place closed tomorrow night, he would go. He would have to let go this business of killing Tim. But remembering Martha's face with the soft sweetness in it, the bitterness left him, all the bitterness. Monk would understand - where ever he was, he would understand. Johnny put out his hand and pushed open the door of Thirteen.

"Come in, Johnny darling," Jinny said.

He started to back away, but Jinny smiled at him.

"Want me to scream?" she said. "I can scream very loud. You let that girl go, didn't you?"

"Yes," Johnny said, "I did."

Jinny stretched out her arms to him. She was wearing a terry cloth robe. It was belted at the waist, and it had fallen, or been pulled, Johnny thought miserably, open at several places. "I'm glad," she huskily, "I'm glad you let her go. I couldn't have stood it – otherwise. . . ."

"Jinny," Johnny begged, "get out of here. Don't you know what you're doing?"

"Yes," she whispered, "I know." Her arms swept up around his neck. Her lips were soft and warm, and wonderfully expert. Johnny brought up his hands to break her grip, but they wouldn't work that way, somehow. They were stealing around her, tightening . . . He made another effort, a wild, angry surge to break free; and it was then that he felt Tim's big hand on his arm.

"Tim," Jinny gasped, "I . . ."

"I know," Tim said. "I know it's yore doing. That's why I ain't gonna kill th' kid. I'm just gonna muss him up a mite, so's as to remind him to keep his paws offen what's mine!"

Then he brought his big first up and slammed Johnny along the side of the jaw so hard that when he hit the wall the whole cabin shook. Johnny tried to bring his fist up, but for the life of him he couldn't. Tim hit him again, short chopping blows, that broke two of his ribs, and sent him sliding downward along the wall. A pleased grin spread over Tim's face. He caught Johnny by the collar and held him up.

Johnny could see that huge hamlike fist, rising until it glinted sweatwet in the light, then it whistled downward into his face, and he felt the small bones in his nose breaking, making a curious crumpling sound like stiff cardboard. Tim hooked his right hand and drove Johnny's face to the right then to the left then back again, grinning all the time, and when his hand went up this time it was scarlet rather than tan, and made a wet swishing coming down. Johnny lost count of how many times the big fist rose and smashed downward, hitting just hard enough so that it hurt like the pangs of dying and not hard enough to make him lose consciousness while Jinny watched with something very like to awed admiration on her face.

He wasn't sure it was real when he heard the bored, weary voice saying:

"That's enough, Tim." It spoke very clearly, so that through all the ringing in his ears, Johnny could hear it, but it was also curiously soft and peaceful.

"The quality of courage is a very strange thing, isn't it, Tim?" it said. "When you beat me like that I whimpered like a whipped hound. I begged for mercy, I went down on my knees. But the Kid's a man, Tim. You wouldn't understand that - would you? Look at him Tim. Look on the quality of courage and the shape of decency. Look upon a man. It'll be a nice sight to take with you to hell - if they even let you in there."

Tim's three hundred pound bulk seemed to be gathering itself in for a rush.

"Don't jump me, Tim," the Croaker said. Johnny could see his tall figure coming clear through the wavering mists. "I'm quite sober. And I'm not at all nervous. Stand back there alongside of Jinny. Dear Jinny. Don't flatter yourself, my sweet, that I'm killing Tim because of you. I don't fight over such as you. I'm killing him because of what he did to me, and what he tried to do to the Kid."

He lifted his left hand to his mouth and took the cigarette out, and dropped it to the rug, still holding the pistol steady in his right hand. He smiled softly, gently.

"Oh yes, Jinny darling," he whispered, "I forgot to tell you - but I'm killing you, too."

The red haze crashed down again over Johnny's head, but through it thinly, he heard Jinny's screeching, and afterwards, short and heavy, like someone breaking boards across, the shots.

When the haze lifted, he was moving. His hand came up and touched the bandages that covered his face.

"You've had a good rest," Croaker said. "We're here."

Johnny looked up and the neon sign above the car spelled out words. Roseland, it said. Roseland Hotel.

Johnny turned back to Croaker.

"How'd you know?" he whispered.

"You raved. Get on out. Let's see if you can walk."

Stiffly, painfully, Johnny got out of the car. He wavered a bit, but he made it. Croaker smiled at him.

"You'll find five hundred dollars in your coat pocket. Have a nice honeymoon."

Johnny hung there on the sidewalk, watching him drive off. But he drove no further than the corner where the policeman was. Johnny saw him stop, beckon, and the policeman came over, walking tiredly. The blue cap bent down toward the window, then it jerked upward, stiffly. Croaker slid over on the seat and the policeman got in beside him and took the wheel. Johnny watched the car move off until he couldn't see it for the bright film of his tears. Then he turned and walked into the lobby and all at once he saw Martha. She came running toward him, consternation whitening her face. Johnny smiled and caught her as she hurled herself, sobbing into his arms.

"It's nothing," he whispered, "nothing at all."

But it was a long time before she could stop crying long enough to kiss him.

Danse Macabre

Kathleen looked at her husband, sitting with his back toward her, then upward into the mirror where she could see his face. He had a little hairline of a mustache and his hair was like black lacquer above his round, swarthy face.

Greasy, she thought, his skin, everything about him – even his mind.

He glanced up at the mirror, then turned toward her, his tiny mouth, half lost in the great full moon of a face, spreading ever so slightly into a smile.

"Lo darling," he purred.

Kathleen ignored the greeting.

"Give me a cigarette," she said coldly; "I'm out – as usual."

Rod got lumpily to his feet and brought a monogrammed gold case out of his pocket.

"You looked marvelous just then," he said. "You always do when you're thinking up a safe method of murdering me."

"Don't be stupid," Kathleen said.

"I'm not. That's why I'm alive." He smiled again. "Don't flatter yourself, Kathy; I wasn't thinking of you. I have much more formidable enemies."

Kathleen inclined her head toward the lighter which he had snapped into flame.

Then she bent back, blowing twin streamers of smoke through her thin nostrils.

"Now you look more like one of the Furies than ever. But which one? Alecto, Tisiphone, or Megaera? It's a difficult choice. I should think . . ."

"Don't be erudite," Kathleen said; "it's tiresome."

He took a cigarette himself, and placed it carelessly in the corner of his absurdly small mouth.

"How's Margaret?" he said.

Kathleen frowned.

"Reminding me?" she said.

"No, I'm really concerned."

"No better. I think she's going to die. And when she does . . ."

"But the doctors said Arizona – the dry air. . . . ."

"Doctors are often wrong."

He looked at her, smiling. All but his eyes, Kathleen thought suddenly; they never smile.

"You don't seem very grieved," he said.

"I'm not. She's suffered enough. And when she's dead and at peace, I'll be free to leave you, my dearly beloved husband."

"You won't," he said. "You might be able to leave me, but all this money – no."

"You're a swine," Kathleen said evenly.

"Perhaps - but such a rich swine, my dear."

Kathleen looked at him.

"I don't care about the money," she said, "not any more. I married you because I couldn't let Margaret die without doing everything I could. But I will leave you, Rod. I want you to know that. I'm telling you now, so you won't be shocked when I do."

Rod took the massive ring with the vulgarly large diamond from the pudgy finger of his left hand and transferred it to an equally pudgy one of his right. This was a ritual with him. He always did this before leaving the house.

"Must we have these unpleasant conversations?" he asked plaintively. "Can't we let the future take care of itself?"

"It will," Kathleen said grimly; "Oh it will!"

He took a half step toward her, then he stopped, staring at her, and the expression upon his face was very like to horror.

Kathleen's eyebrows rose.

"I must say," she began.

"That dress!" he spluttered; "A <u>black</u> dress, Kathy! You know I told you never . . ."

"Oh all right," she said wearily; "I'll change it. But why a man as intelligent as you are should be so blamed superstitious -- Black dresses, changing your ring, entering side doors – That alone is enough to make me want to leave you. And when you top it with your animal grossness and your women. . . ."

"If my wife," he said coldly, "were a little more responsive, there wouldn't be any women. Go change that dress. I'll wait."

Kathleen shrugged and left the room.

When they came out of the house, Kathy was wearing white. It becomes me, she had to admit, but I do like black. The fat fool! I'll be free of him soon enough. She stopped a moment, frowning. Poor Mag. She's the one who must pay for my freedom, Kathy thought bitterly. Such a small price, too. Merely her life.

Morton was waiting with the convertible as they came down the steps, but Rod dismissed him.

"I'll drive," he said shortly. "You take the night off, Mort."

"Thank you, sir," the chauffeur said.

Watching him stride away, Kathleen was troubled. Rod wasn't a good driver. In fact, he was rather a poor one. She began to feel the little prickling sensation of nerves almost at once.

"Where are you taking me?" she asked.

"Sepia Club. New show there. Dancers – damned good. You'll like them."

"I hope so," Kathy said.

The walls of Sepia Club were all mirrors. When Kathleen and Rodney came in, there was a dancing team on the floor. Before their eyes had become accustomed to the subdued light, they had a hard time distinguishing the real dancers from their reflections.

All the entertainers at the Sepia were Negroes. Rod looked at the girl. He said: "Pretty, isn't she?"

She was: dark, curly hair, soft brown eyes, café au lait skin, a lithe, graceful body.

Kathleen answered: "Very. But look at her partner."

Rod turned toward the man. Then the look of bland disinterest left his heavy face. The fatty lids rose over his little pig's eyes.

The male dancer was striking. He looked like some ancient tribal god. Long, lean, and black as jet. He had a menacing kind of beauty about him. Rod's great bulk shivered a little, as he watched him.

"He's from Haiti," Rod said. "You can tell he's not an American Negro."

"I would have said Africa," Kathleen declared.

A waiter appeared and bent slightly, his pencil ready on his pad.

"Eight martinis, George," Rod said, "Dry."

"Eight!" Kathy said.

"Yes. Six for me and two for you. I don't feel very hilarious and I'd like to. Quickly."

"You won't know what hit you," Kathleen told him.

"Don't underestimate me, my dear."

The waiter bowed and disappeared. The dancing team left the floor. The orchestra began to play a low, dragging tune. It sounded like the wailing of a score of amorous tomcats. A smooth brown boy came to the microphone and began to sing a lament about his 'Heavy duty mama, who treats me oh so mean!' He had a nice tenor voice.

Kathleen asked: "How'd you know he was from Haiti – the dancer, I mean?"

"I asked the manager. That's why I wanted to bring you here. I wanted you to see them. I think they're great."

The brown boy sang: "She won't give me no money, she's stingy to boot. If I look at nother woman, she cuts up my best suit. . . ."

Kathy looked around. At the table on their left was a woman and an elderly man. The woman appeared to be very nervous. She kept drumming on the table with her fingers. The rest of the people at the table were just the usual night club crowd. Kathleen turned back to Rod.

"She's the meanest woman," the brown boy sang, "I ever hope to see

"She spent half her time tantalizing poor me. . . ."

The waiter appeared with the martinis. Rod rowed them off in front of him, toying at them with his pudgy fingers. Then one by one he gulped them down. Kathleen turned away from him.

"Set them up again," Rod said thickly.

Swine, Kathleen thought, greasy swine.

"If I ever gets rid of her, I hope I never find

"A – nother woman like that heavy duty mama of mine!" finished the brown boy plaintively.

Rod kept on drinking. His little pig's eyes reddened, so that Kathy could see the bloodshot veins in their whites, despite the semi-darkness. His flabby little mouth loosened. He breathed through it noisily.

The master of ceremonies stepped to the microphone and announced that Rosita would now do a little solo number. Rosita was the name they gave to the feminine half of the dancing team. The Haitian Negro was called Ramon. Ramon and Rosita. It had a nice Spanish ring to it. Spanish enough for Harlem, anyway.

They darkened the place still further and threw a spotlight on the floor. The girl came in. She had on a few gossamer wisps here and there at the necessary places. Rod drew his breath in sharply.

The girl danced out between the tables chanting the words to a mildly risqué song in a deep, husky voice. When she was close to their table, Rod reached up suddenly and pulled her into his lap. Kathy sat still, frozen with disgust.

The Haitian Negro darted out from the wings and started toward them, but the manager headed him off. They gesticulated violently for a moment; then the Negro went sullenly back to his corner. The girl struggled helplessly in Rod's grip and twisted her face away from his loose lipped, wet kisses.

Kathleen stood up.

"I'm leaving," she said clearly. "Enjoy yourself, Rod."

Rod looked up, and his grip upon the dancer relaxed. Instantly she tore herself free and went on with her dance.

"Kathy," Rod said, "please. . . ."

Kathleen looked around her. Every person in the club was looking at her, even the dancer. Wearily she sat down.

"I'm leaving you, Rod," she said slowly. "Nothing matters anymore. Not even Mag . . ."

The orchestra sent up a final blare as the girl took a bow and left the floor.

"Kathy," Rod said, "I. . . ."

The blare of the orchestra interrupted him and the lights went out again.

The Haitian Negro appeared in the spotlight. He was dressed entirely in black. For a moment, the orchestra continued to play a low, elusive tune. Then it stopped altogether. Without the usual announcement he began to dance.

It was a strange dance. It was a sort of tap, and yet not a tap. It had only one rhythm that was repeated over and over. It would rise to a crescendo and then settle to a low monotonous tone as the floor itself resounded to the taps.

Rod's little eyes widened. "What is it?" he whispered, turning to Kathy.

Kathy didn't answer for a moment; then a malicious smile curled the corners of her lips.

"You remember "The Emperor Jones"?"

Rod's face darkened.

"Rot," he muttered, "utter rot!"

Kathleen kept looking at him and smiling. His hand went into his pocket and came out with a handkerchief. He rubbed his forehead. Then he crumpled the handkerchief into a damp ball. Kathy noticed that he kept it there, closed in his fist. He had forgotten to put it back into his pocket.

"The tom-tom," he muttered, "the drum of death. But this is civilization – not the jungle. And people don't believe things like that anymore. Do they, Kathy?"

"No," Kathy said; "no, of course not."

Rod shivered as though he were cold. The dance sounded like someone whispering the same word over and over. Over and over it came; over and over. Rod looked at Kathy, his fat face loose and working.

"Death!" he said aloud suddenly; then he began to chant it in tune with the rhythm of the dance; "Death, death, death. . . ."

"You're drunk," Kathy said, a smile of amusement on her face.

He leaned forward suddenly and gripped her arm. His fingers were tense, rigid. All the other people were leaning forward, rapt, intent, puzzled by the strange dance. This was something new. This was rare. But it was also good, very, very good.

And still the sound came. Never varying, never ceasing, the whispered, sybilant chant of one word. "Death!" Rod said. "Death, death, death!"

Kathy laughed.

"You're insane," she said.

"Am I? Look at that woman over there!"

Kathy turned. The thin woman who had been drumming nervously on the table all night was standing up, her eyes wild blobs of fright. Suddenly she screamed: "Stop it! Stop it! For God's sake, stop it!" Then she fainted. A confused babble of voices broke out. Rod looked at Kathy. His fat face was chalk white and his lips were trembling.

"Thought she was a hysterical type." Kathy said.

The waiters picked the woman up and bore her toward the dressing rooms. The manager followed wringing his hands. But the dancer didn't miss a step. Rod stood up.

"Let's go," he said.

Some of the people were laughing, but most of them were puzzled. Kathy shrugged and reached for her bag. Then she looked up at Rod. He was standing still, his face frozen.

She half turned and saw that the Haitian dancer was advancing, step by step until he was almost upon them. She looked up at him, holding her cigarette in her gloved fingers, a little glow of amusement lighting her eyes. When the dancer was close, he stopped for a moment, then he started to dance again. But this time he increased his tempo. His feet sang out the word, chanted it, roared it until it was a combination of the crack and roar of thunder. He lifted up his arms, and his black cape trailed, until the shadow that fell across Rod was that of a vulture, hovering.

Rod turned and fled, rocking his elephantine bulk across the dance floor. The audience roared with laughter. Kathy stood and followed him slowly, with great dignity. And as she went, she smiled over her shoulder at the dancer.

Rod was waiting at the car, trembling with fury.

"Why didn't you come on!" he said. "Damn it! Why didn't you come on!"

Kathy got into the car.

"You fool," she said. "You poor, pitiful superstitious fool."

Rod slid under the wheel, pushed down on the clutch, and touched the starter. The engine purred into life. He swung out of the lot into the street and went through the red light, the horns of the cars which had the right of way setting up angry choruses. He shifted into high and was off, the accelerator flat on the floor. Behind him, a police siren sounded, and in one corner of the rear view mirror, Kathleen could see the little white car swinging in after him.

"Fool," she whispered, "fool."

It had started to rain, but Rod made no move to start the windshield wipers. Under his hand the wheel spun and the ribbon of the street whirled backward under the wheels, the fat new tires sending up circles of spray. But the green and white car spun with him, closer now. The needle of the speedometer whirled past sixty, the big car whining down the car tracks between the El pillars that spun backwards so fast they made a solid blur.

"Fool!" Kathy taunted.

Rod glanced down at the speedometer then he brought his eyes up again, and his breath came whistling out of his lungs. The streetcar was coming, ballooning up in front of him, growing in every direction at once until it seemed to be filling all space. He yanked the wheel to the left, skimming by the car by inches, roaring down the wrong side of the street. The little Ford loomed up in front of him before he knew it, and try as he would, pulling the wheel all the way back to the right, the best he could do was to sideswipe it so hard that it rolled over on its back on the sidewalk and lay there like a wounded bug with all four wheels spinning. The Buick lunged to the right, clipping three pillars and smashing squarely into the fourth.

Kathy sat very still in the smashed car, feeling the numbness in her right leg and the warm, sticky wetness on the side of her face. She could hear the sirens of the police cars, coming from everywhere – North, East, South, West, the sound riding in upon her through the falling rain.

Then she started to laugh. And all of the two hours that it took the police to cut her free of the wrecked car from beside the mangled body of her husband, she continued to laugh, a low, rich sound, warm with pleasure.

The Italian Ghost of Monte Carlo

He put the valise on the baggage stand at the foot of the bed and opened it. The gun lay there on a stack of shirts. He stood there looking at it a long, slow time. Then he picked it up, and slid the clip out. He knew before he did it that the clip was full. He had bought the shells the same time he had bought the gun, crossing over to San Remo in Italy to make the purchase. The Italians were less fussy about such things. He didn't want some excessively polite Agent de Police dropping by his room to inquire: "And to what use does M'sieur intend to put his little weapon?" Not before he had put it to that use. Afterwards, it would be too late.

He stood there, holding the gun and sweating. It wasn't hot. The wind came down from the Moyenne Corniche hard enough to make all the yachts in La Condamine basin roll; and the palm trees in front of the Casino bowed before it. But he sweated.

He could feel his elbow bending, bringing the gun up. His mouth had the taste of ashes in it. There were pieces of sand between his eyelids and his eyes. He had the gun up now, level with his temple, pointing. He held it like that, his tongue thickening against his breath; his finger lying there against the trigger; but he couldn't do it. He brought the gun back down again, hanging loosely in his hand, and it was then that he heard the knocking at the door.

He stuffed the automatic under the shirts, and went to open it, repeating the already prepared speech over again in his mind: "Yes, I'm John Bridges. I took the money, and it's gone now. You've got me, and I'm glad." But it was only the garcon with the fin of cognac he had ordered half an hour ago.

He stood aside and let the garcon come into the room; then walked into the bathroom where he had left the cigarettes. He took one out of the pack and lit it, dragging the smoke into his lungs. He could hear the boy behind him in the room, making a noise with the ice and the pitcher; but he didn't come out.

"Est-ce- que il-y-a quelquechose de plus, M'sieur?" the garcon said.

His mind translated slowly: "Is there anything else, Sir?" and he growled, "No," over his shoulder before it came to him that the rattling of the ice and pitcher, the polite question itself were only the boy's way of reminding him of the tip he had forgotten.

"Attend," he said; "Wait!" And searched in his pocket for change. He brought out a handful of coins, and looked among them for some Monacoan pieces; but they were all French francs. Then he remembered that French currency was equally acceptable in Monaco, and came back into the bedroom; but the garcon had already gone.

He crossed to the bed and lay down upon it, staring at the ceiling. He lay there like that for perhaps ten minutes before he noticed the draft. Raising up, he saw that the boy had left the door open. He got up and closed it; then came back again and lay down on the bed. Lying there, like that, staring at the ceiling, he went over it all again in his mind, all of it, the way it had happened, why it had happened - which added up to the fact that he had been a fool, and that wasn't a thing he could help, because he had been one all his life.

In the first place, having drawn the money for the pay envelopes of the Trait Company's employees, he should have taken it back to the office and put it in the safe. Of course, it would have meant a taxi ride across Paris - why the devil wouldn't B.P. bank with one of the many banks near the office? - but he could have put in an expense voucher for that, and B.P. would have honored it without question. Just laziness, he thought bitterly, simon pure laziness.

But it had been more than that, and he knew it. For instance, he had not taken a taxi home to his pleasant little flat as he ordinarily would have done, but had started walking aimlessly in the general direction of the Seine, winding down several little streets after leaving Barclays on the street of the Fourth of September, until he had crossed the Pont Du Carrousel under a sky turned silvery with the dusk, standing there a long moment, staring at the equally silvery waters of the Seine, feeling the old impatience rising in him; and knowing quite certainly and finally that he couldn't go home again to the emptiness and futility of his existence, he had turned and started walking down the Quais.

Even then, he had had a chance. He could have made a short detour, stopped off at his flat and left the money there. But he didn't think of that. He did not think about the money at all. And it was this simple negligence which had started the long chain of circumstances that had come to an end now, in a room over looking the Parc of the Casino, at the Hotel de Paris in Monte Carlo.

He had had the first drink at the Café of the Two Magots. He always had his first drink there. Les Deux Magots is large and dingy and a little vulgar; but he had stumbled upon it his first day in Paris and drunk the first fin he had ever tasted there, so that afterwards it became a ritual with him. Besides, he loved the name. The imaginative boldness of naming a café restaurant the Two Magots appealed to something in him, and always he ate the quite bad food there with great gusto. The first brandy called for another and another until he lost all count of how many cognacs he had had.

He never remembered afterwards how he had gotten to the Dôme. Perhaps he had taken a taxi; for the next thing he knew he was sitting at a little table alone in all that crowd of bearded youths in dirty blue jeans, and girls with horsetail hairdo's and no make up, and the air blue with cigarette smoke, and a silhouette artist cutting lacework designs out of paper towels, and the hat being passed, and an accordion player wandering in and playing badly, terribly, excruciatingly, so that they passed the hat again, and a tall youth with an hairline beard coming down from his ears, and running around under his chin like a line drawn by a theatrical makeup pencil which perhaps it was, took the money and gave it to the accordion player with the remark that it was given on the condition that he wouldn't play anymore, and the musician leaving, grinning; and after that more noise, laughter, confusion, until it, going on, continuing, died for him; his ears rejecting it, his eyes, his mind, so that there was nothing there for him but silence.

And in the midst of that silence, there she was.

He knew at once that she was American in spite of the existentialist costume she wore. She had on a red off the shoulder blouse and a black skirt. He guessed that his two hands could span her waist, and afterwards he found out that they could. She was a very small girl with soft brown hair, and her face was like a flower. She was very small and neat and pretty so that even the outrageous clothes became her, and the ragged espadrilles on her feet, and the quite visible grime about her ankles.

He sat there watching her, and the silence grew and grew, rushing out from the place where she sat in the very vortex of that silence engulfing the Dôme and all the people in it, until he, himself, broke it. He got up, meandered over to her table and said:

"Buy you a drink." It seemed to him, at that moment, the most logical thing in the world to say.

"All right," the girl said. "But first you'll have to buy me a sandwich. Can't drink on an empty stomach. I get mean."

He peered at her owlishly.

"When did you eat last?" he said.

"Yesterday," the girl said; "No - the day before. Or maybe even the day before that one. Can't remember. Eating is a habit I've had to break myself of . . ."

It didn't surprise him. It wouldn't have, even if he had been sober. When an American surrenders to Paris, the capitulation is apt to be complete. He knew very well that if he were given the choice between starving in Paris, and living in comparative comfort elsewhere, he'd starve in Paris. It would be no choice at all. It was a very simple and uncomplicated emotion like being in love with a capricious mistress: no matter how much she tormented and betrayed you, you went on loving her, because you couldn't help it. It was as simple as that.

"No," he said; "We'll go somewhere else. A Dôme sandwich would kill you. What you need is decent food."

"All right," the girl said.

He took her to Le Tour d'Argent. The Maître d' took one look at the girl and shrugged his eloquent shoulders.

"Have you a reservation, M'sieur?" he said. "No? I regret infinitely, but we are complete . . ."

But John could see the expanse of glistening white tables behind him, and on four or five of them the little reservé cards. The rest of them had none. There were only a few occupied tables. The others were vacant. It wasn't yet tourist season.

"I think you are mistaken," he said with drunken gravity. "Maybe you'd better check your list."

The Maître d' raised his eyebrows. His mouth hardened.

"I am never mistaken," he said; "I assure you, M'seiur, it is as I have said. The crowd come late tonight . . ."

"How late is late?" the girl said, speaking very rapidly is perfect, accent-less French; "it is twenty three hours now, and we have hunger. Why are you giving us this tour du carrousel, M'sieur?"

The Maître d' looked at her, and his eyes were ice.

"There are certain rules, Mademoiselle," he said. "We have a reputation to maintain. And when a young gentleman, obviously ivre appears avec sa petit souris, the question of reservations becomes of importance . . ."

John took a step forward, his fist clenched. He knew Parisian argot. The obviously drunken young gentleman was perhaps just; but when a Parisian called a young woman a little mouse, he wasn't talking about rodents.

"No," the girl said; "Don't make trouble, John. It's not worth it."

"I should push his face in," John growled.

"Is it that you are forcing me to call the police?" the Maître d' said.

"No," the girl said in English. "Come on, John."

They ended up finally in a small restaurant-bistro called Chez Mere something or the other. The food was wonderful. At least the girl said it was. John didn't touch it. He seldom drank, but when he did, he was serious about it. Food only occupied the space you could put another cognac in. He sat there, drinking very steadily, until the girl had finished a meal that would have swamped one of the enormous porters in le Hall, men with shoulders a meter wide from carrying two hundred pounds of produce on their backs. She scraped away the last visage of a soufflé that had been a culinary miracle; mountain high, yet light and delicate as air. Then she looked at him, bleakly.

"My place is near here," she said. "Probably nearer than yours."

"All right," John Bridges growled.

They got up and left the bistro, John knuckles white around the handle of the brief case that had the money in it. Then in one of those alcoholic fading out of time, they were in her room. His two hands could span her waist. That much he did find out. But, beyond that, nothing more. For, in the airless closeness of that drab little room, all the cognac he had drunk gathered itself into solidity, and came crashing down upon his head.

When he awoke the next morning, in that unspeakable agony which one of his waggish friends had labelled: "The time when you need an Alka-Seltzer so damned bad, but you can't stand the noise it makes"; and lay there cursing the flies stamping their hobnail booted feet across the ceiling, she was gone. And the brief case. And the money.

It wasn't the kind of a thing you could explain to B.P. Lying there in the grip of a terror so icy that even that monstrous, monumental hangover vanished, he remembered suddenly the first time he had been to Monte Carlo. He had had a run of beginners luck, and departed richer by an hundred and fifty thousand francs - about five hundred dollars - vowing never to play again. But now he seized upon that. Maybe I've got the touch, he thought.

But he hadn't. Nobody had. He knew that now. The old wives tales of the born gambler had been shattered in all the salons de jeux along the blue coast; but people believed it still for the same reason that they believed in gods and magic and myths and enchantments. Because they needed to believe; because disbelief would have robbed their pitifully befouled, besmirched and disjointed lives of the last saving grace of hope.

So now, lying there on his back, staring at the singularly uninspired ornateness of the ceiling, he knew he had come to a dead end; that it had all been for nothing, the flight down to Nice, the frantic taxi ride all the way from the Aeroporte to Monte Carlo, the inexorable whirl of the little ball which had drained away in two days nearly all of the few hundred thousand francs he had managed to save from his salary.

There remained only the final act of grace, if he had only the courage to perform it: the alternatives were unthinkable; disgrace, prison, the ruination, final and complete, of a career that was just the beginning to bud into promise. He had no family to mourn for him; no woman either; for his devotion to his work had precluded his forming any deep or lasting attachments. Nothing prevented him, then; but an instinctual shrinking from the act of self murder primordially deep; a last wild surge of love for living; and these even - now, finally, served for nothing.

Swearing, he leaped up from bed, and dug into the pile of shirts. Once more his fingers closed about the gunbutt; once again he raised it; but the voice stopped him.

"I wouldn't do that, if I were you," the voice said.

It was a wonderful voice, clear and sweet with undertones of solemn music in it like some grave, priestly chant. He whirled, seeking the source of it; but the dusk had come into the room while he had lain there, and deepened, so that he saw nothing - nothing at all.

I'm mad, he thought wildly; That's it - after all the trouble and worry, naturally, I'm -

"No," the voice said gently, "You're not mad. Here I am. . . ."

And then he saw her sitting there in the armchair near the window, which he would have sworn by his life and his sacred honor had been empty a moment before. The light was so poor that he reached toward the lamp; but she stopped him with a gesture.

"Please," she whispered, "no light - I don't like light very much. We have so little of it where I come from . . ."

"And where is that?" he said, forcing the words out through lips gone suddenly dry.

"Ah," she laughed; "That is one of the things you must not try to know. There will be others . . ."

"How'd you get in here?" he demanded; then he remembered the door the garcon had left open.

"Through the door," she said; "Or, perhaps I have always been here - who knows? It is not important. The important thing is that I came on time . . ."

"But you've solved nothing," he told her. "I'm still going to be branded a thief, sent to jail, and - "

"No," she whispered, and got up; floating up from the depths of the chair as though she were weightless, drifting like luminous smoke towards him across the room, and though he saw her tiny feet moving, her footsteps made no sound. When she was close, John Bridges saw that she was incredibly beautiful.

Her hair was the essence of darkness, the complete negation and absence of light; and her eyes were blacker still, so that his mind groped heavily for a word to describe them. He gave it up, finally, realized there was none.

She was very close to him now, and her perfume, a strange scent which tugged at his senses for recognition, rose about his head. But he could not place it. It was too odd, too - strange . . .

"You are not to kill yourself, Johnnee," she said, "For tonight your luck will change - I swear it."

He stared at her. Then he said darkly:

"You can arrange things like that?"

"Yes," she told him with the same sweet gravity; "You see, I have influence . . ."

"Hah!" he snorted; "To do my any good, your influence would have to extend up to the throne of God, Himself . . ."

"Perhaps it does," she whispered; "Perhaps, even up to there . . ."

He stared at her.

"How did you know my name?" he demanded; "Why did you come here?"

She laughed then, a quiet, liquid sound.

"Again too many questions, Johnnee," she said.

"I can ask your name?" he said; "Or is that defendu also?"

"No - that I can tell you. It's Maria - Maria Vignalli."

"Italian," John said; "I thought that accent was familiar. But you speak English so beautifully . . ."

"I don't really," she smiled; "It is only that you think I do . . ."

She moved closer to him. The odd perfume stirred him. He had the feeling that on anyone else it would have been unpleasant. It smelled like- like seaweed, he decided suddenly. He started to ask her about it; but there was not time; for suddenly her lips were there, floating inches below his own.

Afterwards, he was to remember how often the idea of floating, of bouancy had been associated with her in his mind; but at the moment, he was incapable of analysis; all he could do was hang there, hearing her voice, strangely not in his ears, but somewhere deep inside his mind, whispering:

"Now you will please to kiss me, Johnnee to seal our bargain. Then I must go . . ."

Her lips were ice. They tasted of salt.

He recoiled from her wildly; but she clung to him, saying:

"In one hour, Johnnee- in the Salon Privée. Bring all you have . . ."

All he had was ten thousand francs. Not enough to pay even a part of his hotel bill; not enough to get back to Paris. He was finished, couldn't she understand that? Finished . . .

But she was drifting out and away from him, her slippers wisps of moon-light caressing the carpet, her oddly old fashioned dress a floating luminosity, smoke like eddying out through the doorway; and he, standing there, rooted to the floor, thought:

It's not true. I'm imagining this. Or dreaming, But I'm awake! I am awake...

He rushed to the door through which she had passed, half expecting what he would see. For though less than half a heart-beat had elapsed since Maria Vignalli drifted through that doorway, the long corridor was empty. In both directions. That corridor down which, he knew, a man almost running would need a full five minutes to reach the end.

But he went down to the Casino all the same, crossing the rounded drive in front of the garden where the wind whipped palm trees were made ghostly by the concealed lights at their feet. He went into the private salon without formalities, because already they knew him, so no longer did he need to present his passport, but paid very simply the hundred forty franc fee, and went through the faded gilt and rose Victorian rooms with their enormously high ceilings and their air of genteel shabbiness, so that the general effect was sad, as though they reflected somehow, faint but immutable, the tens of thousands of tragedies they must have witnessed.

He searched for her among all the tables around which the players sat, but he could not find her. He felt, despairingly, that she had failed him; for, among the habituées of the Private Salon, of whom it had been said with justice that they no longer felt any normal call of nature, so that they could sit hour after hour, with their eyes glittering like those of some nocturnal animal, without moving; their faces robbed of expression, of humanity even, it should have been easy to distinguish her cool, haunting beauty.

She's gone, he thought; and without her I haven't a chance. . . .

"Ah," she laughed; "but you are wrong, Johnnee- on both counts you are wrong ..."

And he turning, saw without wonder or surprise that she was beside him now, her arm though his, the faint seaweed scent of her perfume rising up to him, elusive and faint and a little maddening.

"Come," she said gaily; "We will go to table thirteen which foolish people think is unlucky. And we will play number thirteen on the black which is the color of death and gloomy things ..."

"Number thirteen on the black?" he said.

"Yes," Maria said firmly; "All you have. But I must warn you: You are to play only until you have regained the exact sum you need. If you are greedy, you will begin to lose; and you will lose and lose until it is all gone ..."

"Does that exact sum include my hotel bill and incidentals, and my fare back to Paris?" he mocked.

She stood very still, and closed her eyes. He could see her lips moving; but they formed words in some language he could not understand. Then she smiled at him.

"Yes," she said gravely; "It does include those things; but not one sou more ..."

"Very well," he said, and went up to the table.

The croupier regarded the two of them with his prehistoric, reptilian eyes.

"Faite vos jeux, Messieurs, Mesdames," he droned; "Make your plays!"

"Thirteen black," John said in English; and the croupier who, like croupiers everywhere spoke all known and unknown languages repeated after him; "Treize, noir - " and pushed the ten thousand franc chip onto the thirteen.

He gave the wheel a lazy, negligent spin; the tiny white ball whirling above the number slots, the wheel slowing now, the ball dropping.

"Treize, noir," the croupier called; "Thirteen on the black!"

John stared at Maria.

"Let it rest," she said quietly.

All the glittering black bastlik eyes turned upon him - this young American who was letting this already considerable pile of chips rest there on that one number. When again, the thirteen came up, by some mysterious alchemy of communication, a little wave of excitement began moving through the salon, and the crowd about the table doubled, then tripled, as the tall young man stood there imperturbably and let all his winnings remain on the black thirteen while the ball came to rest there again and again. He alone was playing now. The others having withdrawn to watch with deathstill fascination the charmed action of the wheel the ball always coming to rest on thirteen, black.

"Encore treize noir!" the croupier said, even his glacial voice betraying emotion.

It was a thing they would be talking about twenty years from that night; it gave them a feeling of exaltation, of near ecstasy to even have witnessed it. They were not even breathing now, standing there ten deep about the table, all the rest of the play having stopped, bacarrat, chemin de fer, roulette, craps, everything - while they crowded about, wolves on the scent, vultures awaiting the kill, to witness the legend taking the form it would have for all time; the American Who Broke the Bank at Monte Carlo.

But long before that could happen, long enough, however, for it to already have become an authentic miracle. The little white ball having come to rest on the black thirteen, thirteen times in a row, Maria touched his arm and whispered;

"Enough, Johnnee - you have enough...."

He nodded to the croupier, and the chips were raked in. He gathered them up, tossing a handful of them to the croupier for a tip, and dashed off saying:

"Wait, Maria, I'll be back . . ." paying no attention to how the watchers gaped at his words, hearing, too, an instant before he was out of earshot, the croupier intoning: "Sept, rouge - seven, red! Manque et impair, premier douzain - Lack and uneven, first dozen - "And he knew that the run of black thirteen had been broken.

He watched, too stunned to even feel joy or relief as the cashier stuffed enormous packets of ten thousand franc notes into a sack for him.

"M'sieur desires a guard?" the cashier said. "To carry so many millions alone is perhaps dangerous. By now half the criminal element of the Côte is aware of M'sieur's good fortune . . ."

"No," John said; "Not now - later, perhaps . . ."

He went back to the tables, then; but she was not there. He searched for her frantically through out the salon, even sending the maid into the ladies room to look for her; but she was not there. He came back finally to table thirteen and demanded of the croupier:

"The lady who was with me - have you seen her?"

And now, finally, the last icy wall of the traditional reserve of croupiers was broken through. The man stared at John Bridges in helpless astonishment, his jaw dropping, for a long, slow time, before he recovered.

"It is that M'sieur does not feel well?" he said smoothly; "The shock, perhaps, of such brilliant luck? I should be happy to summon the house physician . . ."

"What are you talking about?" John roared at him; "I ask you about a girl, and you blabber about doctors and sickness! What nonsense is this?"

The croupier looked at him with grave concern.

"Calmly. M'sieur," he said; "I think that truly the doctor should be summoned - You see, M'sieur, there was no young lady with you. The entire evening, M'sieur was - alone . . ."

John stared at him, then into the faces of the others. From their eyes alone, he knew the futility of further questions. Clearly each man and woman there thought him mad.

"Sorry," he muttered; "I - I have been ill. I am at the hotel de Paris- you might ask them to send the physician there. I - I'll go there at once . . ."

"With pleasure, M'sieur," the croupier said; "Your name, please?"

"John Bridges," John said.

But he did not go back to the Hotel. Carrying the money, he went down into the garden; and there, far ahead of him, he saw a gossamer wisp of silver drifting in the moonlight. He started running then, wildly toward it, until he saw that she waited for him under the palm trees.

"Maria!" he wept; "Why didn't you wait? Oh, my darling, I -"

She laid a finger then, as cold as her lips had been, across his mouth.

"I cannot be your darling," she said; "Though I would like very much to be. But, if you are not bitter; if you can think with kindness even of that poor girl who robbed you -"

"How can you know so much?" he gasped.

"About you, I know everything," she said; "Even your future, Johnnee . . ."

"Tell me," he growled; "Are you in my future?"

"No," she said.

"Then to hell with my future," he grated; but going up on tiptoe, she stopped his mouth. This time, there was a trace of warmth beneath the ice and the taste of salt.

"Keep your eyes closed, Johnnee," she whispered; "Please to keep your eyes closed . . ."

He obeyed her, finding his will powerless against hers, impervious to the force that coiled deep inside his brain itself, holding him there. When he opened his eyes, she was far away from him. Drifting like moonsilver, like fairy gossamer down the collines toward the sea. He went after her, but his feet weighed tons. He could scarcely lift them; but he kept on, doggedly. The Plage was before her now, deserted, with no swimmers there in the moon-light; the off shore raft bobbing uselessly in the swell, the twin hulled pedaloes rocking as the surf boiled under their sterns. On the edge of the beach, she stopped, and turning, waved to him.

"Goodbye, Johnnee," he felt her voice inside his mind; "Goodbye, my Johnnee- forever more - goodbye . . ."

Then she walked out into the water, straight out into the moontrack on the water, the silver of her dress becoming one with the moonsliver; her hair's blackness, blending with the night. And he, standing there on limbs which refused to obey him, watched her go, standing there trancelike, unliving, until a cloud veiled the moon. When it passed, she was gone, and he was free.

He was prepared for anything, when he walked into B.P.'s office: rage - to be discharged, even to be arrested; but he was not prepared for what he got: B.P. greeted him in stoney silence; grated the single word, "Well?" and waited.

He found himself blurting it out - all of it except that part about Maria; for he had no intention of being condemned to sessions with B.P.'s psychiatrist.

"You see," he finished lamely; "I didn't know what else to do, so I flew down to Monte Carlo, and -"

B.P.'s eyes were deadly.

"So," he said; "That's what you did with the Trait Company's money! Lost it gambling! Why you unprincipled young scoundrel - and you had the nerve to come back! Did you think I'd gotten soft in my old age?"

John Bridges tossed the package on the desk.

"Count it, B.P.," he said.

B.P. looked up from the stack of bills.

"Sit down, boy," he said. "So you won it back. My God, but you must have a system! For twenty five years I've been trying to do it again. I did it once, you know, twenty five years back . . . Broke the ruddy bank; but that was because of Maria . . ."

"Maria?" John whispered.

"Yes. Italian girl I knew. Sweet little thing. Real aristocrat. Maria Vanessa, Contessa Vignalli. As long as she was there, I couldn't lose . . ."

John felt a wild surge of something like pain: Jealous pain.

"What happened to her?" he said.

"Poor thing," B.P. muttered. "She killed herself. Lost her last cent the night after I left. Walked out into the sea and drowned. There was some talk, too, of an unhappy love affair; but I wasn't the guilty party . . ."

He started at the young man, interest in his small, blue eyes.

"I should fire you," he growled; "It was a damned fool trick, letting yourself get rolled while you were drunk. And the gambling was worse. But, under the circumstances -"

"Thanks, B.P.," John began; but B.P. was staring at him.

"That girl!" he roared; "That little American girl who's been coming around asking after you! By God, I'll have the police on her neck quick enough -"

"Please, B.P.," John said; "After all, you got your money back . . ."

"That's true enough," B.P. growled. "In love with her, eh? I could understand that - she's pretty enough . . ."

"No - yes," John whispered. "Can I go now, B.P.? It's been an awful strain . . ."

"No," B.P. said, interest mounting in his little eyes; "About this system of yours -"

"I haven't any system, B.P.," John Bridges said.

Supper for Louie

Annie May sat in the little one and a half room kitchenette up in Harlem and looked at the clock. It said ten after eleven, so she looked at her wrist watch and it said the same thing. She got up and walked to the window and looked out. The street was full of people, for up in Harlem there are always more people out at night than there are in the daytime, but none of them were tall enough or well dressed enough to be Bill, so she blinked back a couple of tears that felt like droplets of live steam under her eyelids, and turned away from the window.

"What can I expect," she said to herself; "little old black girl like me."

She had been saying that most of her life. And when she didn't say it, other people said it for her. Her sisters, whose dusk-rose and copper complexions looked appetizing enough to take a bite out of; her father, who used to take her on his knee and bounce her up and down and say with a grin:

"Little girl, your old lady sure musta tipped out on me!"

All but her grandmother, who would snap at them, saying:

"Hush! She the spittin image of her grandpaw, and you know it!"

But her mother, whose skin was the color of the keys of a piano that has been used for several years, would smile sadly and say:

"Now, Henry, don't make the child feel bad." And that, of course, made her feel worst of all.

When she was growing up, she was a very smart child. She read all the books and magazines and newspapers. And every time she came across a picture of a girl who had won a beauty contest or had got a contract to go to Hollywood she would look at it hard. Each time the girl would be tall with skin the color of the snow in Central Park when the first dawn sunlight was falling on it, and hair that was like ripe wheat, or corn tassels in the moonlight, or honey and taffy, or like sunlight itself; and Annie May would look into the mirror at herself and sigh. It made a kind of sickness in her finally, so that she got to be very quiet, and took to staying in her room when company came to her father's house. She noticed that her mother and her sisters seemed quite relieved when she did this, so she kept to herself more and more until finally she only came out to eat her tiny, bird like meals.

Her family wasn't very religious. Nobody read the Bible but her grandmother, and she never read the Song of Songs. So nobody ever pointed out to Annie May that there was once a Queen named Sheba who was as black as she was, yet so beautiful that the wisest man in all the world fell in love with her. Nor did anyone ever tell her that the Patriarch Moses, the great liberator of his people, loved an Ethiopian woman so well that he defied his brother and his sister in order to marry her. So Annie May grew up without knowing these things. And since all of the boys and girls whom she grew up with read the same books and magazines that she did and saw the same movies, none of them ever noticed that her tiny little body was as perfect as a statuette, and that her skin was like rick black velvet under a midnight sky.

When she got older, she couldn't stand it any more, so she got out and got herself a job taking care of the children of a rich white family. Then she was lonesome, but she was happier than she had been at home. But there was the problem of boys. The better looking ones had the idea that Annie May should give them all the money that she had worked so hard for, or go out and buy them a "hard set of threads," by which they meant a flashy suit; but somewhere in her reading she had picked up the idea that a woman should be loved for herself alone, and not for what she could give a man. So the better looking ones didn't linger. The uglier ones were willing to pool their resources with hers, but she soon discovered that this pooling included moving into her apartment without benefit of clergy. Now Annie May was instinctively as clean in her person as a cat, and this cleanliness was of her mind also, so she never had the slightest intention of messing up her life like that. Therefore, most of the time, she was lonely. Of late she had lessened the loneliness somewhat by her friendship with Bill, a big, good looking boy who looked like Joe Louis, and paid her careless attention, only coming around when he didn't have anywhere else to go, and breaking dates without explanation whenever he felt like it.

"But I got enough," Annie May said to her reflection in the mirror. "I ain't sitting around here waiting on him no more. I'm going down to the Savoy and have myself a time. I been a fool long enough."

She picked up her tiny hat and adjusted it atop her glossy upsweep that looked like black lacquer and which cost her more per week to keep like that than she spent for food. Then she went downstairs and hailed a taxi.

Inside the ballroom, she stood off by herself and watched the dancers. There is probably no feeling in the world worse than that: to stand by yourself in the dimness and watch happiness swirl by in syncopated time. The music crawled along her nerves. After a while she couldn't stand it any more, so she whirled and started toward the cloak room, her eyes blinded with tears that she ran straight into the tall young man before she saw him. It was like butting into a post. When her breath came back she heard him saying:

"Crying! What's the matter, little girl? Cute little thing like you ain't got no business crying."

Then she looked up at him and she couldn't say anything at all, because of all the men she had ever known, this one was by far the handsomest. He was copper. He was golden. And his hair was black silk so fine that he had to keep pushing it out of his face with his hand. Then, suddenly, she was sad again. Any man this good looking could have all his bills paid gladly by a dozen hard working women. His bills paid, his clothes bought, and pocket money to boot.

"Come on, dance with me, little girl," he said. "Tell me what's making you so sad."

They moved off to the music. But for the life of her Annie May couldn't keep step. But the man moved like he was drifting before a little wind.

"You upset," he said. "Let's get a table and then you tell me all about it."

Time I answered him, Annie May thought; time I said something to him – anything. He be thinking I'm dumb next.

"What's your name?" she blurted.

"Louie," he grinned; "what's yours?"

She gulped a couple of times before she got it out.

"May," he laughed. "All American girls named May. Annie May, Susie May, Josie May, Tessie May .... why your people name you like that?"

"Don't know," Annie May said. "Just do, somehow. Where you from?"

"Antiqua, BWI. And I ain't seen nothing like you since I left home."

"Please," she said; "Don't jive. I ain't in the mood."

He lit a cigarette and studied her through the smoke.

"Now," he said; "tell me what the crying was about."

Annie May looked at him and all she could think of was the truth.

"Because I was lonesome," she said.

His eyebrows moved upward.

"Lonesome?" he said. "American boys forever and ever fools!"

Annie May's fingers gripped the edge of the table so tight that they hurt.

"Please," she said.

"Well, you don't be lonesome no more. I'm coming around, little girl. Dance with me?"

She got up, and this time it was better.

"What your girl friend say to that? You coming round, I mean."

"Ain't got none."

"Please," she said again, "good looking boy like you . . ."

He looked over her head and his eyes were very clear.

"Back home, boys like me tupence ha'penny the dozen. I sat on the beach for twenty years and a fortnight before I come here. Plenty of time for thinking. And I thought up that the best way to be was free. Right?"

"Right," she said, "but still. . . ."

"American girl like a man, she want to give him stuff. Suits, money, buy his wine. Well, I ain't for sale. Cripes! Woman think I ain't worth no more than a suit. Give it to you, see you talking to another girl, come and cut it off you. What kind of life is that?"

"No kind," Annie May said, and missed a step, because her heart was singing so loud she couldn't hear the music. Then another thought struck her. "But I ain't goodlooking," she said.

"Not goodlooking? Don't talk foolishness, little girl."

Annie May dropped her head down upon the hollow of his shoulder and floated. The night moved off in a bright haze.

"See you home, little girl?" he was saying, and she nodded her head very fast. She put her arm through his and they walked off the floor together. On the outside, the cabs were waiting for the dancing crowd so they had no trouble getting one. Annie May thought that they had got the fastest driver in New York. Certainly she had never gotten home this quickly before. She wanted to tell him to slow down, or to drive through the park, but of course she couldn't.

When they got there, Louie told the driver to wait and walked across the sidewalk with her. Then he lifted his hat like an English gentleman in the movies and said goodnight without even trying to kiss her. Annie May caught a deep breath.

"You – you can come up for a minute if you want to," she said.

"No," he said; "It's too late. Give me your phone number and I'll call you."

After he had got back in the cab and driven away, Annie May stood in the doorway for fifteen minutes looking down the darkened street. He won't call, she thought bitterly, he won't.

But when she came home from work the next day, the landlady met her in the doorway.

"Some man been calling you all evening," she complained. "Sound foreign – like a Monkey Chaser, if you ask me. Lemme tell you child, stay away from them West Indians! My second husband was one and he was the meanest damn man what ever drew breath. Jealous! Why he'd . . . ."

"Yes," Annie May said. "Yes, I know. But what did he say? Did he leave any message?"

"Said he'd call –" the landlady began, but the shrilling of the phone cut her off. "Betcha that's him now," she said; but Annie May was past her, running down the hall. Her hands shook so lifting the phone off the hook that she almost broke the connection, then Louie's voice floated over the wire.

"May I come around?" he said. "I've been wanting to see you all day."

"Yes," she said, "Oh yes! But not right now. Give me half an hour. Give me an hour. I just got home and I look . . ."

"I'll be there in twenty minutes," Louie said. But it was only fifteen minutes later when he rang the bell. Annie May was standing up in the middle of her room, fighting to get a slip over her head. She kept him waiting outside in the hall for ten minutes longer before she opened the door.

"That wasn't fair," she wailed. "I look a fright! Why'd you come so quick?"

"Wanted to see you with the polish off," he grinned. "Now I'm gladder than ever. Come on."

"Where we going?" Annie May said.

"Out and around. I want to show you off."

"Ain't nothing to show. Know what they'll say?"

"No – what?"

"What little old black girl like that doing with that good looking man? He must be drunk – or crazy."

"Crazy is right," Louie said. "Crazy bout you. Come on."

They went down the stairs and out into the street. Annie May had on immensely high heels but she still came up only to Louie's shoulder. He strode along with a short pipe stuck in his mouth and blew a fragrant blue-grey cloud back over his shoulder. They went down the street until they came to a corner where a crowd of men were hanging out. Seeing them, Annie May started shrinking into herself until she looked even smaller than she was. Louie looked at her and frowned.

"Chin up," he said. "Walk tall! Walk like a queen. Walk like you know you the finest lady in all the world and nobody daren't say a word."

"Can't!" Annie May wailed. "I'm scared."

Louie slowed down and started talking. He didn't say anything about the men on the corner or about Annie May's being scared. He said:

"There's an old African man in Antiqua who carves statues out of wood. He look all over the island til he finds the right kind of wood. Then he makes things out of it. Little figures: birds and animals and people. Sometime he use ebony. When he get through he take oil and rubs the little thing he carved all over with his hands. Two, three days maybe he sit there rubbing one little figure. And when he get through, it glows – not shines – glows."

He looked at Annie May.

"You like that," he said. "Little statue out of ebony – glowing."

And when Annie May went by the men on the corner, her tiny little nostrils were flaring, and her head was up like a queen's.

"Wheeeee – un!" the men whistled. "Little lump of dark chocolate, steppin high!"

Annie May's heart beat very fast, for nobody had ever whistled at her before.

Louie came every night after that. Annie May was so happy she couldn't talk. All day she went around listening to the singing in her heart. And sometimes she just had to let it out in clear little wordless soprano runs and trills that tinkled like spring water.

"Annie May's in love," her white people said. "Now we're going to lose her." They were sad because Annie May was a very good girl. Her work was always done just right. And all the time she was going with Louie she worked harder than ever, doing little, tender, extra things that only a woman in love would think of.

"Let's don't go out tonight," she said to Louie on Sunday night. "I fixed supper for you. The landlady let me use her kitchen. But she didn't help me. She wanted to, but I wouldn't let her. I wanted to fix it for you myself."

Louie looked at her and smiled.

"You sweet," he said.

The supper was perfect – just perfect. There were hot rolls and fried chicken and green peas and chips and potato salad and apple pie and coffee. But Louie didn't eat much at all.

Annie May watched him picking over the good food until she couldn't stand it any longer. The tears spilled over her long lashes and down her cheeks. In the candlelight – for she had bought candles, too, thinking them romantic – they looked like silver streaks on ebony. Louie bounced up at once and caught her hands.

"Sorry," he said. "It's good food. It's wonderful food. That's the trouble. I just don't like American food. When you want to cook for me, just get an egg and some oil and an onion. That's all."

Then he took her in his arms and let her cry her disappointment out upon his shoulder. After a minute she straightened up smiling and blinking her eyes. She freed herself and pulled up the huge easy chair that filled up most of the space in the little half room that she used for a parlor. Then she put a footstool in front of it. The chair and the footstool were both new. She had bought them for Louie.

"Sit down," she said, smiling at him.

Louie sat down and stretched his long legs across the footstool. Then she loosened his tie and opened his collar. Afterwards she knelt down beside him and took off his shoes.

"Take your ease," she said. Suddenly she ran off and came back with the new pipe and the jar of tobacco. Louie didn't have the heart to tell her that nothing in the world is worse than a new pipe before it has been broken in, and that the aromatic tobacco was far too sweet. He sat back contentedly and let her light it for him and drew in the soft, gurgling smoke. Annie May curled up on the floor beside him like a black Persian kitten and rested her head on his knee. He put down his hand and stroked the back of her neck. They sat very still for a long time, not even talking until finally Louie said:

"I'm going down and get us a license tomorrow. Then we go and get us a blood test. That way we can be married on Friday by the judge."

Annie May sat there trembling for a long time. When she looked up her eyes were tearbright, brighter than diamonds, brighter than twin evening stars in a night sky.

"Louie," she said; "You sure you ain't making a mistake?"

"Quite," Louie said, and took the pipe out of his mouth to kiss her.

But on Thursday night when Louie came in, his face was bleak. Annie May gave one look at him and her hand flew up to her throat.

"Something happened," she said; "Something bad. I knew it. I knew nothing good could happen to me."

"Ain't that bad," Louie told her. "Looks like we have to put off getting married for a little while. I lost my job."

Annie May's face was stricken.

"Don't take it to heart, little girl. I'll get me another. Or I'll think of something. It was the war being over so quick. They couldn't keep everybody."

Annie May walked up close to him so that her face was half hidden by his tie.

"Louie," she whispered.

"Yes?" he said. "Yes, Annie May?"

"Don't let's put it off. I – I still got my job. We could make it til . . ."

Louie's jaw was iron.

"No!" he said.

Annie May looked up at him, and her perfect white teeth came together tight. For the first time in her life she was going to fight for something. And she was going to keep on fighting until she won. She caught him by both his arms and tried to shake him.

"Look," she said; "I lend you the money. I keep account of every penny. I even charge you interest! But we don't postpone it. I ain't going to wait no six months or a year til they finish reconverting every blame plant in the country. I ain't gonna wait til you get hooked by some other woman! I love you, Louie; you understand that? I ain't never loved nobody or nothing like I love you and if you go away I'll just curl up and die. We got a little date with that judge on Friday, and we gonna keep it, you hear me!"

Louie looked down at her fierce little face, and suddenly he began to laugh.

"All right, hon," he laughed; "we keep that date all right."

Annie May snuggled up against him, like a kitten.

"I'm gonna be dressed in white," she whispered. "I know I'm gonna look like a fly in a bowl of buttermilk, but I always wanted a white wedding. And I'm gonna make you so damn happy you never look at another woman. You watch."

"Suppose I take to drink," he teased; "Suppose I beat you?"

"I'll hit you over the head with the mop handle til you behave. Oh Louie, we gonna be so happy!"

They had a two day honeymoon, but on Monday Annie May had to go back to work. She walked around all day in a complete daze, but she had done her work so long that she got most of it right from force of habit. And her employer smiled over her lapses, saying:

"You'll get over it! Six months or so and he'll be grunting at you over the top of his newspaper and forgetting to kiss you when he leaves the house. You just wait."

But Annie May just smiled at them for she had her Louie now, and there wasn't another man like him – not anywhere in the world.

When she was going home that night, she stopped at the grocers, and carefully counting her pennies, for they had to last all the way to next Saturday, she bought an egg, a bottle of olive oil, and an onion. The grocer put them all in one bag together, and Annie May went skipping down the stairs to the subway with them.

It was late in the rush hour and the crowd had thinned out a good bit, but she couldn't find a seat. So she stood there, hanging by the strap and thinking about Louie. The train went uptown very fast and rocked around the curves. And each time it rocked more and more olive oil spilled out of the loose cap of the bottle until at last it weakened the bag and it and the egg and the onion fell out on the floor. The bottle and the egg both broke.

All the people on the car were white people except a few, and they all started laughing not even excepting the few. Annie May stood there looking down at Louie's omlet running back and forth across the subway car with the onion rolling through the green and yellow pool, then back through it as the car rocked the other way until the doors hissed open at the next station, then she ran out although it wasn't her station. When the doors closed she could see the people still laughing.

She went upstairs and caught a bus the rest of the way home. I'm late, she thought. He be mad with me sure. I ain't got no supper for him. Three days married and I ain't got no supper – Never did have no sense in my fool head . . .

She unlocked the front door to her flat and went up the stairs on tiptoe. Then she pushed open the door to her flat and Louie came toward her, grinning. She caught a deep breath.

"I ain't got no supper for you," she blurted. "I bought something and I dropped it. And we ain't got but a little money left cause we spent too much on our honeymoon. Oh Louie, what we gonna do?"

"Do?" he said, and his grin never wavered. "We go out, that's what. Best restaurant in town. You ain't troubling yourself about a little thing like that."

"But Louie we can't! We don't have no money! We got exactly five dollars and. . . ."

He shook his head from side to side.

"All this talk before she even kiss me," he said; "what a wife!"

She went up on tiptoe, and he bent down to her.

"Now," he said, "change your things cause we going out!"

"But Louie . . ." she began.

"No arguments! You just get dressed."

"But Louie, honey – what we gonna use for money?"

"You think I'm one these American boys in the big hats and long coats and baggy trousers? I worked on a war job nearly three and a half years. I got money saved. And I got everything fixed up for us right now."

Annie May's eyes widened but she didn't ask any more questions. She ran into the tiny stall shower, drawing a bathing cap over her lacquered curls. She handed her clothes out to Louie who put them away and brought fresh things. A few minutes later, powdered, perfumed and exquisite, she stepped out of the room.

Louie looked at her and his eyes brightened. Then he took her arm and they went down the stairs. A few blocks away, Louie stopped her before a diner. It was fairly well kept, and the fixtures seemed to be in good shape: counter, stools, coffee kettle, grill.

Annie May looked at it trying hard to keep the disappointment from showing. This was what Louie called the best restaurant in town! But she smiled up at him bravely, taking care that he would not know.

"This ain't where we going," he said. "I wanted to show you this. I – I bought it from old pop this morning. He was getting too old to run it and I thought. . . ."

"Louie," Annie May said, "you the smartest man in the whole world! People gotta eat. And eating here won't cost much, so we'll always have business, no matter how hard times get! Oh Louie, Louie. . . ."

"I thought maybe you wouldn't like it. We start in day after tomorrow, so you better give your people notice. Come on now, let's go eat, I'm starved."

"NO!" Annie May said. "We eat right here! In our own place, Louie – just like home!"

Louie smiled down at her.

"Pop cooks terrible," he said; "but if you want to – come on then."

Sitting next to Louie at the counter, Annie May couldn't eat for watching him. She stretched out her hand and caught his.

"You the handsomest man in the world," she said, "and the smartest and the best. There's just one thing I can't figger out . . ."

"What's that?" he said.

"Why you married me."

Louie put down his fork.

"Because you're beautiful," he said. "You're like night – night without stars."

Then he leaned over and kissed her, right there, in front of everybody.

The Invasion on Chauncy Street

The boy, Woodrow, stopped the two wheeled chip cart beside the turret lathe, and stood there watching Ernie Stahlheim turning out the valve stems. Ernie grinned at him, then bent forward spinning the two handled rod so that the pointer showed a full thousandth instead of a half. Then he started the machine going, the piece whirling in the chuck at full speed. He turned the other wheel gently, the merest fraction of a turn at the time, advancing the triangular shaped blade on its bed until its point engaged the whirling piece. It bit, and a flat ribbon of steel whirled up from the lathe, curving like a living thing around Ernie's oil soaked hands.

The boy went closer, his black face alive with interest.

"I could do that," he said; "I could do it jus as easy!"

"Schure you couldt, keedt," Ernie said; "It ist nodt hardt. See – now ist enough!" He leaned forward, whirling the rods rapidly so that the blade pulled away from the piece. Then he stopped the lathe and loosened the jaws of the chuck. Pulling the piece out, he wiped it gently with a cloth, and set the points of a micrometer over the O. D.

"On der nose!" He grinned. "Dots how t do it, fest!"

Woodrow was looking at the micrometer.

"One point six twenty five," he read.

"Dots rightd. You can read der mike!"

"I ain't no square, Jack! Th ole man knocked me down t th mike n a couple o machines, too. He run a internal thread cutter up at <u>Siskins</u>."

"Goot place, Ziskins. I vorked vunce dere. Vell I go smoke now. You klean him goot."

Woodrow took the little metal rake and began to scrape up the ribbons of steel and the little blue burnt chips from the turned parts out of the tray of the machine. Then he lifted up the great pile of oily steel scrap: chips, ribbons, and filings, and dumped them into the deep belly of his two wheeled cart.

"I could run it," he muttered; "I could run it jus z easy!" he took up the can of mixed sand and sawdust and sprinkled it over the oil splotches on the concrete floor. Then he swept it up into the scoop shaped dust pan. When it came up, it took the oil with it so that no worker would slip in the oil puddles and perhaps break an arm.

Woodrow stood staring at the mess in the cart. His frown deepened.

"Think I'm some blam from Alabam. Th original square from Delaware. I show em I'm hipped t th jive. Definitely and as of now!"

He left the cart standing by the machine and stalked toward the doorway. He pushed it open so hard that it swung back and forth on its hinges several times. Then he was gone down the stairs that led to the superintendent's office.

The decorative blonde pushed the wad of chewing gum over to one side of her mouth with the tip of her tongue.

"Whatcha want?" she demanded.

"Nothin you got, Toots!" Woodrow said and walked on pass her.

"You can't go in there!"

"Well twist my joints and call me pretzel!" the boy growled; "I'm doin it, ain't I?"

He pushed open the inner door and marched in.

The heavy set man with the heavy brows looked up.

"Who let you in?" he growled.

"Lissen jack," the boy said; "climb down! I feel f yuh, but I can't reach yuh. Me n you gonna do some straight gum beatin – right now."

"You got a pass to leave your department?"

"Naw n I don't need one. Store that off beat gab, buddy; I'm layin it t yuh, straight – eight t th bar. I been here four months. I took that jerk broom pushin job because I was promised a better one in a couple weeks. I don't know how you greys tell time, but right now I'm letting yuh in on what th score is. Do I git upgraded t th machines or don't I?"

"You don't. Now git th hell outa here. I got work t do."

Woodrow unpinned his picture badge and held it in his hand for a moment. Then he flipped it on to the superintendant's desk.

"Take that n pin up your back pants wit," he said. "I ain pushin no more brooms f nobody. Greys come in here. Start right off as trainees on th machines. Eighty five cents a hour. Onliest thing you give us is sweeper, chip puller, erler. Thas high z I kin go. Well pull in your flaps, brother, cause you're definitely off th beam."

The big man pushed a button.

"Gimme Plant Protection," he said, "Two guards t my office right away."

Woodrow waited quietly until the two big men in the blue uniforms came in.

"Take this boog," the superintendent said, "out th South Gate, and see that he don't come back! Tell th time keeper t give him his time and have them call up the paymaster's office to make up a special pay and mail it to him so he don't even have t come back for that. Now git him th hell outa here!"

"Come on, boy," one of the two plant guards said; "Git a move on you!"

When he came down the stairs from the El on the corner where he lived, Woodrow's shoulders sagged a little.

"Ole man gonna blow his top, when he find out I done lost that job. Well he don't hafta know til they mail me m pay n that won't be til next week."

He looked up at the windows of his flat. A light showed, so he knew that somebody was at home. The El tracks cut across the two front windows so that the sunlight came in only between three and five o'clock in the afternoons. After that, it was dark. Before that, in the mornings, in the flat the light was grey, so that Lucy had to keep the lights burning all day when she was home. The back windows opened out over the alleys where the neighbors dingy clothes blew on the clothes lines for full five storeys down to where the garbage lay piled up in two months old heaps.

He looked at the windows again, then he straightened up and walked across the street to the building. He climbed the steps slowly instead of bounding up them two at a time. On the landing opposite his own door, he stopped. He could hear his mother's voice coming through the door.

"Jesus, I'm tired," she said.

Then his father's voice, with laughter bubbling up between the words like spring water:

"Lucy, honey – betcha can't guess what I done!"

"I'm too tired t guess, Tom – so I reckon you better go on n tell me."

"I done bought us a house!"

"You done what?"

"I done bought us a house. Up on Chauncy Street."

"Chauncy Street? Where's that?"

"Way, way uptown. A long damn ways from here! Ain'tcha glad, honey? You always useta want a house."

"Yeah, I guess I'm glad, Tom. I jus stay so tired that nothing don't make no difference no more."

"But this make a difference, honey. You quittin that damn job as of now!"

"Tom!"

"Yessir, I mean it. This ain't no way t live. Th baby farmed out to one relative or another. Woodrow eatin outa cans n livin in th street. N when lil Tome come back from overseas, he gotta have a place t stay."

"He gonna wanta git married, Tom. He ain't gonna wanta live wit us."

"Then he kin have th apartment upstairs. Thas th good part about it, Lucy; it's a two family n th rent we gonna git from th upstairs flat will pay f the whole place. Thas why you ain gotta work no more!"

Lucy put her plump brown hands up to her face all of a sudden and started to cry.

"Well I be damn!" Tom said.

"I can't help it, Tom," she wailed, "I'm just so happy I gotta holler!"

"Then holler, honey, holler all you wants tuh."

"Whas th matter, maw?" Tom turned. Woodrow was standing in the door-way, his little eyes bleak and fierce. "Doan tell me them greys done walked out agin, paw!"

"Naw," Tom said; "they done got useta seein me on th machine. They ain gonna strike no more."

"Then whas maw drippen them solid drops fur?"

"I done bought a house, son."

"But thas what she always wanted. That ain no reason t flood th jernt!"

"Wimmen is funny, son. Sometimes they crys when they's happy."

"Doan be such a square, maw!" Woodrow grinned; "Them drip-drop doan git yuh nowhere!"

"What kinda talk is that?" Tom demanded. "An lookit them clothes! Jes like a damn jitterbug! Lucy, you let him buy that junk?"

"He worked f th money, Tom – so I sorta thought I'd let him buy what he wanted tuh."

"Well don't think no more! From now you go wit him t pick out dome decent clothes!"

"Ain nothing wrong with these rags, paw. This here's a solid set o threads!"

Tom looked at the maroon loafer jacket with the checkered yellow and maroon sleeves. Then he looked at the big hat with the low squashed in crown, and the four and one half inch wide brim, pulled so far down on Woodrow's head that only his eyes and half an inch of forehead appeared beneath it. Woodrow turned uncomfortably under his father's steady gaze, and Tom could see the long hair that had been konked until it was glossy and twice as straight as a white boy's.

"I be damn," he said almost to himself, "t think a chile o mine be such a fool!"

"Cut th chin music, paw," Woodrow said, "An les make with th fork n knife!"

"Don't talk that fool talk t me, boy! Or by Jesus I whup you t a inch o yo life!"

"Les don't fuss, Tom. Right now I feel too good. Don't let nothing spoil it."

"Awright, honey. You go wash up, Woodrow!"

Lucy was bending over the table, pulling at the strings on the two small packages.

"Look what I got, Tom," she said.

Tom took the opened packages and looked inside the cheap wrapping paper. One contained a picture frame of glass on which was painted two crossed American flags. Above the flags was an opening for the picture to show through; below them was the legend: "In the service of our country." The other was a white silk flag with a red border, and a single blue star in the center.

"Swell! Lil Tom's pitcher look grand in that frame sittin up on th mantelpiece. N we hang this in th front winder – let th neighbors know what kinda boy we got!"

Lucy's full lips drooped and the corners began to quiver.

"Oh Tom!" she wailed.

"Hush, honey. He be awright. I come back th las time, didn't I? An lil Tom jes like me. He's smart – smart z a steel trap!"

"Jus like you, Tom?" Lucy smiled, a slow crooked smile, wavering through her tears. "You know, you kin act awful dumb sometimes!"

"Awright, awright! Les go eat."

Lucy busied herself with the can opener. She dragged a few thin pork chops out of the ice box and threw them in the frying pan. In a few minutes the dinner was ready.

"Beans again," Woodrow said; "They eat better at Father Divine's."

"Be different now, son," Lucy said gently; "I'll be home where I kin cook you some good grub."

"Bout time," the boy growled. "Done forgot how it feels t scoff ace-deuce round th chiming Ben."

"Bow you head, boy," Tom said, "an don't lemme hear nother word o that fool talk!"

"Aw paw, that lame in th sky don't git yuh no place. He jus like th bear, jus ain't nowhere!"

"Woodrow!"

"Aw awright, paw. Make with th mumbling if it make you feel any better."

Tom glared at his son, then launched into the lengthy blessing. Afterwards there was silence except for the clinking of the knives and forks, and the gurgle of the coffee. Eating was a serious business. Finally Tom pushed back his plate and sighed.

"Hope you got enough," Lucy said, "cause thas all they is."

"Plenty," Tom declared; "Now I go over t Susie's n git Sissy. Wanta come wit me, Woodrow?"

"Naw, paw," Woodrow grinned; "gotta go do some gum beating with th cats down on th Ave. But you kin slip me a dead president cause my glory roll's flatter n las year's beer, n I'm really sufferin with th shorts!"

"What you talking bout, boy?"

"Why don'tcha git hipped, paw? All I want is a single off that horse choker you got in your back pocket."

Tom's hand went into his pocket and came out with his wallet.

"Here," he said; "give you a couple more when you learn t talk sense!"

"Thanks, paw!" Woodrow said; "you ain't no square; you're all there for fair! Well, plant yuh now, n dig yuh later."

"You be back early," Tom said; "you got t help yo maw with th movin t morrow. I won't be home til late."

"Solid, paw!" Woodrow said and went out the door. He slammed it behind him and went down the three flights of stairs turning at the landings where the smell of stale cooking and old clothes and unwashed bodies came through the doors. Then he was out in the street under the El tracks where the night came down with double blackness, so that the dim lights made round grey yellow blobs in the dark, under them no faint gleam showing.

The others were waiting for him on the corner.

"Jee sus," Sheeny said, "Jee sus it's hot!"

"Wish them Franklin Street lugs would come down here now," Woodrow growled. "I'd whupp em all. By myself, too!"

"Oh yeah?" Skeetr said. "You n what army?"

"Take it easy, greasy! I feel like layin a solid knock knock on somebody's tick tock, n it might z well be yours!"

"Aw f Chrissakes, Woodrow," Sheeny said, "it's too blame hot fur fightin. Leave Skeeter be."

"He got too much lip. Fur a little square he got too much lip."

"What we gonna do?" Skeeter piped.

"Like t go t th Savoy, but ain got that much legal lettuce."

"Les make with th feet up th Avenue," Woodrow said with elaborate care-lessness, "I wanta case th lay one more time, since I'm takin a powder t morrow A.M."

"What!"

"Yeah, I'm leavin you cats what don't know where you at. Th old man done knocked us a pad up on Chauncy Street."

"Chauncy Street?" Skeeter said; "I bin up there. Don't nothing but greys live up that way. They got in behind me n I beat th El back t Harlem!"

"I ain't runnin," Woodrow said. "I'll make with this shiv, not my feet!"

His hand came out of his pocket with a lightning like movement. The blade of the knife, already opened, gleamed dully in the street lights.

"How you do that, Woodie?" Skeeter asked; "That ain't no switch blade!"

"Ketch th point in the corner o my pocket. It pulls itself open coming out. Hafta keep it erled. N yuh gotta practice. Pays t be fast."

"Look," Sheeny said, "thas better n a chill!"

The three boys stopped, snub noses pressed up against the glass. Overhead, the three brass balls clinked slowly in the barely moving air. Inside, on their cushions, the revolvers and automatics glowed in all their malevolent beauty.

"Boy!" The word came out of the three mouths in one breath, blended in perfect unison.

"One o these nights," Woodrow said slowly, "I'm gonna come back here real late--"

"N that ole Jew'll have th iron doors cross th front, then what you gonna do?"

"C'mon through this alley n les case th jernt from th back." The three of them stole into the thick midnight blackness of the alley. Behind the pawnshop, a gleam of light stole out from around the edges of an old wooden door.

"See!" Woodrow said, "what did I tell yuh? Locked wit a padlock n a staple! Any ole piece o iron could prize it loose!"

"Yeah," Sheeny said drily, "n set th burglar larm off th minute you git inside!"

"I fix that," Woodrow declared; "Jus cut them wires n it won't go off - it work by electricity don't it?"

"Yeah," Sheeny said dubiously, "but --"

"When yuh gonna do it, Woodie?" Skeeter begged. "T night, huh? Huh, Woodie?"

"Naw, not t night. Later maybe. I let yuh know."

"A real gun," Skeeter breathed; "Maybe a tommygun! Like Edward G. Robinson! Like Jimmy Cagney! Like Gawge Raft! Look at me! I'm Gawge Raft -- naw! I'm Humphery Bogart! Youse guys is th coppers! Rat tat tat tat tat tat! A rat tat tat tat tat tat! Fall! Gawddamnit doan you know when yous kilt? You n Woodrow's daid. You spose t fall!"

"Lookit th lil jackass," Woodrow said. "He really think he got a rod. Now I can't do it."

"Why, Woodrow, why?"

"Cause you cain't keep them flappers o yourn buttoned. You shoot off your mouth now, whatcha gonna do afterwards?"

"Aw Woodrow, I ain't gonna spill! I swears I ain't! Ain'tcha gonna git us them rods? Aintcha, Woodie?"

"Maybe. Dig youse cats. Gotta go knock me a wee bit o shut eye. Stashin out early in th A. M. See you in a deuce o haircuts--"

He turned back up the street in the direction of the El shadowed flat.

"S'long, Woodie," they called after him, "Be seein ya!"

The next morning, while Woodrow was helping the moving man bring the furniture into the new house, a little turbulence ran up and down Chauncy Street. It was a fierce little turbulence, and it traveled fast. It leaped over the back fences all over Chauncy Street, and cackled dismally over the telephone wires going even into offices far downtown.

Mrs. O'Mallery started it. She leaned over her back fence and called out to Mrs. Fishbein:

"Have yez seen th new neighbors?"

"No I ain't. What are they like, Mrs. O'Mallery?"

"They're niggers!"

"Ach mein Gott! You don't say so!"

"That I do! Ain't it awful?"

And Mrs. Fishbein, who should have known better, since blood kin of hers had perished in Germany of a malignant growth of just such turbulence, passed it on:

"And they have such an awful lot of children," she said to Mrs. Martin; "and they steal everything what isn't nailed down --"

"They smell awful," Mrs. Martin said to Mrs. Roberts, "and all of em carry knives, even th kids!"

In the afternoon, when the men came home from their offices, the talk grew fiercer:

"Should run th black bastards out!"

"Ruination of a neighborhood. Property values depreciate like mad."

"We'll have to move, if they're allowed to stay."

"I say chase em out!"

The teen age boys stood around their elders and listened. Then very quietly they began to drift together until there was half a hundred of them standing in the street, watching the house.

"We don't want no niggers here!" one of them chanted. And one by one they all took it up until they were all chanting it, roaring it out at the top of their lungs.

Woodrow put the chair he was carrying down, and started out the door, the long bladed knife already opened in his hand. But the minute he stepped out, the first stone crashed against the doorframe, not an inch above his head. He ducked, but the next stone caught him in his stomach, knocking all the wind out of him. Then the stones were hammering against the house without ceasing, and all the windows came crashing in. Woodrow slammed the door.

In the middle of the floor, little Sissy stood up and howled.

"Oh Jesus!" Lucy said, "Oh Lawdy, Jesus!"

Then a stone came through the window and grazed Sissy's cheek. It brought blood. Woodrow gave one quick look then dashed for the door. He jerked it open, but Lucy had him by the feet, dragging him down. She sat on him and kicked the door shut.

"Git off me, maw!" he yelled, "Gawdamnit! I'm gonna kill them bastids! I'm gonna kill em!"

Lucy got up.

"You git upstairs, son," she said.

"Naw, Gawdamnit! I'm gonna --"

Lucy's hand moved so fast that it blurred, but the sound of its striking was clear and sharp like a pistol shot.

Woodrow stood there holding his jaw, his eyes widening; then he turned and dashed up the stairs. Lucy followed him, hard on his heels. The minute he was inside the room, she turned the key in the lock. Then she sat down on the stairs and cried like a child. The stones were coming less frequently now. Finally they stopped altogether.

It was nearly an hour later when Lucy heard Tom's steps coming up the walk. She dashed down the stairs and tore the door open. Then she threw her plump arms around her husband and shook all over with convulsive sobbing.

Sissy grabbed him around the knees and added her howls to the noise.

"Hush!" Tom said sharply, "pull yourself t gether. What happened?"

"Why didn't y tell me, Tom? Why didn't y tell me they wasn't nothing but white folks up here? They say we got twenty four hours t git out! Say they burn us out if we don't move! An they called us awful names – like ---"

"I know, I know," Tom said softly. "N I thought I was outa Mississippi. I thought this was th Nawth. Ain't they nowheres a man kin go?"

"Oh Tom, les move! Les go!"

Tom's heavy jaw set stubbornly.

"Naw," he said, "Naw, Lucy; I ain runnin!"

"Tom, we be kilt! They kills us all!"

"Then our time done come," Tom said grimly, "but I'm gonna take five o them f erver one o us! We gonna have lotsa company in hell!"

"Tom, don't talk like that! That's wicked talk, Tom!"

Tom ignored her.

"Where's Woodrow?" he demanded.

"Upstairs. I had t lock him up. He crazy mad, Tom. He wanted t fight em all – by hisself."

"Good!" Tom said and started towards the stairs.

"Tom," Lucy called, "Look, Tom!"

Tom turned. In her hand she held the new picture frame. It was shattered into fragments. One of them had passed through the picture slashing through the face so that it was ripped in half. Tom looked at the mutilated picture of the handsome brown lad, splendid in khaki with the stripes of a sergeant showing on his arm.

"An I doan even know where he is," Lucy moaned; "He might be daid right now! Why they hafta break his pitcher, Tom? Why they hafta?"

"Hush woman!" Tom growled and went on up the stairs. He unlocked the door. Woodrow sprang up from the bed, his little eyes red and swollen from weeping.

"Lemme at em, paw," he said; "lemme go git th grey bastids!"

"Naw, son," Tom said, "that ain't th way. But I got a job f you. A job that call f nerve. You do it f me?"

"Yassir," Woodrow said, "Yassir!"

"I want you to go down t th corner drugstore n call up th po leece. I be settin on th steps wit m shotgun to see that nobody don't bother you. C mon now!" He went into the attic where he had told Lucy to store the things not often used and came down with the shotgun and two boxes of shells.

Lucy was still sitting there holding the broken picture when they came down the stairs. When she saw the shotgun, she set up a fresh wailing. Sissy clung to her skirts and howled with her.

Tom and Woodrow went by them without speaking, then Woodrow was off, flying down the street toward the drugstore. A gang of white boys spotted him at once. But when they came out of the alley, they saw Tom sitting there with the shotgun in his lap. Instantly they broke and scattered.

Woodrow reached the drugstore and dived into the phone booth. The nickle clanged home, and he spun the dial madly. Then having shouted his message into the mouth piece, he came out again. For a moment he hesitated. Then from the other side of the drugstore, hidden from Tom's sight, a voice called softly:

"This way, boog!"

Woodrow leaped for the voice, his eyes blinded with rage. Then from the alleys and from behind the hedges, from above him on the telegraph poles the white boys jumped down upon him. Woodrow got the knife out and whirled it just once, laying open a white face from ear to mouth. The others fell back in a circle. Then one of them picked up a rock and threw it, and another, and another until they were all throwing rocks. Woodrow ran up the street ducking under the shower of stones, running away from his house to the place where the El curved around into a new station. Then he was flying up the steps and under the turnstile. The door of the train was almost closed but he jammed an arm through and forced it open. Then the train was moving off, just as the first of his pursuers reached the platform.

"Got t git a rod," he muttered as the train roared downtown. "Got t git a rod! Got t!"

When the train pulled up to the old stop, Woodrow went out of the door and down the steps in a dead run. As he came down the steps, Sheeny and Skeeter who had been standing dejectedly by an El pillar looked up and saw him.

"Look who's back!" Sheeny grinned. "A deuce o haircuts! I knew them grey's chase yuh out in a pair o minutes!"

"Got t git a rod!" Woodrow chanted, "Got t! Go git your flashlight, Skeeter. Make tracks! Got t git a rod! Got t git a rod! Got t!"

Skeeter looked at Woodrow and his little jaw dropped open. Then he was off, around the corner to his flat.

"Be dark after a little now," Sheeny said; "What happen, Woodrow?"

"They wrecked th house. They threw bricks at maw n Sissy. Got t git that rod now, Sheeny, got t!"

Skeeter came down the street with the flashlight. Then the three of them moved off until they came to the little pawnshop. They crossed the street and went down an alley behind the vacant store with the For Rent signs in the window, and lay down in the tall weeds and rubbish behind it.

The hours crawled. The dusk deepened into blackness, and between the ties of the El tracks, they caught the pale glitter of a star. Still the light stayed on in the pawnshop. Then at last, the fat little Jew was coming out, extinguishing the lights one by one as he came. When he reached the sidewalk, he drew the hinged iron gates across the windows, leaving the pistols in their show case, and locked them with a clang.

"Now," Woodrow whispered, "Now!"

The three of them dashed across the street. In another instant they were gone, moving up through the black alley, shadows within shadow, their feet soundless on the gravel.

"You stay here n watch!" Woodrow told Skeeter. "C mon, Sheeny!"

Back of the pawnshop, Woodrow climbed up the gutter until he reached the lead wires. A few minutes sawing and pounding and they fell. Then he pried the lock off the door and went inside.

Out on the sidewalk, Skeeter was trembling. He could hear Woodrow stumbling around inside the shop, and here where he was, it was night: the dark falling through the El tracks in patterns of blackness, broken here and there with the gleam of a neon sign, and the occasional twin beam of a truck, butting its way between the pillars.

Then Woodrow and Sheeny were coming out. Before he even straightened up, Skeeter could see the white teeth gleaming in a grin.

"Got em!" Woodrow panted, "nuff f all o us. C mon now, we gotta be a long ways from here when that bull pass by!"

Sheeny was off in an instant, his long legs blurring with the speed.

"Cut it!" Woodrow called; "You wanta let everybody dig you're pullin sumpin? Walk slow like you on your way home from th Swing Shift."

Sheeny stopped running. Skeeter and Woodrow came up to him, and the three of them walked down the dark streets, turning aimlessly this way and that, looking back over their shoulders.

"We's safe now, Woodrow," Skeeter said, "les see th guns."

"Awright." He dragged them out. "Th forty-five's f me. This here thirty-eight's f Sheeny, n th twenty-two is f you, Skeeter - jus your size." He reached in his pocket and came out with a handful of bullets of all sizes.

"Jeee sus!" he growled, "I got more thirty two's than anythin n they don't fit none o these rods!"

"Whatcha gonna do?"

"Lemme think --- Tell you what --- spread your handkerchief out on th walk. You, too, Sheeny. Now here's mine. Now look. I put th forty fives on m handkerchief n th thirty eights on Sheeny's n th twenty two's on yourn, Skeeter. Th thirty two's I throw away. Awright, heah goes."

The sorting went on briskly.

"Sheeny's," Woodrow said; "Skeeter's. Mine. Throw thisun away. Mine. Skeeter's. Skeeter's agin. Sheeny's. Throw away. Mine --"

Afterwards, Woodrow loaded the guns.

"C mon, now," he said; "we go teach them grey skunks a lesson!"

"How we goin?"

"Th BMT. They might be watchin th El."

"But we ain got no dough --"

"F Chrissakes! Ain you never ducked under? C mon now!"

The three of them sprinted down the subway steps and ran up to the turnstiles. Then all at the same time they ducked down and were through running along the platform.

"Hey!" the man in the change booth called, "Yuh lil bums! C'm back here!"

But the door of the train hissed open, and they were inside, mingling with the crowd. Through the closing door they could see the platform guard sprinting towards the train, but the doors came together and the train moved off, rocking through the tube.

"Whew," Sheeny said, "that was a close one!"

A young white woman looked up. A quick glance took in the huge furry hats, the loud loafer jackets with the big, loose patch pockets, and the pants with knees as full as harem skirts, and cuffs hugging the ankles above long pointed toe shoes.

She nudged a companion.

"Look at the Zoot Suiters," she whispered.

Woodrow's little eyes moved in his dark face. Then he was moving forward, dragging the huge army colt automatic out of his hip pocket.

"White ho!" he screamed. "Git outa heah! All you grey bastids git out! This is D Day f th cullud folks, n you white trash better start moving!"

The passengers started up out of their seats falling over one another. The young woman fainted, going down in a crumpled heap on the floor. One of the men, a big muscled laborer, stopped. He turned and started toward Woodrow.

"Lissen fella," he began; "this won't git youse nowheres --"

The pistol roared twice, the butt slapping against the palm of Woodrow's hand. The man sat down abruptly on the floor, holding his thigh where the two slugs had smashed the femur, and staring at the little spurts of blood leaping up between his fingers. Then a woman started screaming and another took it up and another until all the women were screaming.

Then the train was grinding to a stop and the doors hissed open. The people surged forward all at once, using their elbows and their fists to beat a path away from the automatic waving wildly in the boy's hand. When they were all gone from the car except the man Woodrow had shot and the young woman who had fainted and an old man who had been trampled into unconsciousness by the stampeding passengers, Woodrow came through the door, still waving the gun. Sheeny and Skeeter were behind him, their black faces ashy with fear. They bounded up the stairs and scattered in the crowd on the street.

Woodrow heard the shrill cry of the whistle behind him. A dozen fingers were aimed straight at his back.

"That's him!"

"Git 'im!"

"Kill th Boog!"

He could hear the heavy pounding of police brogans on the sidewalk. He fired twice over his shoulder and dashed away to the corner. The light changed just as he got there and all the cars stopped. Woodrow stopped too. For there, in front of him, next to the curb was the car – a long, red forty two Buick convertible, heavy and massive as a streamlined locomotive, glistening in the rain, its wipers wigwagging contemptuously.

Woodrow put his hand on the handle and pulled it down, hard. The door swung open. Then he was inside, next to the fat well groomed man with manicured nails and big rings on his fingers. The man's mouth dropped open, so that the cigar he was smoking dropped down into his lap and showered ashes all over his expensive suit.

Woodrow put the muzzle of the forty-five against his side, feeling it sink into the too soft flesh.

"Git out," he said. The man hesitated. The boy jammed the muzzle of the automatic into the flesh. The man released the wheel and bounded out into the street. The engine gave a coughing choke and died.

Woodrow slid under the wheel, pushed down on the clutch, and touched the starter. The engine purred into life. Before him the light had already turned green, and the horns of the cars behind him were setting up their angry chorus. He shifted into first and was off, the accelerator flat on the floor. Behind him, the police sirens were sounding, and in one corner of the rear view mirror, he could see the little white cars swinging in after him.

Under his hands the wheel spun and the ribbon of the street whirled backward under the wheels, the fat new tires sending up circles of spray. But the green and white cars spun with him, closer now. The needle of the speedometer spun pass sixty, the big car whining down the middle of the car tracks between the El pillars that spun backwards so fast they made a solid blur.

"C mon, baby," he whispered, "show em some speed. Always wanted a car like you. Now I got yuh n ain nobody goin t tek you erway – not nobody!"

He brought his eyes up from the speedometer, and his breath came whistling out of his lungs. The streetcar was coming, ballooning up in front of him, growing in every direction at once until it seemed to be filling all space. He yanked the wheel hard to the left, skimming by the car by inches, roaring down the wrong side of the street. The little Ford loomed up before him before he knew it, and try as he would, pulling the wheel all the way back to the right, the best he could do was to sideswipe it so hard that it rolled over on its back on the sidewalk and lay there like a wounded bug all four wheels spinning. The Buick lunged to the right, clipping three pillars and smashed squarely into the fourth.

Woodrow tumbled through the opened door and ran up a side street. There was a warm sticky wetness on the side of his face. He could hear the sirens of the police cars, coming from everywhere – North, East, South, the sound riding in upon him through the falling rain.

They were turning into the street now, passing the smashed Buick without even pausing. He bolted into an alleyway between two dwelling houses, scrambling over the board fence at the back. Then he stood quite still, the cold rain hissing down into his face.

There was no way out. The two apartment buildings were joined at the back, forming a blind alley. There was a door through which the garbage was pushed, but it was locked. There was a small door in the fence over which he had climbed; but in front of it the squad cars were shrieking to a stop. So he stood there in the rain and waited until he heard the policeman's voice calling:

"Awright, Boog, come outa there!"

He lifted the automatic slowly and pointed it at the fence. Then he held the trigger back until it clicked empty, shrieking through the gunfire:

"C'm n git me, yuh grey bastids!"

Outside in the street, the police stood behind patrol cars and let the slugs splatter against the warehouse across the street. Then they started firing, the little black pattern of holes going up and down every board in the fence; then across, then diagonally crisscrossing, the big splinters flying up from the impact, falling, and drifting away in the little stream of rain water that was flowing from under the fence.

They stopped shooting then, and waited. There were no answering shots from behind the fence. Instead, the water creeping across the sidewalk got pink in it, then streaks of red, then it was all red, moving thickly across the walk, dropping into the gutter.

The tall police sergeant stepped from behind the car and strode forward to the little door. Holding his gun ready, he kicked it open and stepped inside. They could see him through the half opened door, bending over, looking down. He straightened up.

"Aw right boys," he called, "you kin come n git him."

The other cops were moving forward now from behind the cars, swaggering carelessly, putting their revolvers back in their holsters as they came.

Drink the Evening Star

"My wife," the artillery captain said, "is, of course, a lovely woman."

Tad had the odd notion that he could see the words floating in the air above the captain's head like the balloon script of a comic strip character with the expression "of course" slightly italicized. He sipped his warm beer and said nothing.

"Intelligent," the captain said, "oh, very!"

And damned strenuous, too, I'll bet, Tad thought; but he didn't say it. What the captain needed was a sympathetic ear. He kept looking steadily across the table at the faintly blurred outline of the artillery captain. The captain was a large black man with a Hitler mustache and a bald head. Before the war he had taught mathematics at Howard University. He had a plentiful supply of ribbons: the Pre-Pearl Harbor, the African Theatre, The Mediterranean, Italy, Tad guessed, and the European. He also had a thin sprinkle of bronze battle stars, a unit citation, and the Purple Heart.

"Smith," the captain said, "thirty seven."

"I didn't know they let colored girls . . ." Tad said.

"Oh they accept a few. A quota - carefully selected."

"I see," Tad said.

A few soldiers came into the little juke joint. They looked at Tad queerly. PFC's don't usually drink beer with artillery captains, or any other kind of captains for that matter. Tad felt an idiotic impulse to get up and explain: It's just that we're both from New England. And we're both college men. A man gets starved for talk, you know. Real conversation - literate and connected. Not grunted monosyllables and jive talk. But he didn't do that either. There were so many things you couldn't do.

He downed the last of the tepid beer and studied the foam still clinging to the inside of the glass. The silence elongated. What the devil could he say now? Avoid the obvious remarks about the state of democracy America. No good, that. The captain was an intelligent man, and realism could get to be such a hellish bore. Tad cast a sidelong glance at the ribbons.

"Nice lot of confetti," he said.

"Yes," the captain said. He laid a finger on one of the small bronzed stars in the middle of the European ribbon. "This is for Bastogne . . . it and the unit citation."

"Really?" Tad said. The tone was just right, just casual enough. Too much interest and the captain would have retreated into his shell of Bostonian privacy. But Tad was interested. Bastogne, with McAuliff's Battered Bastards. That was a good show.

"We lowered the muzzles of the long tom's until we were firing at point blank range," the captain said. "First time we ever hit the beggars in plain sight. Usual range is ten to fifteen miles. Rum show, that."

"You were in England too, I see."

"Yes. More beer?"

"Don't mind if I do."

"Waiter," the captain called. "What was I saying?"

"You were talking about Bastogne," Tad said, "Sir . . ."

"Oh yes. McAuliffe mentioned us in his dispatch. That's how we got the citation. But the papers didn't. Not that I give a damn, personally; but it would be nice if somebody knew we were in this war."

The waiter came shuffling up with the beers. They were even warmer than before. And the waiter was a horribly dirty man who smelled worse than a goat. In New England, Tad thought, the hills are cool and green, and all the lawns are neatly clipped. While here, here . . .

"My wife," the captain was saying, "has no nerves. She is an absolutely fearless woman."

"Yes?" Tad said.

The captain touched his battle stars again. "I've got enough points," he said sadly. "My discharge should be along any day now."

"You don't seem very happy about it," Tad said boldly.

The captain smiled wryly. "I'm not," he said.

Tad grinned.

"Go on," he said; "get it off your chest."

"It's just that she's so damned fearless. Brilliant - absolutely brilliant, but no – no . . ."

"Common sense?" Tad suggested.

"I was going to say motherwit. A person can't be really intelligent who can't be frightened. That and the refusal to believe that she could ever conceivably be wrong about anything." He sipped the warm beer slowly. Then he smiled half to himself. "She doesn't pray," he said. "She <u>argues</u> with God."

"Strenuous eh?"

"Quite," the captain said. He looked at the fine chronometer he wore on his wrist. "Got to be shoving off," he said.

Tad had an impulse to detain him. Even to tell him about Anna. But he wasn't that drunk yet. He put out his hand.

"So long," he said. "Thanks for the beer."

"Don't mention it," the captain said.

Now, Tad thought, watching the thick form of the artillery captain walking away, a little unsteadily, now I can get down to some serious drinking.

That morning his company had gone on a twenty-three mile hike with full pack.

Disciplinary matter. Some of the boys had got drunk up in town and slugged a policeman. The policeman couldn't positively identify his assailants and nobody else would so the whole company got it. There hadn't been any wind, and the sky was white with sun. The sky in Georgia in the summertime is always white. The sun burns the blue out with solid waves of heat. No wind. When the men marched down the dirt road the dust that their feet made hung all around them like a cloud, thick and stifling. They had their tunics open down to their navels, and the dogtags smacked wetly against their black chests. Behind them the brick red dust stood up for fifty feet in the still air and the road was outlined in all its windings through the fields by the unmoving clouds. The trucks came up after them pounding up a mountain of dust, rounding the last of the curves, and roaring down upon the marching men in a five mile long avalanche of massive metal, blasting the heat back into their faces.

Tad looked straight ahead into the back blasted torrent of exhaust smoke, heat and Georgia topsoil. His lips formed the single syllable, "Damn!" But he didn't say it. That would have taken too much energy. The heat was a whiteness on the land. Everything swam in a metal bright blur of sunglare, except the little green bottle flies. They were motionless, suspended like hot, bright notes between earth and heaven.

Now that the artillery captain had gone, some of the GI's who were hanging around the entrance of the juke joint came in. They went by the table where Tad sat without saying anything and crowded around the bar. Then one gigantic ex Georgia plowhand walked straight up to the table and his little pig's eyes were filled with meanness.

"High cotton," he said, "runnin with de heavy brass."

Tad opened one weary eye and looked up at the big black man.

"You get the hell out of here," he said, speaking coldly, quietly, spacing his words with deliberation. The big man went. That always gets them, Tad thought. They're so damned used to being kicked around. . . . He looked over to the bar where the big farmhand lounged and he shuddered. With one hand, he thought, he could have broken every fool bone in my body. The whiskey bottle was half empty now. Tad held it firmly between his two hands. Somebody put a nickle in the jukebox. The music blared out.

"Oh God, Oh God, Oh God," Tad groaned. "That thing again! No melody. And it's not modern. Not even good dissonances. It's not music. Not anything. Just plain damned noise."

He lurched to his feet. But, as if by a signal, the girls were coming in the door and all the black soldiers set up a wolf howl. Tad sat back down again. They would dance now. He liked to watch that.

The music pulsated loudly. It beat in upon his brain in a weird deluge of noise. The GI's pulled the lean, hard muscled black girls to them, and the heavy soled shoes began to shuffle over the floor. Tad could see them through a soft multicolored haze, their outlines blurred and shifting. The big plowhand was dancing with a little gingercake colored girl with soft black hair that swung damply about her shoulders. Pretty, Tad thought, damned pretty. And he was sick, suddenly, remembering Anne.

For some unknown reason the opening movement of a Chopin Etude was running through his head. The gingercake girl was having a struggle with the great male animal. Tad could see his wide nostrils flaring, his hot breath stirring her hair. Tad was humming the Etude aloud as he stood up. It couldn't be heard against that pulsating wall of noise. But he kept on humming it as he swayed toward the dancers.

He put out his hand and touched the big GI on the shoulder.

"Cut," he said crisply. The man stood stock still in astonishment. The girl whirled free of his arms and threw her arms around Tad's neck. He got the smell of cheap perfume, powder, and bodysweat. They moved off raggedly to the beat of the music.

"Let's get the hell out of here," Tad said.

"We better," the girl said. "He kill you sho."

"Oh him?" Tad said airily. "Come on. It's too damned hot in here."

They danced by the table, and Tad dipped suddenly. When he came up, he had the almost empty bottle by the neck. When they went out the door, Tad could see the big plowhand peering over the densely packed crowd, looking for the girl.

Outside the stars hung inches above the treetops. Tad could feel them burning into his brain. They walked down the last dark street beyond the last dim blob of the street lights burning feebly atop the pine poles until they came to a black top road that ran into a pine wood. They turned away from the road until they came to a place where there was a hole in the pine trees and great stars blazed through. Tad sat down upon the pine straw and opened his tunic. He mopped his bare belly with a handkerchief and picked up the bottle.

"Gimme a shot," the girl said.

Tad passed over the bottle. The girl's eyes were small and they had a slant to them. She reminded Tad of something out of Rimsky-Korsakoff. He could remember the music, the beat of it; he could even hum it, but he couldn't remember the name. Odd. Deuced odd.

The girl snuggled up close to him in the darkness. Tad bent down and kissed her experimentally, then decided he liked it, so he kissed her again. Then he reached for the bottle. He lifted it to his mouth and the stars danced crazily above the tree tops. Then suddenly he thought about Anne.

"My wife," he said gravely, "is the most beautiful woman in all the world. She is slim and very tall and she has lovely white teeth."

The girl's eyes widened in the darkness.

"She is the color of dark chocolate and she wears her hair on top of her head like a queen."

The bottle was almost empty now. He sloshed the contents around inside and listened to it.

"She's a hell of a good fellow. She's very affectionate with good normal appetites and a talent for the bed. There's nothing neurotic about her. She's very good to me and she knows when to leave me alone. I miss her like hell."

"You love her, don't you?" the girl said.

"We live in a little town in upstate New York," Tad said. "We've got a little white house with green lawns and hedges. There's a rose bush by the door. There aren't any flies and it's always cool and there aren't any fields. No damned cotton."

The girl didn't say anything. She lay back in the darkness with her eyes luminous and listened. She was a weight against his shoulder but Tad hardly knew she was there.

"We've got a piano. A baby grand. I used to play it every night. For hours. Music – real music. No blaring bastardized noise! No heat. No flies. No dust. No high pitched nasal whining voices. No Goddamned, hellborn, misbegotten bigoted ignorance."

"You're sweet," the girl said.

"Her name is Anne. Her voice is a soft contralto like organ music. I miss her so much that I'm half out of my mind. Her and the green and ordered hills of New England."

He lifted the bottle to his mouth and held it there until it gurgled empty. Then he hurled it away into the underbrush. It made a great crash among the leaves.

"I'm lost," he said. "I don't exist. I'm black and there aren't supposed to be any blackmen like me. We're all supposed to be like that big animal you were dancing with."

"Kiss me," the girl whispered. "She won't ever know."

"No," Tad said savagely, "Goddamnit, no!" He could hear her breathing in the darkness. "Sorry," he said. The stars reeled and danced above the trees.

"I've got nobody to talk to. . . . except the captain; and he's got troubles of his own. I can't forget how to speak English. I don't give a damn about the baseball scores. And I give even less than that about the stinking, bloody, bastardizing war."

The trees were beginning to reel a little bit now.

"If only I could go home. Just for one night. Home to New England. I'd kiss my wife until she couldn't breathe, and then I'd sleep with her and everything would be all right. And in the morning I'd play the piano."

He fumbled in his pocket for a sodden pack of cigarettes. He drew them out at last and passed one over to the girl. Then he lit them both. The match made a brief flameglow in the night.

"Piano," Tad said. "If I could just play a piano for a little while. I'd feel better. Even here I'd feel better."

At his side the girl spoke suddenly.

"I know where there's a piano," she said.

Tad's hands were gripping her shoulders like iron.

"Where?" he said, and his voice was high and breathless, almost like a sob.

"Yonder," the girl said; "in the church. They's havin services tonight though."

"Where?" Tad said. "Where?"

"Bout half a mile down the road."

Tad yanked her to him, and kissed her suddenly, savagely. Then he was off, his GI boots pounding against the soft blacktop. Behind him the girl leaned against a pine trunk and her eyes were tearbright, and glistening.

The stars swam in great circles above his head. The wind stirred the pine tops. His body was sweatsoaked, but he kept on running. When he reached the door of the church he didn't even pause, although the lampglow shone through the windows and ancient sopranos and rusty basses quavered out a hymn. He came running up the aisle, straight toward the ancient, battered piano.

"Move!" He growled at the pianist, and flopped down beside her, shoving her half off the seat. The whole congregation was locked in open-mouthed silence. Tad didn't even look around. He spread his long black fingers wide, and the keys swam in a soft, alcoholic haze. Then he brought them down upon the keys in a crash like thunder and the angry music of the Chopin Polonaise echoed through the church. His GI cap fell off and lay upon the floor. His head bobbed with the music and his fingers were a dark blur upon the yellow white keys. The music sobbed and thundered all the way through to the end.

Without even pausing he swung into the Grieg Concerto. The congregation was swaying with the music now, staring at the thin black boy with his tunic open to his waist and his dogtags clinking as he swayed above the piano. Then the Hungarian dances, the fury within him lessening. Then the soft Forest Murmurs from Seigfried, and the Album leaf, and last of all, sweetly, gently played the Brahms Lullaby.

He stood up suddenly, swaying upon his feet. The congregation brought its hands together and the clapping crashed through the church.

Tad made them a deep bow, almost falling over.

The preacher leaned down from the pulpit.

"Please son," he said; "just one more. Somethin we know, this time."

Tad sat down again and spread out his fingers. His brows furrowed with thought.

Then he brought his hands down upon the keys and the music soared up.

"Goin home!" an old sister sang out happily. He played half of it and then they started singing. A hundred voices singing beating upward in waves against the rafters. "Mother's there beckoning – father's waiting too . . ." Soprano, alto, baritone, bass swelling out, mingling. The windows vibrating with the sound.

"Anne!" Tad said, and the sob in his throat was brine and blood. His fingers crashed into silence, a broken, dissonant chord. He stood up and weaved toward the door.

"Son!" the preacher called out, "Son!"

But Tad went on out the door and down the black top road. The stars were red and close. They were white fire, as bright as tears. I could hold them in my hand, he thought, I could drink them down. . . .

"Tomorrow," he said, "tomorrow, I'll be home again."

Land of the Pilgrims' Pride

In the late afternoon the light had a quality of stillness about it. It lay on the green lawns of the campus as though it had been painted there, so that even the students crossing the quadrangle were like figures in a landscape arrested for a moment by the eye's fixation point and held there waiting until it should move again, releasing them into motion and to life.

Hank Morrison – Doctor Henry Morrison, PhD, English Literature, Nineteenth Century Romanticism – took off his heavy rimmed glasses and looked over toward the edge of campus where the silver birches were. The sunglow lay upon them and their white trunks threw back the light in a kind of soft blaze. He heard the put-put of a motor and turning his head a little he could see Karl riding the seat of the motorized grass cutter, leveling the grass into a velvety carpet.

Damned scoundrel, he thought suddenly, completely impervious to logic – completely. Hide like a dinosaur's. If only he'd stick to his landscaping ---- His hands tightened behind him as Karl chugged past looking up at the window of his office and the letter crackled between his fingers. Slowly he put the glasses back on and lifted the letter again. Phrases leaped out at him:

".... about fifteen, but looks twelve, due no doubt, to pure starvation ... The authorities were very kind .... The mother died in our hospital ... Her body was covered with bruises, and so starved that not even the amino acids would do any good .... Well, he's ours now, and Hank if ever a child were in need of love ...."

Damn it! Hank thought bitterly. He looked toward the grasscutter moving over the knoll toward the tennis courts. You went through the world like that, he thought, leveling it until only you towered. And now you've been leveled too, and I'm stuck with one of the results of your ethnological experiments. Quite an experiment. Total extermination of a racial and cultural strain. He looked toward the sound of the grasscutter which was out of sight now, over the knoll.

"Arrogant scoundrel," he said. "Don't see why they keep him."

He turned and crossed the office, folding the letter, and went down the stairs. Crossing the campus, walking heavily, lumpily, his brow furrowed with thought, he looked older than his fifty years. He went wearily up the steps of the cafeteria, thinking: Why the devil doesn't Ella come home? The dadblamed war is over; and this food is ruining my stomach. Then he sighed and pushed open the door.

At once, with a curious, jerky tightening of his nerves, he heard the bass voice begin to hum that tune again, the words printing themselves out in the air ahead of him, "Da – da – da – the girl I left beee – hind – me!" Damn it, doesn't he know that a joke repeated ten thousand times isn't funny, no matter how good it was at the start? But he turned to Coach Walker, and smiled wanly, waiting for what he knew he was going to say.

"Hiyah, Hank!" the coach boomed. "How's the morale on the home front?" And Hank tried not to wince. He resisted again the impulse to explain: I tried to get in. Could I help it that I was too late in my forties; and that a complete, detailed, and documented knowledge of the Romantic Poets is of no use in wartime? Where there should be anything comical in the fact that Ella, his wife, fifteen years his junior, and already a graduate nurse could now wear ribbons for the African, Mediterranean, Italian, and European campaigns, the twin silver bars of a Captain on her shoulders, and five battle stars, while he sat home in mufti and tried to explain the significance of "She Walks in Beauty As The Night" to a group of giggling female sophomores who were perversely interested in Byron's relationship with his half sister, Augusta, and not at all interested in his poetry? Ella, God bless her, was doing her job magnificently. And he was doing his. But would it never occur to Coach Walker, or indeed to anyone, that there was something perhaps a trifle amiss with a world that for fourteen ugly years had had no time for Keats and all possible time for smashing young men into bloody rags which Ella and others like her must try desperately to patch into something that remotely resembled humanity?

"Well," he said, "pretty good. You've ordered, Joe?"

"Sure. How's Ella? Heard she's been decorated."

"Yes," Hank said, trying to keep the pride out of his voice. "The silver star. She was up near the perimeter of the line when Von Rundstedt came through in December of last year. And she stuck until the Mark Fours were in plain sight, excavating the wounded. But she won't wear it. Seems that she overlooked six lads in the excitement. Jerry shot them. One bullet apiece through the back of the head. Damned economical. When Ella found out about it, she went to the commanding officer and attempted to return the medal. She felt that she's failed because she didn't get them all out."

"He wouldn't take it, of course?"

"No, but Ella won't wear it just the same."

Coach Walker looked at Hank.

"Quite a girl, Ella," he said.

"Yes," Hank echoed; "Quite."

The pretty young student waitress was at the table now, and Hank ordered. Fruit juice, soup, toast, a pot of strawberry jam, black coffee.

"Trying to reduce?" Coach Walker grinned.

"No. Stomach's acting up. I never could eat anything except Ella's cooking."

Joe Walker threw back his head and laughed aloud.

"Good thing they took Ella instead of you," he chuckled. "She always was the man of the family."

Hank looked at him and smiled slowly. He said: "That's what I like about you, Joe; you're so tactful."

"Sorry," Joe said, "but it's the truth."

Hank sipped his fruit juice. It was very sour and tied up his jaws. He stopped suddenly, looking at Coach Walker. Then he put his hand in his pocket and came out with the letter.

"Here," he said, "read this."

The young coach stretched out his hand and took it.

"From Ella?" he said.

"Yes," Hank said. "Handed me quite a jolt."

He watched the younger man's eye dancing over the page, stopping in quick little jerks over each word. Poor reader, Hank thought. Fixation points on each word, instead of phrases or sentences. At one place Joe's eyes lingered longer than usual, and Hank knew at once what that was. The coach looked up, frowning.

"My God, Hank," he said.

"I'll do it, of course."

"But, Hank, a Jewish kid!"

He could almost see Joe Walker italicizing the word with his voice.

"So what?" he said irritably, his voice rising. "He hasn't any people. They've all been killed. And we haven't any children."

"I don't suppose," the coach said doubtfully, "that there really are any racial traits. After all, he'll be raised as a gentile. Maybe in a few years you couldn't tell the difference. That is, if he doesn't look Jewish."

"You didn't read the postscript," Hank added harshly.

"No."

"'It was her dying wish,'" he read aloud, "'that Emil be reared in the religion and culture of his people. I promised, Hank. It seemed such a little thing to do . . .'"

Coach Walker stood up.

"When is he coming?" he asked.

"Next week. I'm going down to New York to meet him."

Coach Walker shook his head.

"I don't envy you, Hank," he said.

Fool, Hank thought, as the coach walked away. An educated man, too. What's race got to do with it? What's race anyway? If Ella says he's a good kid, then damnit . . . He got up hurriedly, leaving most of his lunch untasted.

As he approached his neat little cottage, he could see Karl, the gardener, waiting for him. He could feel a little wave of anger moving over him. Arrogant scoundrel, he thought again.

"I cut the hedges," Karl said; "But your lawnmower was locked up. I can't use the motorcutter in this little space. If you will give me the key . . . . ."

Hank fumbled in his pocket, and came out with the key.

"I readt the casualty lists," Karl said. "Such a lot of nice youngt men. And for what, Doktor? So that those Russians can . . . ."

"The mower," Hank said evenly, "is in the corner to the left of the car."

"Thank you," Karl grinned, "Herr Doktor."

Hank turned on him savagely.

"In this country," he said, "Doctor is sufficient."

"So sorry," Karl said. "Sometimes, I forget."

"Well don't again," Hank said, and walked away, leaving Karl smiling after him. Again, he thought bitterly, again he's got the better of me.

Sitting nervously in the outer waiting room at Ellis Island, Hank was conscious of the fact that of all the many times in his life that he had been frightened, never had he been quite as afraid as now. He looked at his watch for perhaps the twentieth time, and put it away again without knowing what time it was. Damn, he thought, why don't they get started? The boat's been in for hours --- Then he started almost out of his seat, for the officer at the desk was calling his name.

He walked over and stood there patiently while the man looked over the sheaf of papers before him, then up at him.

"Doctor Morrison," he said. "Physician?"

"No – professor," Hank said; "University professor."

"I see. Doctor of Philosophy, eh? Well, these seem to be in order. You're well able to support the child. I don't see any real objection . . . You want to take him home, now?"

"May I?" Hank said a little breathlessly, "may I?"

"Of course," the officer smiles wearily. "Everything is done." He turned to an attendant. "Send Emil Goldfarb in."

Hank drew in a breath and held it until his head whirled dizzily. Then the door opened again, and the attendant came back leading the boy. Hank took a step forward. My God! he thought, no wonder Ella . . . . . He put out his hand. The boy was small. Smaller in fact than an American twelve year old. There were great masses of dark hair curling damply above a high, white forehead, and his eyes were big with ten thousand years of terror.

"Emil," Hank said huskily, "Emil . . ."

Shyly the boy put out his hand. But suddenly Hank rushed forward, brushing it aside, and gathered the boy into his arms. He could feel the thin form trembling all over, and then the boy's head dropped forward, and Hank could feel the smooth thin face against his cheek, and upon it, the big wetness of the boy's tears.

"Gott sei danke," Emil whispered; " 'bist gut, Herr Doktor!"

"Hush," Hank said, "hush. You're all right, now. Everything is all right."

He took Emil by the hand and led him down to the landing where the ferry waited.

"You don't speak English?" he asked.

"A leetle," Emil whispered; "Die Frau Kapitan. She taught me. But French, better. I was there long."

Hank frowned, trying to remember a few words. He had had French in college, but language courses in American colleges bear only a remote resemblance to the living, breathing tongues. Emil put out his hand and laid it upon his arm.

"Please," he said "English I want to learn. So good does it not go now, but soon . . ."

Hank nodded. "Come Emil," he said. The boy trotted along beside him, his big eyes filled with adoration.

Sitting in the taxi, after they had crossed to the city, Hank noticed suddenly the clothes the boy was wearing: a khaki pullover, cut down GI pants, a vastly too big army shirt, and enormous paratrooper boots. He leaned over and spoke to the driver.

"Change that destination," he said; "make it Thirty Fourth and Fifth Avenue."

Emil was looking out the window at the building as they went along. Then he looked at the sidewalks where crowds of clean, well dressed people moved along, walking briskly, with their heads up, and no fear in their faces.

"<u>Ach</u>," he whispered, "so beautiful it is!"

Hank smiled at him, thinking, with an odd tightening at the base of his throat: a son, in my old age, a son. The taxi coughed to a stop. They got out and Hank led the boy into the clothing store.

"Everything," he said, "from the skin out."

The boy's eyes kept widening as they brought the clothing out for Hank's selection. Hank thought that soon they would eclipse his whole face.

"Which one do you like, son?" he asked.

Emil's mouth came open. His face twisted, groping for the words.

"It's all right," Hank said quickly. "We'll take this one now. You can send the others."

"His old things," the clerk said; "Shall I dispose of them for you?"

"Throw them away," Hank said, but instantly Emil set up a wail:

"The shoes!" he wailed. "Not the shoes!"

"Bring back the shoes," Hank said, then to Emil: "Why son? They're much too big."

Emil opened his mouth and a flood of mingled English, French and German poured out. From it all, Hank gathered that he had been given those shoes by an American soldier, a hero who afterwards had died in battle and hence he must keep them always. They walked out of the store and up the street, with Emil holding the shoe box containing the paratrooper boots in his arms. Then, as they neared the corner, Emil stopped and Hank heard his breath come out in a little gasp. He dropped Hank's hand and darted across the sidewalk to the window where the violins were, lying side by side in all their satiny beauty. The shoe box fell from his hand and lay upon the sidewalk, unnoticed.

"You play?" Hank asked, but the question was almost rhetorical.

"Yes," Emil said; "yes, oh yes!"

"Come on, then." They went inside the shop and the tall, aristocratic clerk started toward them bending over a bit with bored condescension.

"May I serve you?" he drawled.

"Bring us a violin," Hank snapped.

"For the young man?"

"Of course," Hank said impatiently. "Hurry up!"

The clerk went back in the store and came back with a small violin, obviously designed for a child.

Emil took it in trembling fingers and tucked it under his chin. Then he drew to bow across the strings. At once his clear eyes clouded with disappointment. Hank saw the look.

"Bring him a good one," he said; "the best."

The clerk smiled blandly.

"The best," he said, "is a Stradivarius, valued at eighteen thousand dollars."

"Don't be a fool," Hank said. "A good, workmanlike violin, that's all I want. Not a toy."

The clerk frowned, but he brought another.

Emil picked it up and tested it. Then softly, surely, he began to play the Bach Concerto for the Violin. He played it almost all the way through, but near the end the bow made a ragged screech on the strings, and the boy stood there trembling, the great tear penciling his cheeks.

"I'll take it," Hank said. "How much?"

"A hundred fifty," the clerk said. "And sir . . . ."

"Yes?" Hank growled.

"The boy can play. He needs lessons, of course . . . . ."

"He'll get them," Hank said. "Come, Emil. We've got a long ride yet."

The boy trotted along beside him, holding the violin case under one arm and the GI boots under the other. Hank bent to take one of the burdens from him, but Emil's face was shining with such a concentration of happiness that he straightened up and left the boy with his treasures.

The first person to visit Henry Morrison and his charge when they had reached the University was the Chaplain, Father Cannon. He came into the room while Emil was playing, his back turned to the door. Hank made a motion to rise, but the Priest raised his hand for silence, and stayed there while Emil played a little show piece all the way through. Then he spoke very softly:

"God has granted you a great talent, my son. Use it well."

The boy whirled. Then, seeing the clerical garb, his face broke into a smile.

"A curé," he said. "Like Pere Chaillot . . . M'sieur doubtless works with the CIMADE? Or through the UGIF?"

Hank's eyebrows rose.

"The Comité d'Inter-Mouvement auprès des Evacueés," the Priest explained. "The UGIF was the Union Generale des Israelites. The CIMADE was a Protestant group, and the UGIF was Jewish, but we worked with them both. And the Catholic Church itself was one gigantic resistance organization. The three groups together with some desparate men of the Communist Party saved more than eight thousand Jewish children in France. Strange bedfellows, Henry. But it was God's work."

He took the boy's hand.

"You've been a good boy, Emil," he said; "I'm proud of you." He turned to Hank. "Your wife," he said, "wrote me about him. I've a request to make of you, Henry."

"Yes?" Hank said.

"When he's somewhat acclimatized, I want you to send him to me for instructions. The boy has need of God after all he's been through."

Hank frowned.

"He's Jewish, remember."

Father Cannon's big mouth curved upward.

"So – at least in part – was Our Lord," he said.

Hank hesitated. "There's the matter of Ella's promise to his mother," he said slowly. "I've got to take him to the Rabbi, Father."

"I see. I didn't know about that. Well --" the Priest's voice had genuine sadness in it, "there are many roads to God. I am long past believing that ours is the only way. Still, I would have enjoyed having him, Henry."

"I'm sorry, Father."

"Don't be." He walked toward the door. Inside the doorway, he turned. "I was in Paris last month," he said. "They took me down to see the former headquarters of the Gestapo. There was one room, Henry, that had steampipes – all of them pierced with hundreds of tiny holes. It's a low room, and the live steam softened the walls. They're covered with the imprint of hands. From the ceiling all the way down to the floor. Every size from the big palms of laborers to the tiny fingers of babies – inches above the floor. I can't forget those hands." He shook his head as if to clear it. "No," he said, "I can't forget them." Then he was gone through the doorway leaving Hank staring at Emil's long fingers, so graceful upon the strings.

"Play!" he said, and his voice was so harsh that Emil jumped.

Two weeks spun by, so fast that Hank did not notice their passing. They were bright weeks with no darkness in them until the morning that the bell rang and Karl stood in the door, twisting his hat in his hands.

"Yes," Hank said brusquely, looking up from the papers that littered his desk, "What is it?"

"That boy," Karl said, "Your adopted son. You know where he goes?"

"Of course," Hank snapped, "why?"

"Everywhere, Doktor?"

"Everywhere. What the devil are you driving at, Karl?"

"Nothing – only for several days I have seen him down in H Street. You know, Doktor, nothing lives down there but," Karl's voice dropped to an insinuating whisper, "but Jews, Doktor."

You swine, Hank thought, you filthy swine. But when he spoke aloud his voice was perfectly controlled.

"Emil has every right to go down there," he said, a little note of malicious pleasure creeping into his tone, "since he is of the purest Jewish blood. In fact, I send him. He's studying with the Rabbi."

Karl's mouth came open and worked. Hank looked at him standing there as though the heavens had fallen upon his head and laughed shortly.

"Now," he said, "get out of here. I've got work to do." But Karl lingered, hearing the boy's footsteps sounding clearly on the stairs. Hank half rose, but Emil came bounding into the room, his small face shining.

"Uncle Hank," he began, but his eyes fell upon Karl and he stopped. In the little pool of silence, Karl's voice sounded clearly, saying:

"Of course it's your business, Doktor, but is seems to me after all the trouble and misery that the Jews have cost the world ---"

"Get out!" Hank said evenly. "And don't come back, Karl."

Karl shrugged.

"I go," he said; "but if you love your little Jew, you better keep him out of H Street. There's going to be trouble."

"Karl," Hank said slowly, "if one of your filthy ex-bundists . . ."

"No Germans, Doktor. Good Catholics, like the Herr Doktor himself. Italian boys, and Irish. Not one German. You see, Doktor, other people are waking up . . ."

Hank pushed his chair away from his desk. The scrape of the leg on the floor was a harsh sound. Karl watched him come, smiling a little, then, at the last moment, he turned and went down the stairs.

Emil's great eyes were turned on Hank's face. His mobile, expressive lips trembled.

"Here," he said, "is it starting here, yet? I will go away. I would not endanger you, Herr Uncle Doktor."

Hank put out his hand and rumpled the boy's dark hair.

"No, Emil," he said gruffly; "it's not starting here. It never can start here, praise be to God."

"Good," the boy said. "I learned a new one - a part of a fugue. You want that I play it for you?"

"Yes," Hank said; "I'd like that very much."

Going across the campus, late in the summer, Hank sighed with content-ment. Everything had been good since the boy came. He didn't miss Ella so much. Even his digestion had improved. He looked up at the great stars blazing low and close among the Gothic towers of the University, and his shadow lengthened behind him. The boy would be sleeping now, tired out after his day; High school, then afterwards the Hebrew School down in H Street -- Rabbi Solomon Iser was a good man, Hank reflected, and perhaps the wisest I've known. It was by such wisdom that they have survived, God knows they couldn't have without it.... Last of all, the music lessons under a Jewish violinist named Herskov, whose fingers were a miracle upon the strings.

He looked up in time to see Coach Walker's big form bearing down upon him.

"Hank," he said, "where's the kid?"

"Home," Hank said, "why?"

"Good," Joe Walker said, relief audible in his voice. "There was trouble down in Kiketown. Bunch of young hoods, Irish and Wops, wrecked H Street. They were smashing every store window in the street when I left. They even set the Synagogue afire ...."

But Hank was gone, running toward the house, his heart pounding in his throat, so loudly that his footsteps, running, were drowned in it. He tore at the door twisting the key savagely, and cursing, fluently, forcefully, prayerfully. Then he was falling up the stairs, yanking open the door to Emil's room. It was empty and there on the bed, in a carefully heaped pile of splinters was the boy's violin.

"Smashed," Hank said, and the word stuck in his throat. "Emil!" he called, "Emil!" The name crashed into echoes. He went through the house from the basement upward. At the attic door he stopped, his fingers cold upon the knob. Then he pushed the door open and flicked the switch. The light flooded out, and there before him on the floor was a chair. It was lying on its side as though someone had kicked it over. He stared at it a long time before he could bring his eyes up to where the little feet swung gently in a semicircle as if moved by a little breeze.

"Emil!" he said, "Emil . . ." Then he bent his head and let the huge, stran-gling animal sobs out tearing open his throat as they passed, his eyes tear scalded and blind. He got up, dry eyed from the floor and cut the boy down.

Tenderly he carried him downstairs and lay him down upon the bed, wiping the blood and grime from his beaten face.

Then for the first time, he saw the note. It was half hidden by his own picture on Emil's dresser. He tore it open and read:

Dear Uncle Doctor,

Now again it begins. If you are caught sheltering me, it will go hard with you. And that, never, will I permit. Forgive me this, but it is better so. Pray for me.

Your son,
Emil.

The handwriting was shaky. Hank sat staring at it a long time, then back again at the little face, purple above the slip knot. He got up slowly and walked to the closet. When he came back, he had his duck gun, a twenty gauge repeater, crooked over his arm. He left the house and started walking southward toward H Street. But when he reached it, it was still. The glassless windows looked out of their jagged, splintered frames like great blind eyes, and even the street lamps were smashed and dark. He looked up toward the dome of the Synagogue, where the Star of David bent over at a crazy angle, its supports half burned through. He sat down on the curb holding the shotgun across his knees. Far down the dark street the finger of a searchlight on a police car probed the broken windows, moving from house to house away from him.

He sat there a long time, thinking: What will I tell Ella? What on earth will I tell her now?

A Wake for Reeves O'Donald

There must be a point, a beginning; a moment, an instant, when suddenly what never was before – is. Our minds cry out for that, needing the certainty of it. And, likewise, there must be the point of termination: the moment that time stops, the instant of annihilation. We accept this, too; having imbibed with our mother's milk these necessities: that all things have form, a beginning, a middle, and an end. Only, they have not; and, instinctively, we know it. We go on, chips swirling down a turgid, endless river, caught in the eddies and the whirlpools, drifting out of darkness through a brief space of sun and cloud, back into darkness again. Knowing this, hating our imprisonment in brevity, in meaninglessness, we honor the givers of form, of meaning, of beauty, out of all proportion to their worth. Or perhaps we do not honor them enough. I do not know.

But what else can explain the presence of twenty five such varied people crowded into that cold basement room on the Street of the Dragon, with the rain seeping through the ceiling and dripping down our necks, except that having known Reeves O'Donald, having loved or hated him, we were all somehow linked by a shattering sense of loss? A loss at the same time personal, and transcending personality.

"By God, he had style!" Bob Fellows said.

Nobody answered him. I could see Sweetlips Page's black fingers caressing the keys of his trumpet. Slowly I shook my head. Not yet. Not yet, Sweetlips – the time for the dirge you've made for him, who took you finally out of the prison of your somber hide has not come. Wait, and be still; for it will come.

At my side, Mimi was crying very softly, her hands rubbing the tattooed number they had put on her arm in the concentration camp. She had been ten years old when that happened, in 1943; and the next day the Maquis had raided the camp and saved her and eight other children. They, the Maquis, had been Communists and atheists – and men and heroes, which is a difficult thing to say now, twelve years later, when the gages are down again, and the lines drawn. But they were, and Reeves would never have tolerated

142

the poverty of spirit that cannot admit that any faith engenders heroism, if held firmly enough; no matter how mistaken it is. And they had passed the children along through that underground railroad which had consisted mainly of Parish Priests and the Nuns of small cloisters throughout France. And they, these Priests and Nuns, who often died under torture with grace and dignity and humility and style, screaming as little as was humanly possible, were also martyrs and heroes for their Faith, at opposite poles now, and warring for its very survival against the other. It was a paradox that would have delighted Reeves, who had little respect for human motives; but great respect for the magnificence of the actions which often resulted almost accidentally from them.

But it came to me that the best part of it all was that Mimi would cry. It had been years since she could cry, her tears frozen deep inside her by all the things that had happened to her. But, after Reeves, she could cry; for him, she could; and this was the proof of her healing. And I knew quite suddenly where and how to begin this, which being real, being true, had no beginning, nor has any ending either.

With Mimi.

It was raining that night, too. Paris is a city of rain. The streetlamps and the headlights of the cars made brief rainbows in the oilslicks on the Avenue MacMahon. He, Reeves, had come down the street towards the Etoile, going home, perhaps, because that was one of the times he had money, and he was staying at the Hotel Splendid on the Avenue Carnot; or perhaps simply walking to the corner to look at the white bulk of the Arc de Triomphe glistening in the spotlights through the silvery mist of the rain. With Reeves, you could never be sure.

She came up to him with the phrase that everyone understands at once in Paris, and perhaps in all great cities everywhere in the world; her finger pointed toward the sodden cigarette dangling from one corner of her ravished mouth:

"A bit of fire, M'sieur, si-il - vous plait?" which is the French way of saying: "Give me a light, please –"; and he, searching in his pockets came out with the windproof lighter and lit her cigarette, cupping the flame in his hands, so that when she bent towards that little pool of light (that flame of tenderness, of compassion) he saw the beautiful bone structure of her face, and the dark eyes big with a thousand years of terror; that beauty all the more vivid for the imagination it took to call it back into existence; the loveliness implicit in a face brutalized almost out of humanity, marked only by pain, by a violation of personality that clawed deep into the very tissue of her soul.

"You're pretty," Reeves said.

"Thank you," she whispered; "It is perhaps that M'sieur cares to – "

"No," he said brusquely; "Before the day comes that I have to buy love, I hope I shall be dead."

She stood there, looking at him, and the pain in her eyes deepened. It was very late. There wasn't much chance now that anyone –

"Please," she began; but he cut her off.

"You're cold," he said; "and wet, you haven't had anything to eat. Come along. We'll go to the Monte Cristo, and you can sit by the stove and dry. I'll buy you your supper. What are you called?"

"Mimi," she said. "But I cannot. I must stay here until – "

"Nonsense," Reeves said; "Come along."

"Please, please!" she said; "I cannot . . . If M'sieur will come back in an hour, then, perhaps . . ."

Reeves looked at her.

"In an hour, then," he said; and moved off.

He did not get back on time. It was an hour and ten minutes later when he reached the intersection of MacMahon and the Rue Troyon where he had left her; just late enough to arrive at the exact moment that the black Citroën drew silently to a stop beside her. The man got out of it, and took her handbag from her without a word. He opened it, and played the light of an electric torch into it. His expression did not change. He simply swung the handbag, striking her across the face with it, again and again, with icy viciousness, so that the catch cut the corner of her mouth, bringing blood.

Reeves put his hand on the man's shoulder and whirled him about. They fought, being evenly matched, for half an hour, after Reeves had kicked the springloaded switchblade knife out of his hand. But, in the end, Reeves left the <u>souteneur</u>, as these creatures of unspeakable vileness who prey upon the women of the streets are called, unconscious in the gutter where the <u>Flics</u> could find him, and took Mimi away from there.

Reeves' face was bloody, and his clothes were in rags. So he took Mimi into the Splendid. The concierge looked at her.

"Mademoiselle will have the goodness to give me her card of Identity," he said; "And, M'sieur, I must beg to inform you that the management looks with severity upon the practice of bringing women into the hotel – especially at such an hour –"

"Blast the damn management," Reeves said; "In ten minutes, when I have had time to change, you may descend my luggage. Have the note ready. There are, M'sieur le Concierge, other hotels in Paris . . ."

The Concierge shrugged.

"Perhaps," he said coldly; "If M'sieur knows of one that caters to a clientel which engages in street fights and enters <u>Poules</u>, he is, doubtless, better off there . . ."

Reeves took a step toward him. Mimi took his arm.

"No," she whispered; "Please, no –"

They got a room in the Acropole in Saint Germain de Prés. The manager looked at Mimi a long time. Then he shrugged. They, after all, had luggage. They came down from the room as soon as the bags had been placed in it. Reeves took her to an all night bistro, and sat there, watching her eat. She scraped away the last of the sauce from the plate with a piece of bread; then she looked at him, the pain and terror in her eyes mingled now with awe, with wonder.

"Why have you done this thing?" she whispered.

"You're a human being," he said simply. "I don't like to see people kicked around."

"I," she said flatly, "am a –"

"No," he said gently; "You're not. Not at heart. I've been hungry, too. But not for very long. I don't know what I would do myself, if it went on long enough . . ."

"You're good," she said. "I'd forgotten that there were good people . . ."

She sat there, staring at him.

"I – I," she said; "Cannot go back there, now. Edouard would kill me. I must never enter the Sixteenth Arrondissement again. Perhaps, even here –"

"I am here," he said.

She reached across the table and took his hand. Her fingers bit into his flesh with sudden intensity.

"Come," she said; "let us go back to the room, now . . ."

He smiled at her.

"Yes," he said; "Let us go back – and sleep. Only sleep, little Mimi. I don't want gratitude, nor any kind of payment. You understand that? It would be the same thing. What we do with our bodies must be done only out of love. Anything else, any other reason, dirties it – You understand, Mimi? You have well comprehended this which I have said?"

She stood up, suddenly. He could see her lips moving, as if in prayer.

"What are you saying?" he said.

"I am thanking the Holy Mother for letting me live until now," she said simply. "I have prayed so often, Reeves – first that I could escape that life, that one day I would find a good man who would – do what you have done.

But I had stopped praying for that. All I could ask Her for before tonight was that She would let me die . . ."

He was staring at her bare left arm. She had taken off the sodden Army Trench coat, and he could see the blue numbers.

"Yes," she said; "My name is Mimi Levy – but I was reared by the Sisters of the Sacred Heart of Jesus. I know no other Faith. Does this trouble you? I have heard so many people say that the only good thing the Nazis did was to rid the world of Jews . . ."

He smiled at her.

"I am a Jew," he said; "and a Mohammedan, and a Buddhist, and a Catholic. I believe in all Faiths, and in none. What I do believe in, Cherie, is, I think, only the brotherhood of man. Come . . ."

They lay in each other's arms, and talked until it was light. They did not make love. There would be all the time in the world for that – later, when he had finished her healing.

"I," she whispered to me now, "burdened him so greatly with my sorrows. I even took him to that place outside Paris where they killed my mother and father and little brother. It is only a large room, you know, with pipes running around it at intervals. But they have perforations, those pipes. And when they introduced the live steam –"

"Don't!" I said, shuddering.

"The plaster softened," she went on as though she had not heard me. "You can see the prints of the Hands, Tom. High up, the prints are larger – where the men could reach. Lower, there are the prints of women; and still lower –"

"Mimi, for God's Love!"

"God's Love?" I had ceased to believe He cared. "How could He permit that? All around the bottom, Tom, the tiny palm prints of the children. . . ."

I didn't say anything. She had to talk it out. She had to.

"Perhaps it was so that they could come to Him in their innocence, and their purity. I – I have envied them often, Tom. The pain was soon over. But for me it was never over. It went on and on and I could not die of it. Until I met Reeves, and he took away the pain . . ."

"He was so gay," Jean Aubert said. "Do you remember that affair of the Croix du Guerre with Palms?"

"Yes," Bob said, smiling in spite of himself.

That was how it would have to be now. Always – Do you remember?

"It was a good thing the judge had a sense of humor," I said; and we were back again in the court, being tried with Reeves for lese majestié against the Republic of France.

"But, Your Honor, you do not understand," the Prosecutor said; "It is true that he was drunken, and that he is an American. I know that maintaining friendly relationships with our sister Republic is of the highest importance, now. But I do not think the Americans would permit a Frenchman to insult their flag and their institutions. To glue a high military decoration to the bare breast of a nude dancer in a <u>boîte</u> with scotch tape is, I submit, excessive . . ."

The court rocked with laugher.

The judge peered at Reeves over his glasses.

"This is most irregular," he said, trying to hide his smile; "But I wish to question the young man directly. M'sieur O'Donald, where did you get that medal?"

"Your honor," Reeves said gravely; "It is the disposition of the medal that concerns us here, is it not? It's origin can scarcely be of importance . . ."

"Ah, but it is!" the judge snapped; "If it were established that it were acquired in a fashion which reflects honor upon yourself and upon France, the Court might be more considerate in – ah – judging the manner in which you disposed of it . . ."

Reeves stood there, looking at the Judge. A slow grin lighted his eyes.

"Truly, your honor," he said blandly; "I'd rather not say . . ."

The Counsel for the Defense got to his feet.

"Then, with your Honor's permission," he said drily; "I will. My client is overburdened with modesty and with ideals. It required two days search of the records of the Ministry of War to find the citation, since I could hardly apply a burglar's jimmy to the trunk in which he has his copy of it locked. He refused to let me see it on the grounds that war is barbaric, and his lack of pride in his own heroic part in it. Have I the court's permission to read it?"

"Yes, Counselor," the judge said.

"Soldier extraordinary of the Army of the United States of America," the Attorney for the Defense read, "Who with selfless devotion to duty, and entire disregard of his own personal safety, liberated single handed the village of Vailley in the Aisne Sector; putting to flight an entire company of S.S. Troops with his accurate submachine gun fire; and saving the lives of the Mayor and his family, who had been held as hostages by the Nazis . . ."

I looked at Reeves.

"I was drunk," he said out of the side of his mouth, in English; "and AWOL. Drew a court for that caper. Hadn't been for that fat little Mayor with the chin whiskers and the l'eau de garlic breath, I'd still be in the clinker. The village had exactly three bombed out houses, and a feedstore. There were no more than five Krauts, also drunk and AWOL. And I missed every one of them. Didn't really want to hit them anyhow ..."

He was lying. I knew that. It was his way to play down every praiseworthy thing he did.

The judge had taken the citation and was looking at it. Then he stood up and began to talk. His speech was moving. It was filled with many references to La Belle France, and to Glory. He shook the hand across the sea several times. At the end, he permitted himself a pleasantry.

"To pin an honorably earned medal on the bosom of a daughter of France in appreciation of her beauty seems to me more a compliment than an insult. He might, Messieurs, have chosen to pin it to her derrierre ..."

"What the hell didn't I think of that?" Reeves said; but nobody heard him, or even the Judge's dismissal of the case for the laughter.

"I wonder," Bob Fellows chuckled; "If he ever succeeded in his greatest ambition – to make all the girls at La Nouvelle Eve?"

"Yes," Mimi said bitterly, "he did ..."

"Ah, hell, Mimi," Bob said; "I am sorry. I didn't think ..."

"It's all right, Bob –bee," Mimi said. "He was like that. They were all – so pretty. And he loved beautiful things. But he was never viceux, you comprehend. He was very gay and clean and fine. He loved them all – truly. He was capable of that. I was jealous and I quarreled with him about such things. He said: 'It has nothing to do with you. It does not mean I love you less. I just love life, and we are given so little of it. Besides you are free to do as you like. One human being can never own another. ...'"

"Yet you never looked at anyone else," I said, wondering if my voice sounded to the others as it did to me.

"He was wrong. He did own me. Body and soul and flesh and spirit. There was no one else. It was like looking into the sun and being blinded. I could not see another man. ..."

"Oh hell," I said.

"He was great," Sweetlips said. "Crazy. Gone. Cool. The greatest. ..."

I looked at Sweetlips. He was a tall thin black boy who played a trumpet in a Bop cave in St. Germain de Prés. He had come over to study under the G.I. Bill of Rights, and had stayed. The Jazz Mania of Paris made it possible for him to live fairly well. But he would have stayed if it meant starving. We have gone a long way in America to make life easier for black boys like Sweetlips. But not far enough. I told Sweetlips that once, defensively: desegregation of the schools, the interstate carriers, the restaurants of Washington, the opening of Southern Universities to Negroes – all the improvements –

"Listen, Man," he said; "You just don't tumble. It's the little things, like being sure. I want a room at the Waldorf Astoria, I can get it – maybe. Only I'm not sure. 'Sorry we're all filled up. You have a reservation? Oh, I am so sorry, there's been a mistake ...' Never sure. Want a room at the Georges Cinq, I'm sure. Desk clerk looks at my camouflage job and yawns. Like that, Man, a place where they yawn at a black skin. Go to Maxim's, long as I'm dressed nice, and got my reservation in early, I get a table next to Ali and Rita, or whoever he's married to now. Go to El Morroco in the Big Town where I was born, and they hide me behind a potted palm. Go to the Twenty One or the Stork, and they don't even let me in ..."

"What the hell do you want to go to those crummy clipjoints for?" I demanded.

"I don't. Just want to know I could if I ever get a weird impulse. Don't you know what freedom is, boy? Or ain't you lived in Paris long enough?"

There must be an answer to that one; but I haven't found it yet.

"You didn't always think he was great," Bob said drily.

"I was sick, Man – sick. He cured me. I remember – "

That word again. Would we spend the rest of our lives, remembering him?

He had stopped at the sidewalk café where Sweetlips and two other colored boys were sitting. Hearing them speaking English, he came over to them.

"Mind if I join you?" he said.

"Why sure, Man," one of the others said; "Drape the body. Glad to have you."

Sweetlips glared at him. Sweetlips had not only been born in New York City, but he was a graduate of both Columbia and Julliard. When he was drunk, or off guard, he spoke precise grammatical English. Most of the time he affected Bop talk; except when he felt mean. Then he would drawl like a Georgia fieldhand. He didn't do it very well. He didn't know how.

"Whitefolks," he mocked; "What's the matter? Y'all slumming?"

"No," Reeves said pleasantly, "Just lonesome, I guess. Heard you talking English and knew you were from – home. I miss it, sometimes ..."

"You wouldn't do this back home, Cap'n," Sweetlips drawled; "You wouldn't sit your lil' white body down next to no colored folks. ..."

Reeves looked at him.

"You are a bastard, aren't you?" he said quietly.

Sweetlips grinned.

"Ain't y'all forgetting something, Cap'n? You left out the 'black'. Way I always heard it was: Gawddamn black bastard ..."

"No," Reeves said. "The black has nothing to do with it. The World Federation of Bastards is very democratic. Any color can get in." He looked around for the waiter. When he turned back, he was smiling, peacefully.

"Come off of it, Sweetlips," he said. "Oh yes, I know you. I've heard you play a hundred times. You're one of the greats; so why the hell are you being so petty?"

"That's right, boy," one of the others said; "Give it to him. He needs it . . ."

"Thanks," Reeves said. "All right – so it hasn't been pleasant. I understand that. What I don't understand is why you're cooperating so beautifully with all the nasty little people with wormy souls and underdeveloped hearts . . ."

"Cooperating?" Sweetlips said; "Me?"

"Yes. Why are you making of yourself a grotesque caricature of the thing they presuppose? They've got you half convinced. Right now you really aren't sure that an irrelevancy, a biological accident like your black skin or my red hair doesn't actually mean something. They don't. I'm a writer; you're a musician. Those are the real things. And we're both men, dreaming loving, suffering under the sun. Never have seen any scientific proof that the color of the hide was any protection against the pain the heart can feel, or the joy, or the response to beauty. So come off of it, son. Wake up and start to live . . ."

"I argued with him," Sweetlips said now, softly; "I had hugged my hurt feelings to my bosom so damned long I thought I'd be lonesome without 'em. But I'm not. It's like having a weight off. Couldn't make him mad, no matter how I tried. That boy just naturally had too much sweetness in his soul . . ."

We sat there, considering that. It was almost good enough for his epitaph.

"Tom," Renée Gravoir said to me; "You are also a writer. You have often said that he was a great writer, the greatest. Why then could he not live from the things he wrote? They seemed to me – beautiful. I did not understand all the words, but what I could comprehend was wonderful and terrible and very fine; so why?"

"Because," I said harshly, speaking out of my own bitterness, my own deep hurt, "he was not a whore." I felt Mimi stiffen beside me; but I went on now, recklessly.

"There are other ways of selling one's self beside the minor prostitution of the body. There remains the debasing of what one is, the corruption of the talent given of God, the falsification of one's art. I know this sounds precious; but it is true. He could not do that. He had to write what was in him; all the terrible, lovely things – all the things he knew about people, about life. And because he could accept human weakness, human evil, the hopelessness of most men living, and write about them with understanding, with compassion, he offended a lot of people. The last book, the one they wouldn't take, "Night Cry," was like that. They couldn't see the magnificence rising out of squalor, out of sordidness. They couldn't understand the unspeakable courage of all the little, doomed, damned people of the streets, going on, living, hoping, dreaming, in spite of the knowledge that there is nothing to live for, no hope, and that all dreams are false ...

"They wanted him to pretty it up, to change things. He read it to me. He said: 'Tom, is there anything to change?' He was like that, always humble about his work. I swore at him: "No, nothing! Not one goddamned lovely word! It's perfect you fool, perfect!"

Mimi's fingers tightened on my arm.

"He had that kind of courage. The brave, gay, bright kind. He'd spent every sou from the first book – on us. Feeding us, the parasitical bastards that we are; giving us more than food, wine, music, joy – giving of himself, more than he had to give. So now he's dead, the one true artist among us, the only one who could not be spared. He lies there dead with the laughter in him stilled, lies there in his lonely integrity and his lovely pride – while we –"

I couldn't go on. The thing in my throat was as big as death, stopping my futile words.

"It's all right, Tom," Mimi said.

"It is not all right!" I whispered; "It will never be all right again. . . ."

"Ah, but it is," the strange girl said; and looking at her, I recognized her at last: Simone, to whom Reeves had stuck the Croix du Guerre; I hadn't known her with clothes on.

"It is all right," she said; "because he was not defeated. Even after he had become a clochechard and slept under the bridges of the Seine in the cold and the wet, it was all right. He left Mimi because he would not take the little money from the first decent job she ever had. He was hungry and cold, but he was not beaten –

"We, all the girls at La Nouvelle Eve, took turns visiting him at the hospital. He would not permit us to tell you others about it – it was only by hazard that we knew it, since he collapsed in the street outside the club – and he did not wish to burden you. And the day when le Docteur told him he could not get well, he beckoned to me. 'Get me some clothes, Bébé,' he said; 'and a taxi. If I'm going to die, I'll do it where I always swore I would: In the gutter on the Place Pigalle with all the vulgar neon lights winking at me...'

"I argued with him. But he has this fantastic stubbornness and the discussion did not march. In the end, I did so, because it was what he wanted. It was raining again, and all the girls came out, wrapped in raincoats, and stood beside him, crying. The <u>flic</u> stood there with tears in his eyes – he knew Reeves, too; all the police did – and directed the circulation of cars and autobuses around his feet. And Reeves said – he said –"

We waited while she found her voice.

"He said: 'Tell them for me: that there was one man who was not nibbled to death by the rats of time; and who, when he died, went not with a whimper – but with a shout!'"

It was so right. We had his epitaph now. I looked at Sweetlips and nodded.

He lifted the trumpet. The clean peal of sound was like a sword thrust through the darkness. We could almost see it, like a blade of light.

ABOUT THE AUTHOR

Frank Yerby (1916–1991) was an American author of thirty-three novels. He is best known for *The Foxes of Harrow*, which became the first novel by an African American writer to sell more than a million copies and made him the first African American to have a book purchased for screen adaptation by a Hollywood studio.

ABOUT THE EDITOR

Dr. Veronica T. Watson is professor of English and director of Graduate Studies in Literature and Criticism at Indiana University of Pennsylvania. She is author of *The Souls of White Folk: African American Writers Theorize Whiteness* and coeditor of *Unveiling Whiteness in the Twenty-First Century: Global Manifestations, Transdisciplinary Interventions*. Her articles have appeared in a number of collections and academic journals, including *Mississippi Quarterly* and the *Journal of Ethnic American Literature*.

CPSIA information can be obtained
at www.ICGtesting.com
Printed in the USA
LVHW100935080723
751743LV00004B/688